# THE WAY
# OF THE NORTH

## JAMES B. HENDRYX

SAGEBRUSH
Large Print Westerns

First published in Great Britain by Edwards
First published in the United States by Doubleday

First Isis Edition
published 2015
by arrangement with
Golden West Literary Agency

ISBN 978–1–78541–008–6 (pb)

Published by
F. A. Thorpe (Publishing)
Anstey, Leicestershire

Set by Words & Graphics Ltd.
Anstey, Leicestershire
Printed and bound in Great Britain by
T. J. International Ltd., Padstow, Cornwall

# Contents

# CHAPTER
## ONE

## On Dyea Beach

Young Tom Jorden drew the collar of his mackinaw closer about his neck and surveyed, through the cold, wet fog that eddied and swirled about him, the indescribable confusion that reigned on Dyea Beach. The *Portland* from Seattle and the *Aleucian* from Vancouver, both loaded to the guards, had almost simultaneously dumped their cargoes onto the beach that was one of the main gateways to the promised land of gold.

Men and women milled about, seeking to identify their belongings among the heaps and windrows of goods that had been dumped from the landing boats upon the shore just above the tide reach. Innumerable dogs, begged, borrowed, stolen, or bought by the argonauts who had heard or read that travel in the Klondike was by dog team, sniffed at food packs, fought, yelped, snarled, and barked, adding their voices to the general din of loudmouthed disputes over the ownership of property and loud-bawled curses of triumph or disappointment.

A pair of mild-eyed oxen ambled aimlessly about, and to add to the general confusion, half a dozen horses galloped frantically hither and thither, pursued by a dozen yapping dogs.

Tom turned from the scene to his own pile of duffel beside which the five Indian packers he had managed to hire were squatting about the inevitable tea pail hung above a little fire. Close at hand the foam-crested rollers surged against the shore with a deep, never-ceasing roar, and far away — nearly a thousand miles inland, beyond the mountains and the lakes and down a great river — was gold. Vaguely he wondered, as his gaze shifted from the milling men and women and strove to penetrate the fog, how many of them would find gold — how many would ever reach the Klondike where the gold was reported to be.

A querulous cry reached his ears: "Hey, drop that! That's mine!" And he turned to see a little old man snatch at a heavy "piece" that a larger man had lifted from the ground.

"Who says it's yourn? Leggo, damn you, before I flatten you!"

"It's mine! There's my mark! You can see —"

"Smack the old bastard down, Jack," the larger man growled as another joined him. "Knock his damn block off an' grab holt of one of them other pieces."

Without hesitation the man called Jack swung a huge fist that caught the oldster squarely in the face and he went down among the stones that littered the beach.

Tom Jorden leaped forward, and the next instant his fist crashed against the jaw of the man who had given the order, knocking him down with the heavy piece on top of him. The other leaped in, and as Tom turned to

2

meet the onslaught he tripped on a stone and both went down together, punching, jabbing, gouging as each struggled to regain his feet. Out of the tail of his eye Tom saw the first man he had hit wriggle from beneath the piece and disappear. With a mighty heave he slipped from under the man who pinned him down, and both gained their feet, punching and slugging, as the old man, his white beard red with blood, danced futilely about, his quavering voice raised in cries of "Thief! Thief! Help!"

But no help was forthcoming. Men were too busy hunting their property amid the hopeless tangle of goods to bother about a fight, with a dozen fights going on all about them.

It was then that Tom was aware of the girl — the girl he had seen on the boat. Instantly into his brain flashed the memory of her as she had stood at the rail limned against the afterglow, the keen breeze whipping her skirts about her knees as she stood looking out over the water, one hand resting on the rail while with the other she kept brushing back a stray wisp of auburn hair that persisted in blowing across her face. He remembered that he had thought her the most beautiful woman he had ever seen. Then she turned and her eyes met his for an instant, and Tom flushed deeply at being caught staring at her. And then she was gone. Twice after that he had seen her, but quickly avoided her, for fear of again being caught staring. And now her eyes met his once more, only for an instant, as she stood there beside the old man who was wringing his hands and calling for help. But in that fleeting instant he read

**3**

angry disapproval in the blue eyes. Then there was a blinding flash as the thug landed a blow that rocked him to his heels and sent him reeling backward as the shrill cries of the old man redoubled. As his opponent crowded in for the finish, Tom fought off the onslaught as best he could, guarding, warding off the flying fists with arms that seemed heavy as lead. Gradually his brain cleared, and again he was trading blow for blow, the girl forgotten as he concentrated his entire attention on the man who faced him toe to toe. Presently he realized that the other was tiring. His feet were wide apart, and the air rushed in and out of his lungs in great, audible gasps between lips that curled back to expose uneven, discolored teeth.

Summoning every ounce of his own waning strength, Tom leaped in, bringing his knee crashing upward into the other's groin. The man doubled at the middle, his thick lips writhing in agony, and as he went down Tom's right crashed into his jaw with a force that closed the open mouth with an audible clashing of teeth.

The man lay very still, curled like a grubworm at his feet, and across the body Tom's eyes again met the angry eyes of the girl. Only for an instant their eyes held. Her lips twisting into a sneer of contempt, she hissed the single word "Coward!" And then she was gone, and Tom stood there staring angrily after her until she was swallowed up in the crowd.

# CHAPTER
# TWO

## Sheep Camp

Sue Brandon sat beside her father on the last lap of the twenty-seven-mile trail to Sheep Camp and sipped tea from a tin cup that one of the Indian packers had filled for her from the pail that hung over the fire.

Outfits passed them — stolid-faced Indians, their bodies bent slightly forward under their two-hundred-pound packs, methodically placing one foot before the other with tireless regularity; and white men, most of whom had never carried anything heavier than a suitcase, sweating and panting over the trail under a half load.

"I wonder if they'll all find gold?" she mused aloud, her eyes on the grim, set faces of the men who passed in endless procession.

Sam Brandon smiled. "No. I'd say you could eliminate two thirds of 'em on the first sorting. I've been kind of looking 'em over since we landed — and a little on the boat, too — the few times I managed to go up on deck."

The girl laughed. "You're a rotten sailor, Daddy. If you only knew the wonderful scenery you missed! And the smell of the clean sea air!"

"Yes? Well, I'll get along very well, thank you, if I never see or smell another ocean. By gosh, I couldn't eat — couldn't sleep — just lay there in my bunk wondering how sick a man had to get before he could die."

"Cheer up. There are no more oceans between here and the Klondike — only lakes and rivers and mountains. What makes you think only a third of these men will find gold?"

"I don't think a third of 'em will find gold. What I said was that you could toss out two thirds of 'em on the first sorting — the ones that haven't got a chance. Of the third who are left, maybe one in ten will make good — maybe not so many."

"But why haven't these others got a chance?"

"The first third will never even try to find gold — tin-horn gamblers, thieves, crooks, grafters, parasites of all kinds — they're pouring into the country, as their kind pours into every new country to prey on the successful ones.

"The second third won't make good, for the reason they never made good where they were. They're the failures, the incompetent ones — the beaten, futile men who are making one last play for success. Men whose one hope is that their luck will turn at last. But it won't turn, because in this world I've noticed that a man's luck is pretty much what he makes it.

"In the ranks of the last third will be found the men who will make good — the young men, ambitious, full of high hope — men willing and eager to work and to fight for what they get — and the older men who have

6

confidence in their own ability and who, through the spirit of adventure or the lure of huge profits, are eager to take a fling at something new and big and worth while."

"But there must be luck in it too," the girl said. "Because you just said that only about one in ten of these last would make good."

"Oh sure — there's luck — a lot of luck. One man will dig here and get nothing. Another will dig there and uncover a fortune. But just remember — they're both digging, and digging like hell! They're working, and planning, and figuring every minute of the day to put themselves in line for the luck to strike. The second third, the ones who haven't a chance, are those who are too lazy or too dumb or incompetent to give luck a chance to strike 'em. This mining is a tough game — and it's the tough men who will win. And," he added, his eyes on the girl's profile, "as I told you before we started, I'm afraid it's too tough a game for a girl. This is just the prelude. You haven't seen anything yet."

Sue smiled. "Too tough for a girl, eh? Who was it that laid in a bunk all the way up here? And who was it that suggested we stop for a rest and a spot of tea?"

Her eyes lighted suddenly as she pointed to an old man who, with a light pack on his back, was walking at the head of a line of Indian packers. "Oh, there's the old man I was telling you about! The one who with his partner was attacked there on the beach!" She raised her voice and called to him: "I'm glad you saved your belongings! And how's your partner?"

7

The oldster stepped to the fire. "I never saved it," he smiled. "An' I ain't got no pardner."

The girl look puzzled. "But — your face was all bloody, and you were crying 'Thief!' and 'Help!' — and I saw that man attacking the one who was defending you. When he knocked him down I thought he had killed him — he lay there so still and all doubled up."

The man chuckled. "You kinda got it twisted around, sister. The one that got knocked out — he was the thief. Him an' another one. They was stealin' my stuff, an' when I tried to stop 'em, one of 'em fetched me a clout on the nose, an' the next thing I know'd, this young feller jumps in an' knocks the guy cuckoo that was makin' off with one of my pieces, an' the other one jumped him, an' they had a heck of a fight, an' — Well, you seen the end of it. Hadn't ben fer that young feller jumpin' in, they would of had my stuff — an' I couldn't done nothin' about it. A man could yell his head off down there, an' what with everyone tryin' to locate his own stuff, no one gives a dang what's happenin' to someone else — no one but that young feller. There's some man! Run off before I got a chanct to thank him. But whoever he is, I shore hope he makes a million! Well, I gotta be goin', er I'll never ketch up with them Injuns."

When the old man had passed out of sight, Sue glanced at her father. He was smiling. She frowned. "Oh yes, I know you've always told me to be sure of my facts, and I know what you're thinking — that I jumped at a wrong conclusion — and I did — you don't have to tell me." She sipped the rest of her tea, her glance searching the faces of the men who passed on the trail. "I ought to have known he was no thief," she said, more to herself than to Brandon. "I noticed him on the boat. He had rather nice eyes — and they sure did blaze when I called him a coward back there. If I run across him I'll tell him I'm sorry." Throwing out the tea leaves, she tossed the cup to an Indian. "Come on, let's get going. We want to make Sheep Camp and get the tent set up before dark."

Sheep Camp, the hellhole of the Dawson trail, located six miles from the Chilcoot Pass, was a conglomeration of tents, shacks, and sheet-iron warehouses. Water from melting snow stood ankle-deep in the so-called street, flanked on either side by planks supported on kegs or boxes, behind which monte dealers and shell-game grifters plied their trades, and by tent brothels sandwiched in between tent saloons and tent restaurants — all doing a thriving business. For, added to the hundreds that poured over the trail from Dyea Beach, where they had been dumped by the steamships, were those unfortunates who had been turned back at the Summit by the Northwest Mounted Police because of insufficient supplies. Those with money bought the required supplies at the warehouses, and those without money sought to make up their quota by robbery and theft. In Sheep Camp a man's goods were his own only so long as he could hold them. No semblance of law and order prevailed. Murder was of nightly occurrence, drunken men fought in the street by day, and the nights were rendered hideous by the cries and loud laughter of revelers and the howling and fighting of innumerable starving dogs of all breeds and descriptions, abandoned by their owners when found unfit for trail work.

Tough, sordid, and unromantic, Sheep Camp vaunted unordered humanity at its worst. Sue Brandon loved it — this splotch of blazing color on the long, long trail of gold. During the two days in which her father made the necessary purchases to bring his outfit up to police regulations for entry into the Canadian Yukon, the girl wandered about, never tiring of watching the passing show, fitting the various faces into the classifications Sam Brandon had made back there on the trail — the parasites, the incompetents, and the capable ones — the men who had a chance to make good. And always she sought a face — the face of the young man she had noticed on the boat, the face whose eyes had blazed angrily at her across the man who lay crumpled at his feet there on Dyea Beach. Already she had placed him with the favored third — with the young men full of high hope, willing to work and fight for what they got. For he was not only willing to fight for what he got, but to fight against odds for a perfect stranger because he was old and helpless and in trouble.

Just at dusk on the evening of the second day she strolled beyond the outskirts of the camp, breathing deeply of the keen spring air, wondering vaguely what adventures lay beyond the high barrier of the Chilcoot, that great white wall of rock and snow that towered grim and forbidding to the eastward. Sounds reached her ears: the incessant barking of dogs, an occasional

10

shout, a burst of hysterical laughter, and, blending with the burble of melting snow water that cascaded among the rocks of a swollen creek, the sound of an accordion and a squeaky fiddle where the nightly dance was already getting under way. This was the North — her North. She smiled as the words of her father recurred to her: "Too tough for a girl. This is only the prelude. You haven't seen anything yet." Her lips smiled. "If the main show is as good as the prelude, I'm going to love it!" she exclaimed aloud, and the smile twisted into a grimace of contempt as a fleeting panorama of her life flashed through her brain: school days, then the endless, meaningless round of social events, one day so like another that it seemed futile there should be a succession of days. "In a city you just exist," she murmured. "But up here you can *live!*"

There was a sound close behind her — the sound of heavy footsteps. She turned, and for the first time in her life she felt fear as her eyes met the leering eyes of the thickset, bearded man who confronted her.

"What — what do you want?" she asked, striving mightily to make her voice sound casual.

Thick, lecherous lips grinned. "I guess you know what I want, sister. The ground's good an' dry in under them trees. Come on. What's yer price?" Stark terror gripped the girl as the man's eyes seemed to devour her, to strip her naked before their foul, loathsome gaze. Her eyes darted here and there, seeking an avenue of escape; but there was no trail, and the ground beside the creek was heavily studded with boulders. Divining her intention, the man laughed. "No chanct, sister. I kin git around amongst them rocks a damn sight handier'n what you kin. I've got money — an' I'm askin' you what's yer price?"

"Too tough for a girl. This is only the prelude. You haven't seen anything yet." The words of her father flashed through her brain in letters of fire. Dear God — where was her father? Why had she strayed out here alone? She summoned her voice. "Go away!" she cried, unaware that the words came from her lips in a hysterical scream.

"Oh, so that's it? Yer one of the uppity ones, eh? Well, mebbe I ain't as good-lookin' as some of them high-toned gamblers — but I'm a man as gits what he wants, when he wants it. I'd of played fair — I'd of paid —"

"You're God-damned right you'll pay!" Out of the spruce thicket almost at the man's side stepped a figure, and once again Sue Brandon was staring into the blazing eyes of the young man she had seen on the boat. The next instant she was staring, wide-eyed, her fingers clutched over her heart that was pumping blood back into the face that had been drained of all blood, as the two men fought among the boulders. The fear that had gripped her gave place to a wild singing in her heart as she stared in fascination at the swinging fists and heard the vicious spat of iron-hard fists on bare flesh.

The thickset man was no mean antagonist, and a sharp cry escaped her as she saw her defender go down under a rush of blows. But he was up again, and she watched the pistonlike, almost rhythmic swing of his long arms as he sent blow after telling blow crashing against the face and the torso of the thickset man.

Then it was the other who was down, and again a sharp cry escaped her when she saw the knife in his hand as he rose to his knees. But the next instant the knife flew into the bush as the other's heavy pac landed against the knife wrist, and the man pitched forward and lay still as another kick from the pac caught him squarely under the chin.

The girl found her voice. "Oh — I — I — how did you happen to be here?" The words sounded foolish to her ears. For answer the man pointed toward the thicket of spruce. "I didn't like the camp, so I pitched my tent in there," he said shortly. "I heard what went on."

"Oh, I've — I've wanted to find you — to tell you I was wrong — back there on the beach. I thought —"

"It don't make any difference what you thought."

"I — but I want to thank you. Oh, if you hadn't been here —"

"Never mind the thanks. If you had any sense you wouldn't go prowling around a place like this alone. Better get back where you belong." The man turned on his heel and disappeared into the thicket, and Sue Brandon stood staring angrily at the spot where the spruce branches had closed behind him. For some moments she stood there. Then the anger faded from her eyes, and a peculiar little smile twisted the corners of her lips as with one loathing glance at the inert form on the ground she hurried in the direction of the camp.

# CHAPTER
# THREE

## As the Embers Died

Tom Jorden kindled his fire, and as the little flames licked about his tea pail he sliced salt pork into his frying pan. Presently he heard sounds from beyond the edge of the spruce copse, and then the thud of heavy footsteps which gradually diminished as the man he had knocked out picked his way among the boulders in the direction of Sheep Camp.

A slow grin twisted the corners of his lips as he nested the pan, and he flexed his fingers slowly as he contemplated his bruised knuckles. "Old Doc Leroy was right when he said this was a tough country," he muttered. "He said in a new country a man would find the best as well as the worst. Guess I haven't run across any of the best ones yet — unless —" The sentence remained unspoken, the words giving place to the vision of deep blue eyes that seemed to haunt the dusk beyond the firelight — changing eyes, eyes that had flashed scorn and anger into his own there on Dyea Beach, eyes that betrayed stark terror as she faced the thickset man among the boulders, eyes that had met his own in a hurt, reproachful look as he rudely told her it didn't make any difference what she thought, eyes that had once again flashed angrily as he told her she didn't have much sense and ought to go back where she belonged. "She hasn't got much sense, either," he muttered, in justification of his words. "Damn-fool girl. What's she doing up here, anyhow? She was alone on the boat, and alone on Dyea Beach, and alone here. And if she isn't alone, why in the devil doesn't whoever she's with look after her?" He scowled as he forked over the pork in the pan and caught himself wondering whether or not she were married. "She could be, for all I care," he muttered savagely. "I'll be hitting the trail tomorrow."

Supper over, he washed his dishes, filled his pipe, and propped himself against a tree, his eyes on the glowing coals. His brows drew into a frown as he realized that in the dying embers a vision kept repeating itself — the vision of a girl standing at a ship's rail, the wind tugging at her skirts, a wisp of auburn hair whipping across her cheek.

It was not that Tom Jorden hated women. He distrusted them. His own mother he had never known. Raised by an aunt whose main concern was for her own two children, young Tom had lived much within himself. And now, as he sat there staring into the slowly dying coals, he was reliving the twenty years of his life, or rather the fifteen years that had elapsed since that black day when the father he had adored had suddenly disappeared — disappeared under circumstances that had embittered the lad, driven him behind a wall of defense that had alienated him from the normal existence of the small-town boy and had created within

**15**

him an air of distrust — distrust of constituted authority and distrust of human motives.

John Jorden, a partner of his brother George in a hardware business located in a small town in the Minnesota wheat belt, had been accused of the murder of the local banker and, despite his vehement denial of the crime and his record of sterling citizenship, was arrested. With the evidence all against him, and realizing that he hadn't a chance in the world of establishing his innocence, he had broken away from the sheriff who was taking him to the county seat for trial and disappeared.

George Jorden, professing to believe in his brother's guilt, immediately moved from his rented house into the John Jorden home and, with a show of sanctimonious rectitude, took his five-year-old nephew into his family. And never from that moment on had Tom Jorden known what it was to get a square deal. Always, in the minds of George Jorden and his wife, their own children were right in the petty quarrels that arose between the youngsters. His cousin Billy, a year older than he, could, and always did, lick him in a scrap — and was never reprimanded for it, no matter what the provocation. His cousin Kate, a year younger than he, would tease and plague him until a well-deserved slap would send her howling to her parents, and Tom would receive a thrashing.

The elder Jordens continually harped on John Jorden's guilt in the boy's hearing and never let him forget that he was an object of charity, while George

Jorden calmly appropriated the entire profits from the store.

Among the townspeople only old Dr. Leroy believed in John Jorden's innocence. The others accepted the sheriff's view that he was guilty. Their reactions differed, however. Many held that Joel Stowe, the young banker, deserved killing, and they "didn't blame John Jorden a damn bit." Those were the ones who had lost money in the failure of the Stowe private bank. Others took the view that "murder is murder, and John Jorden ort to be hung."

And as their opinions differed, so did their attitude toward young Tom differ. Many pitied the lad and, realizing that he was in no wise responsible for his father's crime, leaned over backward to be kind to him. Others were openly hostile to him, yelling to their children to come away if they caught them in the lad's company, treating him as something loathsome. And, young as he was, the boy despised both camps. The result was that he lived within himself, trusting no one, making no close friends. For always he suspected any friendly advance as being inspired by pity, and he wanted no pity. He *knew* that his father was innocent. And he hated those who believed him guilty. Dr. Leroy he knew for a real friend — but no other.

So it was that when news of the gold strike in the Klondike reached the village, Tom, who was working for his uncle in the store, made up his mind to go. That evening, when he broached the matter, George Jorden refused to advance him a cent, pointing out that Tom was deeply indebted to him for fifteen years' board, lodging, and schooling. He did not know that the home he had been living in actually belonged to his father. He had often wondered, as he eyed the sign JORDEN & JORDEN on the canvas awning in front of the store, whether he wasn't entitled to more than the five dollars a week his uncle grudgingly doled out to him as spending money, but, never having had any justice, and knowing the attitude of the authorities toward his father, he had kept silent.

The next morning he arose at six, got his own breakfast as usual, packed his meager belongings into a telescope valise, and, with the twenty-six dollars that he had managed to save from his wages, walked down the street toward the depot. There was no hurry. He had three hours to kill before the ten-fifteen train was due.

The feel of spring was in the air that he drew deeply into his lungs as he walked slowly down the tree-shaded street. A robin caroled from the topmost branch of a bare maple, and Tom was conscious of a strange sense of elation. For the first time in his life he felt free — free to go where he pleased, to do as he pleased. Never again would he take an order from Uncle George. He was free of the hated house, the hated store, the whole hated little town. He wondered what Uncle George would say when he reached the store at nine o'clock, as was his custom, and found the door still locked. His lips tightened in a grim smile and he found himself hoping that his uncle would hurry to the depot to prevent his departure. "Get back to the store," he'll say. And I'll look him square in the eye and I'll say, "You go to hell." Yes sir, just like that I'll say it: "You go to hell."

And anyone standing around can hear me, and Bert Rice, the bus driver, will tell it around the hotel, and folks will be laughing at Uncle George behind his back, and Gene Richards and some of the others will kid him about it, and he'll be mad enough to blow up — and I hope he does.

As he walked slowly along the wooden sidewalk he glanced at the houses set back behind neat lawns — the houses of the people he had known all his life, the people who had pitied him and the people who had loathed him because he was the son of a murderer. But his father was no murderer! To hell with 'em! To hell with 'em all! He never wanted to see the town again, nor anyone that lived in it! They all believed his father was guilty, all but Dr. Leroy. Thought of the kindly old doctor turned his feet from the main thoroughfare at the next corner. He had plenty of time; he'd walk past the doctor's house, just so he'd be sure to remember it — it was the only thing in town he cared to remember.

The doctor's horse, hitched to the red-wheeled buggy, was tied to the hitching post in front of the gate, and as the boy passed, the old physician clicked the gate behind him, crossed the sidewalk, and swung the little black medicine satchel onto the seat. He paused with his hand on the hitch rein and eyed the boy with the canvas telescope.

"Hello, Tommy! Traveling this morning — or just going someplace?"

The boy's heart warmed at the homely greeting, and he smiled into the shrewd, kindly eyes. "I'm going to the Klondike," he said.

"The Klondike!" The doctor's eyes widened as he stared at the lad in astonishment. "You mean you're going up to hunt gold?"

"Yes sir."

"Well — dog my cats! What does old George think about that?"

"He told me I couldn't go."

The lips beneath the neatly clipped gray mustache smiled a bit grimly. "But when you told him you were going anyway, he came through with money enough to take you there, eh?"

"No sir. He wouldn't give me any money. He said I owed him for fifteen years' board and lodging and schooling and I'd have to stay on at the store and work it out."

"Did, eh? How long you been working in the store, Tommy?"

"Almost three years. Ever since I finished high school."

"George been paying you pretty good wages?"

"He gives me five dollars a week."

"How much money you got on you?"

"Twenty-six dollars."

"Twenty-six dollars! Know how far it is to the Klondike?"

"No sir. I know it's a long ways. But I'll get there somehow. When my money gives out, maybe I can work my way."

Tom Jorden noticed that the kindly gray eyes were not kindly now. The old man's face flushed until two red spots showed on the smooth-shaven cheeks, and there was a grim set to the thin lips. He pointed to the room at the corner of the house, above the door of which the word OFFICE appeared in gilt letters against a black background. "You go in there and wait till I come back," he said, the words sounding somehow hard and gritty.

"I — I want to catch the ten-fifteen for Minneapolis," the boy said.

"You've got plenty of time. It's only seven-thirty. I've got a call to make first — old Mrs. De Groat has got the bellyache. Then I'm going to have a little talk with George Jorden."

"I didn't open the store this morning," Tom said, "and he won't get down there till nine o'clock."

"I'll catch him at home then. Do as I say and wait till I come back. You'll find some magazines in there on the table."

It was after nine o'clock when the doctor returned. He smiled a bit grimly. "Had quite a little talk with old George," he said. "At that, I'd have been here sooner if I hadn't had to wait for the bank to open." Reaching into his coat pocket, he drew out a huge roll of bills which he counted out onto the table before the astonished eyes of the boy. "There you are, Tommy — five thousand dollars to go with your twenty-six."

The astounded boy stared at the pile of bills. Finally he found his voice. "But I — I can never pay it back, Doctor," he faltered. "I — I can't take it."

"You don't have to pay it back. It's yours — and it ought to be more — a lot more. But that's all the ready cash old George could scrape up — and you bet I

**21**

verified that at the bank! Just sign this receipt and take the money. And," he added with a grin, "I wouldn't worry too much if your uncle don't show up at the depot to see you off. The fact is George isn't feeling any too good this mornin'. He seems a little peeved about something."

"You mean — Uncle George gave me this?"

"Well," the doctor replied dryly, "he didn't exactly give it to you. In fact, he refused to give you a cent at first. So I had to sort of pry it loose from him. It's too long a story to go into now, but a few hints I dropped about the prosecuting attorney and the state prison at Stillwater changed his mind for him."

As one in a dream Tom Jorden gathered up the bills and pocketed them. "I — I don't know how I can ever thank you, Doctor."

"You don't have to thank me, son. Mighty glad I was able to do this for you — and for John Jorden. Good luck to you, Tommy. I believe you're wise in leaving this town. You've never got a square break here — and you never would get one. John Jorden was my friend. I've had my eye on you, Tommy, and I know how you feel about people. I don't blame you. The wonder is that you've kept a level head. You'll find folks a lot different from what you believe them to be. The common run of folks are good, Tommy. Most of the folks in this town are good people. But they haven't got sense enough to know that you didn't want their pity. You know and I know that John Jorden didn't kill Joel Stowe. John was a scrapper when he needed to be, but he was no murderer. And if you ever run across him, tell him I said so."

"Run across him!" the boy cried. "How could I run across him? Why, I — I wouldn't even know him! He's been gone for fifteen years! He'd be changed a lot from the way I remember him. And, besides, he's prob'ly using some other name."

"That's all true, Tommy. But you'll be using your own name. Maybe he'll run across you. I've got a hunch that when John Jorden slipped away from the sheriff, that day, he hit for Alaska, or somewhere up there in the Arctic. An old uncle of his used to sail on a whaling ship. He was wrecked, one time, somewhere along the Arctic coast, and in making his way inland to civilization he found some gold nuggets on a river. Later he showed those nuggets to your father — gave him some of 'em. John wanted to go back with the old sailor and find that river. But your mother wouldn't hear of it. Then you were born, and I guess John forgot the whole thing. But when he found himself on the run, I'll bet it all came back to him — and I'll bet he found some way to get up there, too."

"Gee," breathed the boy, "if I could only find my dad!"

"Stranger things have happened," the doctor said. "There prob'ly wern't many folks up there before this gold rush started. You might locate him among the old-timers. From all I hear and read, that's a tough country, Tommy. And there'll be a lot of tough men piling into it. You're on your own now — you've got to look out for yourself. And from what I hear, you're pretty well able to do it. And remember, Tommy, toughness is a virtue — if it's rightly used. Be sure you're right, then be as tough as the toughest of 'em — and a little tougher. Never hunt trouble. But if you've got to fight, fight to win. Never hit a man easy, Tommy — hit him with all you've got. Remember — in a new country you'll run up against the worst as well as the best. Good luck to you, boy. Jump in the buggy and I'll drive you down to the depot. The ten-fifteen's about due."

# CHAPTER
# FOUR

## Lake Lindeman

Beyond the Chilcoot, Lake Lindeman was still ice-locked. Ever-widening patches of rock and bare ground showed on the south slopes as innumerable freshets discharged their waters onto the snow-covered ice of the lake. A huge camp had sprung up here. In sharp contrast with the chaos that prevailed at Sheep Camp, the Lake Lindeman camp was a camp of law and order, the symbol of which was the British flag fluttering from the top of the pole that stood before the tent of Constable Burns of the Royal Northwest Mounted Police.

The snow, thawed to a sodden slush in the rays of the sun, froze to the hardness of iron at night. All day long men sloshed about, felling trees and whipsawing the logs into lumber. Each night a few sled outfits pulled out onto the lake and disappeared in the darkness — the outfits of the lucky ones who had managed to buy dogs. But for the most part the men at the Lindeman camp were building boats against the time when the ice would go out.

Young Tom Jorden pitched his tent, paid off his Indian packers, and sloshed across a small ravine to

**25**

watch two men, one standing on a scaffold, the other beneath him, whipsawing a log into lumber.

"Gawd," the bottom man grinned as the board was laboriously slabbed off and he paused to wipe the sweat and sawdust from his face, "if I'd only know'd enough to fetch in a portable sawmill, I could clean up more money right here than all the gold I'll ever dig in the Klondike an' be back home come summer."

The old man on top of the scaffold shunted the log into position for another cut and, noticing Tom for the first time, called a greeting:

"Hi there, young feller! Where the hell did you go to, down there on the beach? Knocked hell out of them two damn cusses that was stealin' my outfit an' was gone before I could tell you how I appreciated what you done fer me."

Tom laughed. "Oh, that's all right. Glad to take a crack at 'em. It was a dirty clip that man hit you."

"Yeah — but they didn't git fer. I seen the Mounted turn 'em back at the Summit. Served the damn thieves right. Got yer lumber sawed yet?"

Tom shook his head. "No, I just got here. Noticed forty or fifty of these saw outfits going and came over to see what it's all about."

The oldster chuckled. "You'll know all about it agin you git yer lumber sawed."

"But — what do I want with lumber?"

"Lumber to build you a boat — if you ain't got no dogs an' a sled. Cripes, it's six hundred miles down through the lakes an' down the big river till we git to where the gold's at!"

Tom's brow drew into a frown. "This sawing is a two-man job. I have no partner — and no saw — and no nails to build a boat with if I had the lumber."

"You can prob'ly hook up with a pardner, same as I done. Lot of fellas come in single — but from here on it's a two-man job. You can buy nails fer a dollar a pound, but you can't buy no saw."

He paused and pointed with pride to a pile of newly sawed boards. "We'll finish sawin' by tonight, an' you can have this one. Hunt you up a pardner, an' you can start in tomorrow."

"Okay. I'll buy your saw. Don't sell it to anyone else."

"Ben offered a hundred dollars fer it. I ain't sellin' it to no one. It's yourn. You can have this scaffold too. Cripes — you couldn't buy nothin' off'n me — after what you done down there on the beach!"

As Tom turned away he was accosted by a shrewd-eyed, elderly man who had paused at the edge of the ravine. The man smiled. "Looking for a partner? I couldn't help overhearing what the old man said. How will I do?"

Tom instantly liked this stranger — the humorous gleam in the shrewd eyes, the sound of his voice. He returned the smile. "Ever build a boat?" he asked.

"No. I even get seasick riding on the damn things. And I never sawed any lumber, either. How many boats have you ever built?"

"None. Maybe you better pass me up and find someone who's had more experience."

27

"I'm willing to take a chance, if you are," the man replied dryly. "You see, I overheard what the old man said about that scrap down there on the beach — heard about it from another source too. I have a hunch you're just the man I'm looking for. And seeing you're furnishing the saw and the scaffold, I'll attend to the nails. Brandon's my name — Sam Brandon."

"Mine's Tom Jorden."

"All right, Tom — it's a deal. And I'll bet we'll turn out a damn good boat. See you here in the morning."

"Okay, Mr. Brandon — I'll be here. But —"

"You mean 'Okay, Sam,'" the other interrupted. "To hell with the mister! It's got to be Sam and Tom if we're going to be partners. What was it you were going to say?"

"I was going to say what's the use in waiting till morning."

"Why — these men won't be through with the saw till tonight."

"Got an ax?" Tom asked. "The trees have to be chopped down before we can saw 'em."

Brandon grinned. "I get you," he said. "Be back in half an hour."

It was well toward noon when Tom looked up from his work of chopping a trunk into suitable lengths to find himself once again looking straight into the blue eyes of the girl with the auburn hair. Sam Brandon removed his cap and wiped the sweat from his brow on the sleeve of his shirt. "This is Tom Jorden, Sue — our partner." He turned to the younger man. "And, Tom, this is my daughter Sue."

The girl was smiling. "Oh, Mr. Jorden and I are old acquaintances. It's about time someone introduced us — isn't it, Mr. Jorden?"

Tom felt his face flushing, and Brandon hastened to explain: "She got you wrong down there on Dyea Beach, Tom. But she knows the straight of it now. The old man told us about it on the trail. That's the reason I picked you for a partner. It took guts to tackle those two thieves singlehanded."

The girl laughed. "And you don't know the half of it. I didn't tell you what happened at Sheep Camp. I figured one calling down was enough. Don't worry — we'll get along all right, won't we, Mr. Jorden — even if I haven't got any sense? And by the way, if we're going to be partners, that's the last time I'll call you Mr. Jorden — and if you ever call me Miss Brandon I'll scream."

As Tom searched for a reply it suddenly dawned on him that here was a girl who was neither despising nor pitying him. A lump rose in his throat. This girl was friendly, even as old Dr. Leroy was friendly. And Sam Brandon was friendly — more than friendly — he had spoken words of commendation. The words of the old doctor flashed into his mind: "The common run of folks are good, Tommy," and "You'll find people a lot different from what you believe them to be." He swallowed the lump in his throat and nodded. "Sure," he heard himself saying. "We'll get along."

"Come on," the girl said. "Dinner's ready, and you two must be hungry as wolves."

Tom turned toward his own tent, pitched on the opposite rim of the ravine. "I'll be ready when you get back," he said.

"You're coming with us!" the girl said. "When Daddy came back for his ax and told me he'd found a partner, I made dinner for three. If we three are partners, you bet I'm going to do my share! And if you think I'm going to cook good food and throw part of it away, you're crazy!"

Brandon grinned. "She's right, Tom. It's a three-way proposition from now on. And don't ever try to argue with a redhead."

The meal over, Brandon filled and lighted his pipe and glanced across at the girl. "What's all this that happened at Sheep Camp that you didn't tell me about?" he asked. "And who called you down? And what did you mean about not having any sense?"

Tom felt the blood mounting to his cheeks as the girl replied. "I took a walk one evening out beyond the outskirts of the camp, and a horrible creature must have followed me. Anyway, he started to — to attack me, and then I found out just how good Tom really is in fighting other people's battles for them. And when I tried to thank him, he told me to go back where I belonged and that I didn't have any sense to go prowling around alone. And he was right." She paused and glanced at the younger man. "But you were horrid when I tried to apologize for calling you a coward back there on the beach."

"Well — I — you see — I didn't know you then. I — I thought —"

30

"It don't make any difference what you thought," the girl giggled, quoting his own words, "and now we're even, let's get down to business. In the first place, we're going to move camp this afternoon. We'll pitch our tent there beside Tom's at the edge of the ravine. I'm not going to slosh half a mile through this slush every time I want to call you to a meal."

"But we haven't got any packers," Brandon objected.

"Packers! If the three of us can't move a ton of stuff half a mile in an afternoon, we'd better quit and go back right now!"

Tom nodded. "She's right," he said. "It will be much handier and it'll save a lot of time in the long run."

All during the daylight hours of the rapidly lengthening days the two men worked, adding plank by plank to their pile of lumber. After supper on the evening of the twelfth day Brandon eyed the result of their handiwork. "Guess we've got lumber enough," he said. "We can start building tomorrow."

Tom laid aside the cloth with which he had been drying the dishes as the girl washed them. "How are we going to build her?" he asked. "I've been sort of looking the boats over, and, believe me, they're all shapes and sizes. Most of 'em are square-ended scows sloped up at the bow and stern, with green spruce oars that are heavy as logs. It looks like they'd be mighty hard to handle even in fair weather — and a lake this size could kick up quite a sea in a high wind."

Brandon nodded. "The hardest job will be making her watertight with this rough lumber. There'll be seams half an inch wide to calk — and what are we going to use for calking?"

Sue Brandon threw out the dishwater, hung the pan on a convenient spruce stub, and seated herself between the two. "We'll build her sixteen feet long, and three feet wide at the bottom, and three feet and a half across the top. She'll have to be square-ended, because we haven't got any pattern and darn few tools. But if you plane the edges of the boards so they fit close, the seams won't be very wide."

"Plane 'em!" Brandon exclaimed. "What will we plane 'em with — the ax or the saw?"

The girl smiled. "If I were you, I'd use the plane. I bought one yesterday. Paid twenty dollars for it. I thought it would be worth that much to have a good tight boat. We've got three or four lakes to navigate and some pretty tough river water — what with the Box Canyon and the White Horse and Five Fingers Rapids."

The two men eyed the girl in undisguised surprise. "What do you know about building boats — and how many rapids there are in the river?" her father asked.

"What do you think I've been doing all day for the past couple of weeks while you two've been working?"

"Why — cooking, I suppose. You've kept us well fed, anyhow."

"Thanks for the compliment. But I've been doing a darn sight more than cooking. I didn't believe either of you knew very much about boatbuilding and were too busy to find out, so I've been nosing around looking the boats over, watching the men build 'em. I wasn't very much impressed with most of 'em. There are lots of boats being built in this camp that'll never reach Dawson City. But finally I found two men who really seemed to know how to go at it. One of 'em's a fur trader, and the other's a prospector, and they've been in the country for years — sourdoughs is what they call the old-timers. So I watched them build their boat and asked 'em a lot of questions. They were real nice about answering me — asked me how many there were of us and how much outfit we had, and when I told 'em they advised me what size boat to build. They said that most of the boats being built were either too small or else twice the size they needed to be — and twice as clumsy to handle. We're going to build a double bottom in her — the first one with the boards crosswise, and another one over that with the boards running lengthwise. And we're going to put a three-inch keel on her, and a rudder. We'll have oars — but we are going to depend mostly on the sail."

"Sail! Where in thunder are we going to get a sail?"

For answer the girl pointed to the two tents. "I'm going to rip one of 'em up and make a sail. One tent is enough for three people. I found a discarded blanket that I'll unravel for calking material, and we'll cover all the seams with pitch to make 'em watertight. They showed me how to gather the pitch from spruce trees and how to run it on the seams and iron it in with a hot stone. They finished their boat yesterday, so I bought their plane. They offered to give it to me, but I made 'em take the money, because I had heard a man offer 'em twenty dollars for it the day before."

"Well, I'll be damned!" Brandon exclaimed.

"All right, Captain," Tom said, smiling into the blue eyes. "You give the orders and we'll carry 'em out. It looks like you've got to be boss from now on."

"I don't want to be boss, Tom," the girl said, her eyes on his face. "I just want to help. After all, it's you and Daddy who do the work."

That night Tom Jorden lay for a long time in his blankets staring up at the gray canvas of his tent. And that night he dreamed a dream — a wild dream of two people sailing a boat on a stormy sea; a girl stood in the bow, a girl with blue eyes and a wisp of auburn hair whipping across her cheek, and there were rocks ahead, and white-water breakers, and the girl was shouting orders that he was vainly trying to carry out, and he knew that if he could only carry them out all would be well, but the sail was slatting wildly and the rudder was jammed, and the boat was rushing toward the rocks with the speed of an express train. But he never knew the end of the dream, because he woke up suddenly sitting bolt upright, and the moonlight filtering through the interlacing spruce branches was throwing curious patterns on the canvas.

# CHAPTER
# FIVE

## Tom and Sue Go Hunting

The days lengthened perceptibly. The bare patches widened on the slopes, and the lake ice honeycombed and turned black under the rays of the spring sun. Finally the boat was finished, to the calking and pitching of the last seam, and the following morning, with the help of a half dozen volunteers who were waiting impatiently for the breakup, she was skidded over the frozen snow and chocked on peeled skids ready for launching.

For a week the three had been living in the Brandon tent while the girl ripped Tom's tent to pieces and fashioned it into a sail. With the mast stepped and the sail rigged and furled, Sam Brandon eyed her with approval. "All we've got to do now is to load her, and knock the chocks out, and slide down to Dawson, slick as you please."

Sue smiled. "You always were an optimist, Daddy. From what those sourdoughs told me, there's going to be more to this 'sliding down to Dawson' than you seem to think."

"Nonsense! We've got a good boat, haven't we? And a sail to propel her down through the lakes, and after we hit the river it's all downstream — no current to buck. All we've got to do is sit in the boat and let the wind and the current do the work."

"But there are rapids and canyons to be run, and —"

"Suppose there are rapids and canyons! Other people have run them. And if they can, you bet we can. We've got the best boat I've seen around here. Look at the rest of 'em — damn clumsy affairs — look like overgrown horse troughs, most of 'em. Bet half of 'em'll tip over or sink before they hit the Yukon. Quick as this damn ice goes out we'll be on our way."

Followed then days of idle waiting, during which Brandon curbed his impatience as best he could, playing three-handed cribbage for two cents a point with Tom and Sue, poker with a half dozen other enforced idlers. A cold wave accompanied by snow squalls gave the breakup a three-day setback, but the morning of the fourth day dawned bright and clear, and after breakfast Sue got out a twenty-two rifle and turned to Tom.

"Let's go hunting," she said. "I saw some rabbit tracks out behind the tent and I'm dying for a taste of fresh meat."

As they passed the camp of the two sourdoughs on the outskirts of the big camp one of the men called a greeting: "Hello, Sis! How you comin' with yer boat?"

"It's all finished and ready to go as soon as we load it. We've got it on skids ready to slip into the lake just like yours there." She turned to Tom. "These are the two men who told me how to build the boat. I want you to meet them. This is Moosehide Charlie, a prospector from Dawson, and Mr. Gorman, a fur trader. And this is Tom Jorden, Daddy's and my partner."

The two acknowledged the introduction. "Jack Gorman," the trader corrected with a grin, "not Mr. Gorman. We don't go much on handles to names in this country. Down-river there's a couple of honest-to-God lords that come into the country a year back. First off it was Sir Arthur this an' Sir Lionel that — now one of 'em's 'Art' an' the other's 'Skookum' — an' they eat it up. It don't make no difference who a man was nor where he come from in this country. It's what he is when he gits here that counts."

"Goin' huntin'?" Moosehide asked.

Tom grinned. "Yes. I suppose it looks kind of ridiculous in this country to go hunting with a twenty-two."

"Why?"

"Why — er — this is a big-game country, isn't it? I didn't suppose you fellows would bother with anything smaller than a moose or a bear."

Moosehide laughed. "Most of the cheechakos comes in packin' a cannon, expectin' to find a moose er a bear settin' on every rock. Take it this time of year the bears ain't come out of their dens yet, an' the moose an' caribou are so damn pore an' stringy a man couldn't chaw the meat if he killed one. When it comes to meat gettin', except in the fall, give me a twenty-two every time. The ducks an' geese an' swan will be along pretty quick now — an' there's rabbits an' ptarmigan in the bush. Jest edge along them slopes where the sun hits, an' you'd ort to get a mess of meat in no time."

Heading up a ravine, the two threaded their way among the huge rocks and sparse growth until noon brought them out on a huge flat rock high above the lake. They had taken turns with the twenty-two, and the girl stood the light rifle against a spruce stub and seated herself on the rock. "Whew — I'm kind of tired," she said, eying the two rabbits and five ptarmigan that Tom tossed to the rock beside her. "And famished too," she added. "I wish we'd brought a lunch. I'm hungry enough to eat one of those birds raw!"

"No use eating it raw," Tom smiled. "I'm hungry too. Why not build a fire and roast a couple of 'em? I'll bet they'd be good, even without salt."

"Fine!" the girl cried. "You rustle some wood and get the fire going, and I'll clean 'em. Then we can roast 'em over the flames on sticks!"

The meal over, the two sat with their backs against a rock, enjoying the warm sunshine. "I'm going to love this country," the girl said abruptly, her gaze fixed on the vast expanse of sun-blackened ice and towering heights beyond. "And the people too — the sourdoughs, I mean — like Moosehide Charlie and Jack Gorman. They're so — so genuine — so real. There's nothing put-on or artificial about 'em. When they say something you just instinctively know they mean it."

Tom nodded, his eyes on the girl's profile. "Yes," he said, "I'm going to love it too."

She glanced at him, and he felt the blood mounting to his cheeks as it had mounted that other day on the boat when she had turned and caught him staring at her. "I've lived in a city all my life," she said, "and I'm nineteen, and what have I ever accomplished? Nothing — just absolutely nothing. I've existed, and that's all. I've been through high school and two years of what they call a finishing school where I learned to do fancy needlework, and dance, and play whist, and ride horseback, and which fork and spoon to use with which course, and not to say 'damn,' and" — she paused for a moment, as if trying to remember what else she had learned, then said vehemently — "and not one damn thing that's any good to me!"

Tom smiled. "If you've forgotten the rest of it like you've forgotten about 'damn,' I guess what you learned won't hurt you any."

The girl laughed, then her eyes became serious. "But honestly, I mean it, Tom. I haven't learned a thing that's going to be any good to me in this country!"

The smile broadened. "Well, Sue, when you come to think of it, you'd hardly expect 'em to teach you to drive dogs, and carry packs, and make sails, and build boats in a girls' school."

"No. But they could have taught practical sewing and cooking and things like that. You bet I wished I'd had some lessons in sewing when I was making that sail!"

"You did a good job of it without lessons," Tom said, "and you've done a good job with the cooking too. You don't need to worry, Sue. Whatever you set out to do, you'll do it well. You've got it in you. We're both in the same boat. We've got to learn as we go along. We'll probably make mistakes — plenty of 'em. But we'll learn. And in the long run we'll win."

"Sure we will! Oh, it's a grand country, Tom! And it's doing wonders for Daddy, too. He and his partner owned a machine-tool factory in Indianapolis. But he's been so — so kind of restless and lost ever since my mother died a year ago. He'd always been a good businessman, but he seemed to lose interest in business after her death — seemed not to care. Then this gold strike came, and when he talked of selling out and coming up here, I encouraged him. And it wasn't all on account of the business, either. There was a woman — a horrible creature. She was a grass widow, and blonde. I suppose most men would call her pretty. Daddy met her at a party somewhere, and she'd keep calling him up, and he'd take her out to dinner and to the theater. Everybody could see that she was just after Daddy's money — everybody but Daddy. Why, she isn't much older than I am! If he'd married her and brought her home I'd — I'd have *clawed her!*" She paused for a moment, then asked abruptly, "Do you like blondes, Tom?"

"No," Tom said. "I don't like any women. That is," he hastened to add, "I never liked any women till — till — I saw you that day on the boat."

The girl laughed. "You didn't like me then, either. Why, that day on the beach when I called you a coward you were so angry your eyes fairly blazed. And there at Sheep Camp, when you wouldn't give me a chance to apologize and told me I didn't have any sense, you certainly didn't like me then."

"I didn't know you then. How did you get Sam away from that woman?"

"Oh, I did some inquiring around, and one night I made Daddy take me out and we crashed a party to which he hadn't been invited. He saw plenty — and a day or so later he sold out to his partner — and here we are. And oh, Tom, it's just the grandest adventure in the world! Just think, by this time next year we might all be millionaires!"

Tom nodded, his eyes on the little white dots that were the tents of the Lindeman camp at the head of the lake far below. "Yes," he said somberly, "and then you'll be going back — back to your parties, and your horseback riding, and your fancy sewing. And all the things you learned at that school will seem important again. And this" — he paused and with a sweep of his arm indicated the mighty panorama of vastness — "all this will be just part of your grand adventure. You won't forget it. You'll never forget it. It will be something like this: 'Oh yes, I went to the Klondike with my dad way back in '98 — you remember — the time of the big gold rush. We landed on a beach somewhere and had to walk for miles and hire Indians to carry our packs, and we went in over the Chilcoot Pass and came to the shore of a lake. And the lake was frozen and there were no dogs, so we had to build a boat and wait for the ice to go out. We met a young man — let's see — his name was — well, I can't remember now — it don't make any difference — and we built a boat and went on down to Dawson together, and —'"

"Tom Jorden, I think you're horrid! I'm not going back! I'm never going back! I love this country, and I'm going to stay here always! It's big — and elemental —

and — and worth while!" She paused abruptly, and her eyes fixed on his with a peculiar burning intensity. "Are you going back?" she demanded. "When you've got all the money you want, are you going back where you came from? Doesn't all this mean anything to you — except just a place to dig gold?"

"I love it," he said simply. "I'm never going back. I'm going to stay here till I die."

The girl heaved a deep sigh. "We'll both stay here," she said. Then, abruptly: "Do you know, Tom, you've never told me anything about yourself — why, I don't even know where you came from!"

Tom Jorden was on the point of pouring into the girl's ears the sordid story of his life, of unburdening his very soul, when into his brain flashed a vision of the small town he had left forever — his aunt and his brat of a cousin, the girls who had been his schoolmates, his prim schoolteachers, the women he had served over the counter of the hardware store — those who had pitied, and those who had scorned. Here on the rock beside him was the one girl in the world who treated him as an equal, who appraised him at his worth, who neither pitied nor scorned him. If she knew the truth — Deep down in his heart he knew she would not scorn him, but would she pity? He dared not risk it. "I came from Minnesota," he said almost gruffly. "Come on, we'd better be getting back. The sun will be down by the time we get there — and we've got to shoot a couple of more birds for supper."

42

# CHAPTER
# SIX

## The Sourdoughs Give Advice

The days that followed were days of bright sunshine that rotted the ice and sent the snow water rushing down from the hills in torrents. They were days, too, during which an intangible barrier of restraint grew up between Tom Jorden and Sue Brandon. Twice Tom suggested another hunting expedition, but each time the girl made some excuse. Sam Brandon fretted at the delay and played poker.

Then one morning the whole camp sprang into feverish activity. A strong south wind had sprung up during the night, and daylight showed a slowly widening shore lead. Boats were shoved into the water, some promptly capsizing from top-heavy loads, while in others men bailed frantically to throw out the water that seeped in through ill-calked seams. Shouts and curses filled the air — and bursts of loud laughter. Tents disappeared like magic, and pack-laden men waded belly-deep in the icy water, carrying their goods to the boats.

While Sue busied herself with breakfast the two men hurried to the shore, where a hundred boats of all shapes and sizes already jammed the narrow lead as their owners worked feverishly to load them.

Tom grinned. "You'd think their lives depended on being the first to get away. I'll bet half of 'em didn't stop to eat breakfast."

"Probably not," Brandon agreed. "But they're wise in getting an early start. After all, at a time like this it's 'first come, first served.' Those who get to the Klondike first will get the pick of the locations."

The younger man glanced with pride at their own boat poised on its skids ready for launching. "Yes, but when we get going we'll pass 'em like nobody's business."

"Sure we will. But the sooner we get going, the sooner we'll get there. I'll bet we can load her right where she is, then knock out the chocks and let her slide in. Damned if I want to wade out in that cold water carrying the stuff out to her!"

"Better not stow the whole load till we see how she floats," Tom advised. "I'd say put in about a third of the stuff and launch her, and I'll pack the rest out and trim her up. I don't mind cold water."

"Okay — but let's be getting at it. Come on. Sue must have breakfast ready by this time. If she hasn't, we can take the tent down anyway."

"I don't believe we need to be in such a hell of a hurry," Tom said as he followed Brandon to the tent where the girl was waiting.

"I thought you'd never come!" Sue cried, her eyes dancing with excitement. "Breakfast's all ready. I was just about to hunt you up. Oh, isn't it grand — the ice going out? I can hardly wait to get started!"

**44**

Brandon frowned. "Me too," he said. "But Tom, here, seems to think there's no need to hurry."

"No need to hurry!" the girl cried with a reproachful look at the younger man. "Do you want all these people to beat us to Dawson?"

"I don't think many of 'em will beat us. There are so many boats in the water now we couldn't pass 'em till the lead widens."

"It'll take us half a day to break camp and pack this stuff to the lake," Brandon said. "And if this wind keeps up, there'll be plenty of room to pass 'em. The lead's widening every minute."

"Of course it is!" the girl seconded. "And look all around us! Nearly all the other tents are down, and the men are working like beavers packing their stuff to the boats. And we're just eating our breakfast!"

Tom grinned. "I'll bet a lot of the others will wish they'd eaten theirs before night. And I'll bet a lot more of 'em'll wish they hadn't been in such a devil of a hurry."

"Nonsense!" Brandon snapped. "Here we've been waiting and waiting for God knows how long for the breakup to come so we can get started. And now it's here, you say there's no need to hurry! As I told you a few minutes ago, it's 'first come, first served.' That's an old saying — and a true one. And it certainly applies in a case like this."

"'Haste makes waste' is another saying, and probably just as old and just as true," Tom replied stubbornly. "And it applies in this case too. Didn't you notice the stuff those men were abandoning — leaving

**45**

it there on the beach because they wouldn't take time to load their boats properly?"

Both the others scowled, and Brandon regarded him shrewdly. "What's got into you, Tom?" he asked abruptly. "It was because that old man told us there on the trail how you sailed into those two thugs and saved his outfit for him back on the beach that I picked you for a partner. I knew you had guts. And that first day, when I told you we'd start work the next morning, you pointed out that we could start right then — that the trees had to be felled before they could be sawed. I knew you were up and coming — right on the job. And you've been right on the job every minute since. In fact you've done a damn sight more work than I have. And now — when the time comes to cash in on this work — you hold back. What's the answer? What's the reason? You certainly must have a reason. What's your argument against getting out of here as quick as we can?"

As the two waited for him to speak a flash of suspicion, of vague distrust, flashed into the girl's mind. What did they know of this man they had taken for a partner? Nothing, absolutely nothing, beyond the fact that he was willing to fight in defense of helpless persons. That certainly was a point in his favor, but why hadn't he told her something of himself? During all the days of their acquaintance he had never once mentioned his past. And there on the rock that day, when she had told him something of her own life and had reminded him that he had never told her anything about himself, he had shut her up with the gruff

46

announcement that he came from Minnesota — and not another word had she got out of him. Why? Why was he deliberately concealing his past? Was he a criminal flying from the long arm of the law? Maybe his name wasn't Jorden. They had only his word for it. But even if he were a criminal, what possible motive could he have in delaying the start for the Klondike? If he were trying to elude the law, the more miles he placed between himself and the scene of his crime, the better he'd be off. Could there be some deep, ulterior motive in his strange attitude?

Tom was quick to read doubt in Brandon's eyes — suspicion, distrust in the eyes of the girl. "I have a reason," he said, "but no argument." And at his next words all distrust and suspicion vanished from the girl's mind. He pointed to a little white tent on the edge of the camp. "My reason for not hurrying is that those two men, Moosehide Charlie and Jack Gorman, the men who told us how to build our boat, the only two men in the whole camp who know the country, are not hurrying. They're just as anxious to get to Dawson as anyone. But their tent is still up, and their boat is still on her skids. And they're not falling all over themselves packing their outfit to the lake. Let's go over and talk to them. I'll bet they've got an argument. And I'll bet it's a good one."

"Tom's right, Daddy!" the girl exclaimed. "I've been so excited watching the others that I never noticed what Moosehide and Jack Gorman were doing. They know more than all the rest of us put together."

47

"When in Rome, do as the Romans do." Tom grinned, quick to note the change in the girl's attitude.

Brandon nodded slowly, his eyes on the younger man's face. "You've got a pretty good head on you, son," he said. "Damn it, I ought to have thought of that myself! Come on, let's go have a talk with 'em."

The three found the two sourdoughs squatting on either side of the little fire in front of their tent, sipping tea out of tin cups and regarding the frantic efforts of the swarming men with amused tolerance.

Moosehide looked up and smiled as the girl rounded the corner of the tent closely followed by the other two. "Hello, Sis! Why ain't you sloshin' around up to yer chin in the lake like all the rest of the cheechakos?"

Brandon smiled. "Hoosiers — not cheechakos," he corrected. "We're from Indiana, my daughter and I."

"Indiany, eh?" Gorman said. "Well, that's a damn good place to be from — a hell of a ways from, I'd claim. In this country everyone that ain't a sourdough's a cheechako, no matter whether they come from Indiany er Timbucktoo. At that, I'll bet Sis here'll be a sourdough long before most of these here folks knows what it's all about. She ain't afraid to ask questions — an' by the looks of yer boat, she savvies what you tell her. Me an' Moosehide was lookin' her over yesterday — an' believe me, she's the only boat in the hull damn camp I'd hit out fer Dawson in, except ourn here."

The girl laughed. "We've come to ask you some more questions. Daddy and I were for getting started, so all these others wouldn't beat us to the Klondike. But

48

Tom, here, noticed that you didn't seem to be in any hurry, so we came over to find out why."

"It seems to me," Brandon said, "that the sooner we get started, the sooner we'll get there. With the ice going out, I can't see any reason for delay."

Moosehide Charlie slanted him a glance. "Yeah?" he asked dryly. "Where's it goin' to?"

"Why — why — it's moving away from here. That looks like our only concern. It gives us water to float the boat in."

Moosehide nodded. "That's what these cheechakos thinks. Ever ben to the other end of the lake?"

"No."

"We have — an' the river that runs out of it ain't no wider'n from here to that tree yonder. Do you figger all this ice is goin' on down through that river an' leave the lake clear?"

"Probably not. But — it's going someplace. It's going away from here."

"Yeah? Well, believe me, brother, that ice ain't goin' no place it can't come back from, onct the wind changes. She's shovin' up on the other shore — but she can't only shove so fer. Then she'll hold. That lead's damn near as wide a'ready as it's goin' to be. Then tonight, like as not, the wind'll change, an' the ice'll come back an' shove up on this shore — an' all them damn fools will be onloadin' agin an' tryin' to get their boats out."

Gorman assented. "An' they're goin' to be in a damn sight bigger hurry gittin' 'em out than they was gittin' 'em in."

"But," cried the girl, "won't a lot of 'em be smashed up and lost?"

"Shore they will. Two, three days from now there'll be plenty of them cheechakos standin' around here with nothin' but the clothes on their back. It won't take 'em long to git outfitted, though," he added, indicating the litter of discarded supplies. "Cripes, them damn fools throw'd away enough stuff to take a hundred men to Dawson."

"But — why don't you warn 'em?"

Moosehide grinned and pointed to the boats into which men were stowing supplies. "We did warn thirty, forty of 'em — but that's all the good it done. We give it up when we seen it wasn't no use. They told us that if we was afraid, they wasn't — an' kep' right on with their loadin'."

"They'd ruther learn the hard way," Gorman added. "At that, mebbe it'll stay by 'em longer."

"But that policeman, Constable Burns — why doesn't he warn them?" the girl asked.

Moosehide grinned. "He's a cheechako too. If Corporal Downey was here it would be different."

"How long will this condition last?" Brandon asked. "With that huge field of ice drifting about the lake, shifting direction with each shift of the wind, we might be held here a month!"

" 'Tain't likely," Moosehide opined. "Few days more of hot sun'll rot the ice. She's rotten a'ready, but not rotten enough. She's all in one solid chunk yet. When she gets good an' rotten, you'll see big zigzag leads openin' up all over. Then when a good wind hits her, she'll break all up into icicles an' sink. That's the real breakup."

"It don't sink," Gorman corrected. "It melts."

"Have it yore way," Moosehide grinned. "I shore as hell ain't goin' to dive down to the bottom an' see."

"So you think it's only a matter of days?" Brandon said.

"Yeah — barrin' a cold snap. She'd tighten up, then, an' take longer."

"But in the meantime won't those men get an awful start on us?"

Moosehide laughed. "If a cold snap hits, that lead'll freeze an' all them boats will be worst off than ever. In this country a man learns that it ain't the start he gets that counts — it's how he finishes."

Brandon nodded thoughtfully. "That's a true saying, if ever there was one," he said. "We're mightily obliged to you men. We'll act on your advice."

"See you in Dawson," Moosehide grinned. "An' that's a damn sight more'n I could say to most of them others."

As the three reached their own tent Brandon glanced at Tom. "Well, you got your argument, boy," he said. "How about a game of cribbage? My poker pals have gone."

# CHAPTER
# SEVEN

## When the Ice Went Out

As Moosehide Charlie had predicted, the ice became stationary about noon, and the lead ceased to widen. The flotilla of boats strung out along the shore line and disappeared, leaving only those whose capsizing necessitated the drying of cargos and those which leaked so badly as to necessitate recalking.

All the following day it rained. The wind veered into the north during the night, and the rain turned to sleet and finally to a fine, flinty snow. Then the ice came back. The three were awakened by the sound of it and at daylight hastened to the beach to stare in awed fascination at the four-foot-thick ice, forced ashore by the relentless power of billions of wind-driven tons, reared high among the rocks and broken off in huge slabs that crashed and slivered with the roar of a thousand thunders.

Shielding her cheek from the bite of flinty particles with a mittened hand, the girl pointed with the other to the smashed and twisted planking of the half dozen craft that had been drawn clear of the water for recalking. "Just think," she said with a shudder, "our boat might have been like those if — if —"

"If Tom hadn't had sense enough to notice that those two sourdoughs hadn't broken camp," her father interrupted. "I guess we owe everything we've got — maybe even our lives — to you, my lad," he added, turning to the younger man. "It's a thing we won't forget." The man pointed into the blinding smother that obscured the shore line along which the boats had disappeared. "My God, I shudder to think what is happening out there — misery, suffering — death itself!"

"And in weather like this!" Sue added in a voice that sounded hoarse with horror. "It's terrible! Oh, isn't there something we can do?"

Tom shook his head and pointed to the crashing, grinding ice fragments and the steep, almost perpendicular shore. "Not a thing in the world. Most of the boats are miles away from here, and no one could travel that shore line. Even if he could, there's nothing he could do when he got there."

"That's right," agreed a voice close behind him, and the three turned to see Moosehide Charlie and Jack Gorman. "Them damn fools know'd it all," Moosehide said. "They made their own bed — an' they've got to lay in it, fer all anyone can do."

"We told 'em what could happen, an' they laughed at us," Gorman added. "It's our turn to laugh now — but a man can't laugh at a thing like this. Couple of days from now they'll begin stringin' back, an' there's goin' to be hell to pay when they git to clawin' an' fightin' over this stuff they throw'd away." He pointed to the

53

sleet-crusted litter of goods that lay where it had been abandoned in the wild scramble to get away.

"But — did they throw away food?" the girl asked.

"Shore they did!" Moosehide exclaimed in disgust. "About half them boats was bigger'n what they needed to be, an' tother half was too small. Me an' Jack watched 'em load. They'd start packin' their stuff down to the lake an' dumpin' it in their boats, regardless of what it was er how bad it was needed. An' when the boat would get so full it was damn near ready to sink, they'd leave the balance of their stuff — grub, clothes, tent, even blankets — an' climb in on top of the load an' shove off. By God, if there's a wrong way to do a thing, you bet them cheechakos will figger it out!"

Brandon pointed to the ice barrier that had formed ten to twenty feet high along the beach. "It isn't piling up very fast now. The wind must be letting up."

"The wind ain't let up none," Moosehide said. "The ice has shoved in about as fer as it can git."

"How in thunder are we ever going to launch our boat?" the older man asked, eying the ten-foot ridge of ice that lay between the craft and the lake. "Wait for that ice to melt?"

Gorman grinned. "That would be one way. But it might take quite a while. Better do like me an' Moosehide's goin' to, quick as this snow lets up, an' chop it out. 'Tain't no hell of a chore, rotten as it is. It's honeycombed more'n halfways through. You can do it easy before the ice backs away agin. When it goes out this time, I've got a hunch it'll stay out."

The work of chopping a lane wide enough to admit passage of the boat proceeded as the survivors of the ill-fated exodus straggled back with tales of hardship and misery and loss — and of death — death by drowning, death amid the grinding, crushing ice cakes, and death from exposure. And, as Gorman had predicted, there was hell to pay as these survivors fought among themselves for possession of the sodden, abandoned goods. Constable Burns had pulled out with a pack on his back during the snowstorm to make a survey of the situation and do what he could for the relief of the sufferers. And without the restraining presence of the Law, the Lindeman camp became Sheep Camp on a small scale, as more and more of the impoverished survivors drifted back.

Many of these survivors hit the back trail, some hoping to reoutfit at Sheep Camp, some discouraged by the catastrophe, hoping only to reach the coast and find some means of transportation back where they came from. Abandoned saws were plentiful, and a few indomitable souls went to work getting out lumber for new boats. But for the most part the unfortunates milled about like a pack of wolves, ravishing the abandoned stores, salvaging anything they could lay their hands on and fighting for possession of it.

Not daring to leave Sue alone with the outfit, Tom and Brandon took turns chopping at the ice barrier and standing guard over their goods with Tom's heavy rifle.

Out on the lake the ice got blacker as the sun beat down on it from a cloudless sky. New leads showed — long, irregular lanes and wide ponds of open water.

**55**

Ducks skimmed low over the ice and settled in great rafts on the water, while high overhead huge flocks of wild geese winged northward, filling the air with their honking.

The cut through the barrier was finally completed, and the three waited impatiently for the change of wind that would clear the lake of ice.

Broad daylight grayed the interior of the tent when Sue Brandon awoke one morning. The canvas was shuddering and tugging at its guy ropes, and the girl lay in her sleeping bag for several minutes drowsily listening to the roar of wind in the spruce tops. Suddenly she sat upright. Wind! It was what they had been waiting for — the wind that would move the ice. Her father was snoring on the opposite side of the tent, and, hastily slipping into her clothes, she raised a corner of the square of canvas that served as a curtain partitioning off Tom's sleeping quarters. His sleeping bag was empty, and, stepping hurriedly from the tent, she stood for a moment peering toward the lake. Even in the half-light of early dawn she could see it — blue water, flecked by whitecapped waves stretching as far as the eye could see. The ice was gone! Wildly she raced toward the beach; then suddenly she halted and stared wide-eyed at the spot where the night before the boat had stood on its peeled skids, ready for launching. The peeled skids were there, but the boat was gone! And Tom Brandon was nowhere in sight. For long moments she stood there, her brain groping for the answer. Had Tom launched the boat, and was it riding at anchor in the shallow water, waiting to be loaded? Dashing

**56**

through the ice barrier, she gazed out over the lake. But she saw only the wind-riffled water of the shallows — and in the distance the whitecapped waves. Suddenly her eyes focused upon a tiny speck of gray far out among the tossing waves — a boat — a boat with a sail set disappearing into the north. Whirling in her tracks, she paused only to give one glance in the direction of the camp of the sourdoughs, then dashed for her own tent and fairly tore the flap aside. "Daddy!" she cried in a voice pitched almost to a scream. "Daddy — wake up! The boat's gone! And Tom's gone! Moosehide Charlie and Jack Gorman are gone too!"

# CHAPTER
# EIGHT

## Pursuit

Tom Jorden opened his eyes in the early dawn, and as his senses grasped the import of the dull, all-pervading roar he slipped from his sleeping bag, drew on his clothing, and passed noiselessly out into the dim half-light. As he stood for a moment peering toward the lake, vainly striving to pierce the semidarkness, he was conscious of a sinking sensation in the pit of his stomach — a strange sense of impending disaster. Slipping and stumbling among loose stones, discarded pieces of outfit, and the slash left by the whipsawyers, he came upon the empty skidway where the evening before the boat had stood ready for launching. Dimly, through the cut in the ice barrier, he could see the open water of the lake, and, dashing through, he stood at the edge and strove to pierce the gloom. But within the few yards of visibility was only the wind-riffled water. His brain seemed numb. The boat was gone. The boat that Sue had planned and that he and Sam Brandon had worked for weeks to build — the boat that was to carry them proudly and safely to the promised land of gold — was gone. Over and over in his numbed brain that single word repeated itself . . . gone . . . gone . . . gone.

A sense of utter futility, of utter discouragement, obsessed him. Vaguely he realized that he loved that boat, loved it as he had never loved any other possession, loved it because he had helped to build it with his own hands, loved it because it was his boat — and Sue Brandon's — and it was gone. Sue loved the boat too. She had hovered about, watching the driving of every spike — had collected the pitch and the chinking material and with her own hands had helped to calk her. He visualized the drooping of the sensitive lips, the bitter disappointment in the blue eyes when the girl learned of the loss. Tom's shoulders stiffened as at the thought his sense of discouragement changed suddenly to flaming anger. He could feel the hot blood surging into his cheeks as his blazing eyes sought to penetrate the slowly widening arc of visibility. He could see the tossing whitecaps now, beyond the little riffles of the protected shallows. The boat was nowhere in sight, but he knew that somewhere out among those wildly pitching waves she was sailing sturdily northward — and that the thieves were exulting, chuckling among themselves over their easy conquest.

Tom Jorden had had fights in his life, plenty of fights. His whole boyhood had been one long succession of fights with boys who had taunted him about his father. At first he had sailed into those tormentors, tears of anger blinding his eyes, fists flailing wildly. But as time wore on, and he realized that he was getting licked more often than he won, he methodically learned to fight. Long before he was through high school he was known as the best boxer and the toughest fighter in town, and in the gymnasium no one would put on the gloves with him. And the taunts of his tormentors diminished as his ability with the gloves increased, for he no longer sought to avenge the taunts with flailing fists and tear-dimmed eyes blazing with anger, but rather with eyes that narrowed in cold rage and blows that were driven home with calculating precision — blows that battered, and smashed, and hurt when they landed.

So now the flaming anger of the first few moments crystallized into cold fury, and as he turned away he muttered between clenched teeth, "I'll get her back. By God, if I have to follow 'em clear through to Dawson, I'll get her back! And whoever's got her will never steal another boat."

Hurrying along the shore, he saw, before he reached the spot, that the tent of the sourdoughs was nowhere in sight. Redoubling his pace, he negotiated the slot in the barrier through which they had launched their boat, just in time to see Tom Gorman working at the tiller as Moosehide Charlie hoisted the sail. The heavily laden craft was already in motion, swinging her blunt nose northward as the wind caught the sail, when without a moment's hesitation Tom dashed into the water, waded belly-deep through the shallows, grasped a gunwale, and, with the two sourdoughs staring in wide-eyed surprise, drew himself aboard.

"What the hell!" cried Gorman, shoving the tiller hard around as the sail bellied out in the wind and the boat slowly gathered speed.

**60**

Moosehide Charlie made the rope fast to a cleat and, eying the dripping figure that faced him across the carefully stowed duffel, he grinned. "Goin' someplace?" he asked. "Er jest drop in fer a call?"

"I'm going to get the damn thieves that stole our boat — if we can overtake 'em!" Tom replied.

"Stole yer boat! You mean someone got away with it in the night?"

"That's right. It's gone. I don't know how far they've got. Maybe when full daylight comes we can sight 'em. And if we can overhaul 'em, they'll wish to God they'd never tried to steal her!"

Moosehide peered lakeward over the rolling white-caps. "She ain't nowheres in sight," he said after a prolonged scrutiny. "But that don't spell nothin'. Cripes, they might be miles away, er they might be jest around the first pint — 'cordin' to what time they got started. The wind picked up jest about midnight, an' rotten as the ice was, it wouldn't take long to bust up."

Gorman nodded agreement and eyed the cargo. "We've got a pretty good load aboard," he said, "an' we can't make no fast time. Chances is them damn cusses won't have much cargo in your boat — only what they could rustle amongst that abandoned stuff."

"Hell," Moosehide exclaimed, "there was stuff enough throw'd away to fill forty boats! It's accordin' to how much hurry they was in, er how big hogs they was, how much stuff they tuk along."

"Might be they loaded her," Gorman admitted, "but, by God, if I was stealin' a boat, I'd shore as hell run her light!"

"Even if she is runnin' light, we might overhaul her," Moosehide opined. "If them damn cheechakos don't know no more about handlin' a boat than what they know about anythin' else, they ain't goin' to make no time."

Gorman nodded. "There's more sideslip to her if she is light," he said. "We might cut 'em off in one of the bays. Er they might pile her up on them rocks off'n Caribou Pint."

Moosehide grinned. "If they pile her up on that saw-tooth reef they'll never steal another boat, you can bet yer life on that. But the hell of it is the boat wouldn't never do Tom no good neither."

"I sure hope they don't wreck her," Tom said. "She's our one chance to get to the Klondike."

"She's a good boat," Gorman agreed. "Ever handle a boat?"

"No, nothing but a rowboat."

"Goin' to be quite a chore, runnin' her back single-handed, even if we do overhaul her an' git her back," he opined.

"I'm not going to run her back singlehanded!" Tom retorted between clenched teeth. "Those damn cusses that stole her are going to run her back — or as many of 'em as are able to when I get through with 'em."

Moosehide approved. "That's the talk! By God, you've got guts! An' if we do overhaul 'em, me an' Jack here, we'll step in an' take all but one of 'em off'n yer hands. You might have trouble with yer crew," he added with a grin, "if there was three er four of 'em. But you could prob'ly handle a one-man mutiny."

"How'd Sis take it — the loss of the boat?" Gorman asked.

"She don't know about it. I woke up and heard the wind just as it was breaking daylight and slipped out without waking the others. It'll break her heart to find it's gone."

"No it won't," Moosehide opined. "She's got guts, Sis has — an' she's got a good head on her too. Her old man — he's more like the common run of cheechakos — but not Sis. I ain't makin' no predictions about Sam Brandon. But you two young'uns — you'll git along."

The course held steadily northward, paralleling the eastern shore of the lake. They passed numerous camps of those unfortunates whose boats had been crushed by the ice. Also they passed many boats that had escaped destruction and had been repaired and relaunched.

Toward evening the wind rose and veered into the west. In answer to shouted questions the three received the information from the occupants of some of the boats that a sailboat had passed them several hours before.

Then just at dusk they sighted her. Long and intently Moosehide studied her course. "I don't think she's loaded heavy, the way she's bobbin' around," he said, "an' what with the wind hittin' her crossways, she's got quite a side drift. We're gainin' on her pretty fast, an' if they hold her close-hauled like she is now, we'll ketch up with her agin dark. She's driftin' sideways about as fast as she's goin' ahead."

The boat continued to gain, and at length Tom, who was watching intently from the bow, called out,

"There's two men in her — and one of 'em looks like the damn skunk that tried to attack Sue Brandon at Sheep Camp. By God, if it is, what I did to him back there will seem like a sweet dream to what I'll do to him this time!"

The two in the other boat were plainly visible now. One sat at the tiller, while the other seemed braced at the windward rail holding the sheet. Darkness was rapidly gathering, and with the darkness the velocity of the wind increased, snatching capfuls of icy water from the crests of the whitecapped waves to deluge the three in the heavily laden, wallowing boat.

"By God, if she gets any higher we'll have to run fer the lee of Caribou Pint!" Gorman shouted. "We can't stand no hell of a lot of water in here, with the load we've got!"

It was evident now that the two in the other boat knew they were being pursued. The man amidship seemed suddenly to become active.

"The damn fool's makin' that sheet fast!" Moosehide cried. "Cripes, it wouldn't take much more wind to tip her over!"

"Look out!" Tom called sharply. "He's got a gun!"

Even as the words left his lips the sharp crack of a rifle sounded above the steady roar of the wind.

Moosehide laughed and, picking up his own rifle, sighted it and pulled the trigger. "Ever sence I was in school an' read in the hist'ry books about John Paul Jones an' all them old sea captains, I've wanted to be in a naval battle — an' now, by God, I'm in one!" Again the rifle cracked from the other boat, and, pumping a shell into his own rifle, Moosehide replied with a shot. "This ain't no dangerous pastime," he grinned, "what with the boats poppin' around like they be — an' it gives a man somethin' to do. Damn if I don't feel like old John Paul hisself — only I can't rec'lect which one of them sayin's he got off — whether it was 'Don't give up the ship,' er 'Damn the torpedoes,' er 'I ain't begun to fight,' er he ain't got only one life to give fer his country. Seems like every time there's a naval battle the captain's got to git off some sayin' that kids has got to learn a hundred years later."

With the sound of the next shot Moosehide's cap was knocked from his head and whipped away by the wind. "Hey," he cried, "that one was too damn close even fer an accident! I'd like to plug that son-of-a-bitch right between the eyes!"

Gorman chuckled. "By God, there's one sayin' they won't make no kids learn a hundred years from now! Moosehide, you've lost yer chanct fer fame!"

A few more shots were exchanged at random, the rapidly gathering darkness and pitching of the boats precluding any attempt at accurate sighting. Then a heavy cloud bank suddenly obscured even the little light of the stars, and absolute blackness engulfed them.

"We got to make a lee!" Gorman cried. "Which way's Caribou Pint?"

"How the hell do I know?" Moosehide shouted. "I ain't no owl!"

"Haul in the sheet. I'm easin' her upwind a little. The Pint's got to be upwind, an' it can't be only a few miles ahead."

As Moosehide braced himself and hauled in on the sheet there was a terrific crash that stopped the craft dead and shivered her throughout her length. A single hoarse cry sounded above the roaring of the wind, and then silence.

Moosehide Charlie picked himself up from the foot of the mast. "Tom!" he cried. "Hey, Tom!"

But there was no answering shout — only the roaring and hissing of the elements — that, and the Stygian blackness.

# CHAPTER
# NINE

## Capture

Standing in the bow of the pitching, tossing boat, Tom
Jorden strained his eyes for sight of the craft they were
rapidly overhauling. In vain he sought to pierce the
all-enveloping blackness. Out of the void came sounds
— the soft hiss of curling whitecaps, the splash and
gurgle of the waves that broke against the boat, the rush
of wind about the straining sail, and the voice of Jack
Gorman from the stern.

There was a sudden thud, a crashing jar, and Tom
pitched forward. In that split second he steeled his
nerves against the plunge into the icy water of the lake.
The next instant he landed squarely atop of the man at
the tiller of the leading boat, sweeping him from his
seat and into the six inches of bilge water that sloshed
about the bits of hastily loaded duffel pilfered from the
supplies abandoned on the beach at the Lindeman
camp. Half stunned, he realized that with the release of
the tiller the boat had swung into the wind, and that
from somewhere forward a man was bellowing orders
intermingled with curses; he realized, also, that the man
beneath him lay limp and inert. The boom swung
inboard, and with the sail flapping and slatting above

him he heard the man forward roaring to throw the rudder over.

Instantly Tom's brain cleared. Familiar with every inch of the boat, he rose to his knees, slipped out the wooden key that locked the tiller to the rudder post, pocketed it, and lifted the tiller from the post. Sounds and muttered curses told him that the man forward was scrambling aft along the windward rail. Leaving the inert form awash on the bottom, Tom slipped forward along the lee rail, the stout spruce tiller gripped firmly in his hand. With the sail slatting loudly between them, he passed the man unnoticed and reached the bow, where he tossed out the heavy stone anchor, which found bottom when a third of the hundred-foot line had run out. He slowly payed out the remaining line, and as it went taut he heard the other cursing the inert form in the bottom of the boat. The curses redoubled and rose in shrill fury as the man groped about in the darkness for the tiller, with the boom swinging and the sail slatting loudly as, head to the wind, the boat pitched and tugged at her anchor line.

Stealthily working his way to the mast on hands and knees, Tom located the rifle with which the man had exchanged shots with Moosehide Charlie, then, a grim smile on his lips, he groped about for the cleat and cast off the halyard. The next instant the sail came flapping down, and he crept forward to again take his place in the bow, where he sat humped up with the rifle across his knees and listened to the raving of the man in the stern. "Damn the God-damn luck! Steerin' handle gone, an' now the rope busts an' the sail comes down!

An' hell only knows when this damn boat'll be pilin' up on the rocks! Can't do nothin' in the dark, an' mebbe nothin' in daylight, with no way to steer! An' it's all your fault, you son-of-a-bitch!" he raved, evidently addressing the man who lay on the bottom. "If I've got to drown, by God, you'll drown too! If you ain't drownded yet, layin' there in that water, you damn soon will be! No one knows you was along! No one knows either one of us grabbed off this boat!"

Sounds issued from the dark as the man's voice ceased — straining, grunting sounds, followed by a splash, and again the sound of the voice: "There, you clumsy son-of-a-bitch! You lost that rudder handle! Go find it!" And in the bow Tom realized, with a shudder of horror, that the man had heaved his unconscious partner overboard. He had already identified the voice as belonging to the man who had attempted to attack Sue Brandon on the outskirts of Sheep Camp. His lips set grimly and he fingered the hammer of the rifle as the words of old Dr. Leroy came to him: "Be sure you're right, then be as tough as the toughest of 'em — and a little tougher." "He sure knew what he was talking about," the boy breathed, "when he said I'd run into the worst as well as the best. But I don't believe even he knew a man could be that bad."

All through the night Tom sat in the bow, the cocked rifle across his knees, as the boat rocked and pitched and tugged at her anchor line. She shipped some water, but not much, for, being lightly loaded, she floated high. From time to time the man in the stern muttered

**69**

and grumbled. Toward morning he evidently became seasick, for Tom could hear him retching and cursing.

The first hint of dawn grayed the east, and as the light slowly increased, Tom, whose eyes were fixed on the stern, made out the figure of the other humped on the steering seat, his face buried in his arms which rested on his knees. Presently the man raised his head, and his eyes widened in horror as they fixed on Tom, who eyed him in silence, a grim smile on his lips. The eyes blinked again and again, and as the man raised a hand and brushed across them, as though to rid them of the vision, thick, ropy spittle drooled from his loose-hung lips. Tom spoke no word — just sat grinning into the terror-wide eyes, the cocked rifle across his knees, the length of the boat between.

The man found his voice, a voice that sounded shrill and trembling: "What — who — the hell be you?" Tom remained silent, waiting for daylight to strengthen. The man again brushed a hand across his eyes. "Where'd you come from? Er — ain't there no one there?" Tom's eyes held the other's with a fixed stare. The man's lips writhed and his voice rose in shrill falsetto: "Christ — talk, can't you! Er — er — am I nuts? Mebbe I've went cuckoo! An' they ain't no one there! It's the damn sickness has went to my head!" He lurched from his seat, and at the movement Tom swung the rifle on him.

"Sit down!" he ordered. "You know who I am. You've seen me before — there at Sheep Camp, when you tried to attack that girl."

The man slumped back onto the seat. "But — where'd you come from? How'd you git here?"

"This is my boat. I belong here."

"But — how'd you git here? An' — there in the woods, by Sheep Camp! How'd you git there, too? I follered that girl out there. An' I know'd she was alone!"

"You mean you thought she was alone. But you were wrong. And here in the boat, after you'd dumped your partner overboard, you thought you were alone again — but you're not alone, by a damn sight!"

"By God, I know how you got here! You jumped in off'n that other boat when they bumped! You jumped on my pardner an' killed him! It's murder! That's what it is — murder!"

"That's right. It's murder. And you're the murderer. The man was alive when I came forward last night. You murdered him when you dumped him overboard."

"It's a lie! He was dead, I tell you! Deader'n hell!"

"You can tell that to Constable Burns. In the meantime, you can get busy and we'll sail this boat back where you got her. My partners are anxious to get started."

"Sail — hell! You ain't goin' to sail her nowheres without no steerin' handle! An' with a busted sail rope to boot!"

"I've got the tiller. I slipped it off and carried it forward with me last night when I heard you clawing your way aft. And the rope's not busted. I lowered the sail. Knew we wouldn't be needing it till morning." Reaching down, Tom picked up a tin pail and tossed it to the other. "Take that and bail her out, and we'll be getting started."

The man made no move to comply. "You go to hell! If you figger I'm goin' to help you, you've got another guess comin'. You can't make a man work if he don't want to."

Tom's eyes narrowed, and in them the man noted the steely glint that he had seen there as he faced him on the outskirts of Sheep Camp. Cold fear struck into his heart as the younger man spoke. "No. I can't make you work. But I can damn well shoot you and toss you overboard, as you tossed your partner. You've got it coming." He swung the muzzle of the cocked rifle into line. "And you've got just ten seconds to start either praying or bailing — and I don't give a damn which."

For long moments the man stared into the narrowed eyes.

"By God, you would shoot!" he mumbled. "Yer tough. You damn near killed me when you kicked me in the jaw that time." Picking up the pail, he began to bail out the boat.

When he had finished, Tom issued another order. "Now come up here and haul up the anchor while I ship that tiller. Keep to the right and don't crowd. One crooked move out of you and the wolves'll be gnawing two corpses on the shore instead of one."

As the man made his way forward, Tom slipped aft, keeping the boom between them. The wind had shifted into the northwest and subsided to a stiff breeze. Grasping the anchor rope, the man strained and hauled until the slack was taken up.

"I can't lift the damn anchor," he growled. "It'll take the two of us."

72

"Oh, no it won't. Just keep on trying. That rock only weighs about a hundred pounds."

"I can't lift it. My hands is sore, an' I'm sick to my stummick."

"The sooner you get it aboard the sooner you can quit hauling on it." Retching and growling, the man complied, and after much pulling and hauling the anchor was hoisted and stowed in the bow. "Get busy now and haul up the sail. The way the wind is, we ought to make the camp by night."

The sail bellied out, and as the boat gathered headway Tom settled himself comfortably and watched the shore slip past. A sense of well-being came over him. He had done what he set out to do. He had got the boat back. Vaguely he wondered whether he would really have shot the man had he not started to bail. The scoundrel richly deserved shooting, but ... He remembered the words of old Dr. Leroy: "Toughness is a virtue, Tommy — if it's rightly used." His lips set in a grim smile. "Anyway, I must have looked tough. He thought I'd shoot. But the devil of it is, I'll never know myself whether I was bluffing or not."

Up forward the man growled. "That there's my rifle you've got. An' all this stuff in the boat is mine too."

"That's right," Tom agreed. "Ease off on that sheet. We're running too close to the wind."

"What you goin' to do when you git back there?" the man asked after several moments of silence. "Turn me in fer murder?"

"That'll be up to Constable Burns. I'll turn you over to him and tell him the whole story. He can use his own judgment. If he thinks it's worth while to search the shore for the corpse of your partner, he'll probably hold you for murder. If not, there'll be the boat-stealing charge, and attempted murder, or shooting with intent to kill — or whatever he wants to call it."

"I never figgered to kill no one," the man growled. "All I wanted was to cut the rope so yer sail would come down."

Tom laughed. "Tell that to Moosehide Charlie," he said. "One of your bullets knocked the cap off his head. But there's no half a ton of supplies in here. Burns'll probably just take you back to Summit and kick you out of the country."

The wind held, and all day the two sailed southward, passing outfits heading north in the boats that had been patched up after their encounter with the ice, their occupants toiling at the heavy oars to force the clumsy craft slowly against the head wind. Seated in the stern, Tom wondered how it had fared with Gorman and Moosehide Charlie. Had their boat been stove in or capsized there in the blackness of the night? Or had they sailed on, giving him up for dead? And the Brandons — what of them? What would Sue think when she awoke to find him gone and the boat gone?

Dusk blurred the shore as the craft approached the head of the lake. Tom strained his eyes for sight of their tent among the scattered spruce trees. It was then he caught sight of the solitary figure poised on a high rock that jutted out into the lake — the figure of a girl with her skirts whipping about her knees in the wind. Then the figure was gone.

74

Before the tent Sam Brandon looked up from his task of tending the summer fire to see his daughter running toward him from the direction of the lake.

"Oh, Daddy! Daddy!" Her voice reached his ears, high pitched with excitement. "The boat's coming back! Our boat! And Tom's in her! Tom and another man! And the other one looks like that horrible creature who followed me out from Sheep Camp! You go to the lake. I'm going to find Constable Burns!"

# CHAPTER
# TEN

## The Sourdoughs Head Back

When Moosehide Charlie picked himself up from the bottom of the boat after the crash and received no answer to his call, he shouted to Gorman: "Tom's a goner! He got knocked overboard when the boats hit!"

"Yeah, an' you better haul in on that sheet, er we'll be a goner too! Hold her close in. We got to run fer a lee!"

Hours later, drenched to the skin, Moosehide dropped the anchor into the comparatively placid water of a lee shore. From somewhere ahead came the roar of the waves breaking over the saw-toothed rocks of the Caribou Shoal.

"This stuff got all mixed to hell when we hit," Moosehide said. "But I'm goin' to hunt up my duffel bag an' git into some dry clothes before I freeze stiff."

"Me too. Cripes, I wisht we could land an' git a fire goin'."

"Can't land till mornin'. It's all rocks along here. The boat might get stove up."

After much groping and fumbling about among the jumbled cargo, the bags were located and the two men succeeded in changing into dry clothing.

"This here's goin' to be mighty tough on Sis," Moosehide opined.

"Yeah. She shore set a heap of store by that boat."

"Boat — hell! I was thinkin' of Tom Jorden."

"He was the pick of this year's run of cheechakos, all right — fer's I can see," Gorman replied. "But you got to remember, Moosehide, there's a lot of good men in the Yukon — but damn few good boats."

"But cripes, Jack, them two young folks was in love! Ain't you got no sentiments?"

"Shore I have. But what I mean — take a boat like that there one — double bottom in her, an' all corked up like she was. By God, she ain't goin' to get another boat like that very soon!"

"I feel like hell myself about Tom," Moosehide said. "He was willin' an' eager to learn. He didn't claim to know it all, like most of the damn cheechakos. An' he had guts. He'd of made a sourdough, an' a damn good one."

"Shore he would. But what I mean — Sis can find a lot of sourdoughs in Dawson, ready-made. Hell, there's Bettles, an' Camillo Bill, an' Jimmie the Rough, an' Swiftwater Bill, an' Porcupine Jack, an' Black John — not countin' me an' you, an' quite a few more to boot."

Moosehide laughed. "Yeah, an' believe me, from what I know of them old-timers, I wouldn't want no daughter of mine marryin' no one of 'em — me an' you inclooded."

"Oh, I don't know. Fella's daughter married me one time. An' we didn't hit it off so bad till she broke a leg clumbin' into the fur baler. Damn good fur tromper, she was, too — except she was kinda arkward an' clumsy-like. She'd go better'n three hundred pound, anyways you'd look at her. An' by God, when she tromped a bale of fur, it was tromped! The hell of it was it happened right on the start of the balin'. I was runnin' a post that year, way to hell an' gone up the Stewart, an' I done a good business with them Moosehead Siwashes up in there. I didn't have no fur press — jest rigged up a baler so the woman could tromp the fur down. An' what with her heft an' all, it worked good. But when she broke her leg there, I was left without no help except a damn skinny little Siwash that wouldn't go no more'n ninety pound on a full stummick. Hell, he couldn't tromp a weasel pelt so it would stay flat!"

"Did yer wife get well?"

"No. She had so damn much meat on her leg seems like I never got it set right; somethin' must of went wrong in there. She hung on about a month an' then she up an' died on me."

"That was tough luck."

"You tellin' me! Did you ever try to get a three-hundred-pound corpse out through a door without no help except a ninety-pound Siwash which he was lazy as hell to boot?"

"I mean you must of missed her after she died."

"Oh, I don't know. Chances is she wouldn't never ben worth a damn trompin' fur no more. Prob'ly couldn't never got her into the baler agin. Had a dog onct that stepped in a wolf trap an' got crippled up, an'

I couldn't never get him onto that crick agin. Wimmin an' dogs gets funny notions that way."

Moosehide grinned broadly in the darkness. "I didn't know you was so sentimental, Jack," he said. "But, bein' as you are, you won't kick on headin' back up the lake come daylight."

"Up the lake!"

"Yeah. We're goin' back there to tell Sis what happened."

"But hell, Moosehide! What good would it do to tell her? She knows by now that the boat's gone. Why would she give a damn if two fellas stole it er a dozen? If we could of fetched the boat back, it would be different."

"I mean — tell her about Tom. She'll be wonderin' what become of him."

"Well, hell — so are we."

"Yeah. But bein' in love with him, that way, it might be kind of comfortin' fer her to know what happened."

"If a girl was in love with someone, why would it be comfortin' fer her to hear he got drowned in a lake in the dark?"

"Jest the same, we're goin' back," Moosehide insisted. "It's the only decent thing to do."

"Okay," Gorman said, a note of resignation in his voice. "But we're losin' two hull days."

"We ain't got to be nowheres at no particular time," Moosehide laughed. "Hell, the graveyards is full of folks that was in a hurry."

At daylight they landed, cooked breakfast, and set sail back up the lake. Toward the middle of the afternoon they came upon a boat drifting helplessly in the trough of the waves as its three occupants sat dejectedly amid their belongings. Steering close, Moosehide hailed them: "What's the matter?"

"We lost an oar," one of them explained. "About half an hour ago, it was, when we was changin' off rowin'. It slipped overboard an' floated away. We tried to paddle after it with the other oar, but we couldn't git the boat headed around."

"Okay, it can't be so far off; we'll head down-wind an' pick it up." The oar was retrieved a few minutes later, and Moosehide returned it with a bit of advice. "Better be more careful next time you change — an' the next time you camp, you better make you a couple of spare oars. Hell, if we hadn't come along, you might of drifted clean acrost the lake."

The men thanked him, and one of them asked: "What you fellas all headin' back fer?"

"What d'you mean — all?" Gorman asked.

"Well, you two, an' that other boat. The one that's built jest like that one."

"You mean," Gorman yelled, "that the other boat was headin' back up the lake?"

"Sure she was — she was makin' good time, too. Passed us about noon. Two fellas in her — same as you."

"Haul in that sheet, Moosehide, an' let's git goin'!" Gorman cried, shoving the tiller.

When the boat was once again under way, Moosehide's brow drew into a frown. "I can't figger what the hell them fellas is headin' back fer?" he said.

"Chances is they don't know they're headin' back," Gorman opined. "I'll bet what happened — they got turned around in the dark last night an' think they're still headin' fer Dawson!"

"Cripes — even a cheechako would know more'n that!"

"Like hell they would! By God, if there's a wrong way to do a thing, a cheechako will do it that way every time — an' headin' south here on the lake is shore as hell the wrong way to git to Dawson — so that's the way they'd go. You wait an' see! By God, the way things looks now, we'll help Sis git her boat back!"

# CHAPTER
# ELEVEN

## Supper

With the boat thief safely in the custody of Constable Burns, who was waiting on the beach with the Brandons as the bow of the boat nosed onto the gravel, the three made the craft fast for the night and made their way to the tent.

"Oh, Tom," the girl cried, her eyes alight, "tell us what happened! Tell us all about it! I'm just dying to hear. Oh, when I woke up yesterday morning and found you gone, and the boat gone, and the sourdoughs gone too, I nearly *died!*"

Tom grinned. "Thought I'd pulled a fast one and hit out for Dawson without you, eh?"

"No, of course not! I — I didn't know what to think. I knew someone had stolen the boat, and I knew you'd gone after 'em. Oh, tell us all about it! I can hardly wait!"

"There isn't much to tell," Tom said as they reached the little fire that flickered before the tent, "except that I'm hungry as a wolf. I haven't eaten a thing in two days except what I could dig out of a can with my belt knife and swallow cold."

"You won't have to eat anything cold tonight," the girl said, stooping to tilt the cover of a pot that simmered over the blaze. "Just get a whiff of that!"

"Best grub I ever smelled," Tom said as the savory odor reached his nostrils. "What is it?"

"Duck soup. Three ducks and two rabbits, and rice and potatoes. I spent all day yesterday walking along the shore, looking out over the lake for sight of the boat. I just knew you'd bring her back! And I took the twenty-two along and shot the ducks and rabbits, and today I made the stew. And it's all ready. Daddy and I were just about to have supper, but I ran down for one last look out over the lake when I saw you coming in. And oh, Tom — it was the grandest sight I ever saw — our boat, with her sail set, coming nearer every minute! It was too dark to see your faces, but I just knew it was you at the tiller. And that other — I'd know him anywhere by his squat, thick body — I'll remember him to the last day I live — how he stood there leering at me in the dusk. I was never so scared in my life. And then — you were there." The girl paused, and the shadows of the flickering firelight hid the flush that had mounted to her cheeks. "And again, just now — when I felt so alone and forsaken there on that big rock — again you came to me out of the twilight."

"It seems that Tom has a happy faculty of showing up at the crucial moment," Brandon said. "But come, Sue, dish out some of that stew. Tom must be about famished — and I wouldn't mind a bowl of it myself."

A half hour later the three settled back comfortably, and Brandon tossed more wood on the fire. "And now," the girl said, "tell us all that happened. I'm bursting with curiosity! I want to hear it all — every bit of it!"

"There isn't much to tell. I woke up yesterday morning at daylight and heard the wind blowing, so I went to the lake and found the boat gone. I found Moosehide Charlie and Gorman just getting under way in their boat, so I went along with 'em. We overtook our boat late in the evening, and somehow, in maneuvering around in the dark, the boats collided and I was pitched into our boat. I lit squarely on the man at the tiller and knocked him out. We hove to till daylight, and then the other chap and I sailed her back."

"But — where's the other man? The one you knocked out?"

"Oh, your friend the squat guy pitched him overboard sometime during the night. He says he thought he was dead. I'll tell Burns about it in the morning and let him use his own judgment. The only thing I'm worried about is what became of Moosehide and Gorman. Their boat may have been seriously damaged in the collision."

"Never got a scratch!" said a voice from behind them, and the three turned to see the grinning faces of the two sourdoughs at the edge of the firelight.

"Moosehead!" Tom cried. "By gosh, I'm glad to see you! But what in the devil are you doing back here?"

"It was Moosehide's idee," Gorman cut in, with a glance at the girl who was eagerly awaiting his words. "You see, Sis, the waves was runnin' half as high as a meetin'house, an' it was so black out there a man couldn't see his nose behind his back, an' them boats was rarin' an' buckin' like a couple of broncos, when all to once they hit, an' when me and Moosehide picked ourselves up off'n the bottom Tom was gone. We hollered but didn't get no answer, so we run fer a lee. We set there in the dark waitin' fer daylight to come, an' Moosehide allowed we'd ort to go back an' tell you how Tom got knocked off'n the boat an' drownded. I figgered it worn't no use goin' back here less'n we could fetch yer boat back fer you. But Moosehide claimed it would be comfortin' fer you to know that Tom had ben drownded. What I claim, he's got a hell of an idee of comfort — but he claimed it was our dooty, so we come."

The girl cast an accusing glance at Tom. "You never said anything about what a terrible night it was out there — with the high waves and all!"

Moosehide chuckled. "Yeah. Me an' Jack's ben standin' here a couple of minutes an' couldn't help overhearin' Tom's account of the doin's. Sounded right commonplace an' easy, the way he told it. He never mentioned nothin' about the naval battle where I got the cap shot plumb off'n my head."

Gorman laughed. "The 'Battle of Lake Lindeman,' the hist'ry books'll prob'ly call it. It's too bad they can't set down Moosehide's famous sayin' when that bullet knocked his cap off — but it ain't fit to print, not where schoolmarms an' kids could read it. At that, I'll bet if they set down what them old admirals and generals really said, it wouldn't be fit to print neither. Anyways, it was quite a night, take it first an' last. We were shore glad to find Tom here! When we'd got about halfways

**85**

back some fellas told us they seen the other boat headed this way, an' I figgered them damn cheechakos had got turned around in the dark an' was headed the wrong way."

Moosehide shook his head. "I didn't think that even cheechakos would be that big fools. When them fellas told us about the boat, I figured Tom must of managed to git into her somehow. But gittin' into her was one thing an' takin' her away from them two damn thieves there in the dark was somethin' else agin — an' them with a rifle, to boot."

Tom laughed. "It was simple enough, really. I knocked the tiller man out when I lit on him, and when I heard the other one crawling aft I unshipped the tiller, so they couldn't handle the boat, and crawled forward, keeping the boom between us. Then I heaved out the anchor and lowered the sail. I'd found the man's rifle where he dropped it. The one who crawled aft was so sore at the other for, as he thought, losing the tiller that he picked him up and heaved him overboard. He didn't know I was in the boat till daylight. But I had the rifle, and there was nothing he could do about it. So — here we are."

"Damn if we ain't," grinned Moosehide. "An' by God, there's one cheechako that's a sourdough before he ever seen the ice go out of the Yukon — you bet!"

# CHAPTER
# TWELVE

## Tom Gets a Job

The trip down through the lakes and on down the Yukon was uneventful enough. The two boats held together, and each night the two tents were pitched side by side. They passed dozens of the oar-propelled craft that had been launched at Lindeman, and thanks to the experience of the two sourdoughs, the long journey was made without mishap, and the two outfits arrived at Dawson well in the forefront of the spring stampede.

On the morning of the last day on the river the sourdoughs shoved off while the others were still at breakfast. Moosehide Charlie waved a hand. "So long! See you in Dawson. We'd ort to make it by noon. Good water from here on. You won't have no trouble."

Sue Brandon watched the boat till it disappeared around a bend, then she glanced at the others. "So — this is the last day of our trip," she said, the words coming slowly, a note of genuine regret in her voice. "I've loved every minute of it. But I knew it had to end. I wonder what Dawson will be like?"

"It's been a wonderful experience," Brandon agreed. "Drifting day after day farther and farther from civilization. I never realized there was this much wilderness in the world. Back there at Lindeman, with all the people coming in, I was afraid the country would be overcrowded. But I guess there's no danger for some time to come."

"Plenty of room, all right," Tom said, his eyes on the succession of peaks and ridges that extended back from the river as far as the eye could reach. "I've enjoyed every minute of it too. But of course we couldn't go on just drifting down a river forever. I — I hate to think of it — but when we hit the beach at Dawson our partnership ends."

Brandon cleared his throat. "Well — yes. I — I suppose that's so. What are your plans, my boy?"

"I haven't any plans. I came here to find gold. I don't know the first thing in the world about how to go at it. I guess the smart thing would be to stick around for a while and sort of watch the others — the ones who have been successful — and find out how they do it."

Brandon nodded approval. "A fine idea. But in the meantime, Tom, how are you — er — fixed for money? Prices will be mighty high, I'm afraid."

"Oh, I've got enough to last for a while — about four thousand dollars. Moosehide Charlie advised me to salt the money away for a grubstake and get a job with some outfit till I learn something about the game, then either hit out on a prospecting trip of my own or throw in on some stampede. He says they're always stampeding to new creeks. Someone makes a strike, and when the news gets out there's a grand rush to that locality and the creek is staked from one end to the other. Of course only a few claims on each creek are any good. But the chance of locating one of those good claims sends men swarming into a locality by the hundreds."

Brandon nodded. "Just so. You spoke of getting a job with some outfit till you learned the game. You mean, I suppose, going to work for some outfit that is carrying on a successful operation?"

"That's it."

"The only drawback I can see is that no matter what outfit you worked for, your experience would be limited to that particular locality and to the particular method used by your employer. Whereas it seems to me that in a country as big as this, with conditions varying as they must on the different creeks and rivers, a method that would be highly successful in one locality might well be entirely inadequate in another."

Tom nodded. "Yes, I suppose that's true. But a man can't work on all the creeks."

"He can. That's the point I'm making. He can do just that. I didn't come into this country to dig gold. That is, I do not intend to go dashing about on stampedes, and slosh around in muck, and work with shovels and pans and picks and sluices, or whatever the tools of the trade are. I'm too old for that sort of thing.

"My purpose in coming here is to invest in mining properties. Buy — sell — operate, as the case may be. This, of course, will entail the investigation of properties, many of which will undoubtedly lie at considerable distances from Dawson. It will also demand the ability to apply the technical method that will produce the best results under given conditions. I am too old to cover considerable distances rapidly by dog sled or canoe. And I know nothing of mining. What I need is a young man — a smart young man — a man capable of looking after my interests in the field."

Tom nodded. "What you want is a mining engineer, or at least someone with practical experience in mining. With all the people there are pouring into the country, you probably won't have much trouble finding someone who can fill the bill."

Brandon shook his head. "According to Moosehide Charlie, mining, as carried on in this country — surface mining and shallow shafts — does not demand the services of a mining engineer. About the only engineering jobs necessary are the construction of dams and the building of flumes when occasion demands, and any surveyor can do the engineering work. And as for practical experience — those who have it are either operating on their own account or are otherwise unavailable.

"Another thing, I've got to have a man I can trust with considerable sums of money. Moosehide summed it up very aptly the other evening. 'All a man needs in the Yukon,' he said, 'is a little savvy, luck, and a lot of guts.' I've had my eye on you, my boy. And I think you'll fill the bill."

"Me! Why, I don't know a thing in the world about mining!"

The older man smiled. "But you've got guts. And you've certainly got plenty of luck — or you wouldn't be alive after that night on Lake Lindeman. You have two of Moosehide's requisites — and I'll take a chance on the third. My proposition is this — you go to work for me on a salary. Your job, for the first several months, will simply be to visit operations on different creeks, see how they operate. Ask questions, learn how to appraise new properties — in other words, soak up all the information about mining that you can hold. In the meantime I'll set up headquarters in Dawson and dabble about in small investments, and sort of get the lay of the land from that angle. In that way, when the time comes for operating on a large scale, we'll be all set to tackle it. You can get wider experience in three months' working for me than you could in three years tied down to one locality. What do you say?"

Tom was silent for what seemed a long time. Finally he spoke. "Ever since I graduated from high school I've worked on a salary — and it wasn't much of a salary, either. It was to get away from just that that I decided to hit for the Yukon. It was because I saw the opportunity to do something. To make good on my own account. It isn't so much that I want to get rich. I want to make good. You're offering me a wonderful chance to get experience — much better than I could get anywhere else. But I don't want to be tied down. I mean, if there'd be a stampede, I might want to join it. Or, if I ran across some location that looked good, I might want to work it. If I took you up, I might want to quit at a moment's notice and hit out. That wouldn't be fair to you, because you'd be financing the experience that I might turn to my own profit."

"I see your point," the older man said, "and it seems reasonable enough. I'm willing to gamble on you. Tell you what I'll do. You go to work for me — just as I said. We'll agree that you're at liberty to quit at any time on a moment's notice and go on your own. I'm making just two stipulations — you are not to quit to go to work for anyone else. And if the venture you undertake on your own account doesn't pan out, you'll come back and work for me. For my part, I'll agree to take you back whenever you want to come. That's fair enough, isn't it?"

"It's more than fair," Tom said. "I'll take you up. But I'll make one stipulation, too — if my personal venture is successful, I'll repay every cent you've laid out on my education."

Brandon smiled. "Okay — if your venture should be successful, you could afford to repay me. It's a bargain. And now, the matter of salary —"

"I'll leave that to you," Tom interrupted. "You'll know what I'm worth when I get going."

"All right — we'll leave it that way. I'll pay you what I think you're worth, plus all expenses."

"And where do I fit into the scheme of things?" Sue asked, smiling at the two across the little fire.

"Oh, you'll fit in," her father said. "You'll be one of the main cogs in the wheel. You'll be my office manager. Come on — let's pull down the tent and get going. I'm anxious to see what this Dawson looks like!"

# CHAPTER
# THIRTEEN

## Dawson

Late that afternoon the boat was beached at Dawson, and the three moved, bag and baggage, into the Dominion Hotel. After supper Tom strolled out onto the street and, attracted by the loud jangle of a piano, stepped into the Klondike Palace. The place seemed to be doing a capacity business. The long bar was lined with customers in all stages of inebriation, each striving to outshout his neighbor to make himself heard above the din of the tinny piano. Along one side of the room men sat at round tables playing poker or stud. And toward the rear other men were grouped two and three deep about various faro and roulette layouts.

Threading the crowd, Tom spent a half hour watching with interest as the men, with tense, set faces, placed their bets, risking huge sums on a spin of the wheel or the turn of a card. Tiring of this, he made his way toward the door, pausing for a few moments at the broad entrance to the dance hall to watch men whirling girls scantily clad in tawdry finery about the floor to the accompaniment of the piano placed on a raised dais and lustily pounded by the pasty-faced "professor" clad in an ill-fitting dress suit and imitation shirt front.

Again on the street, as Tom strolled past the warehouses and stores with false wooden fronts, he pondered the fact that the sights he had seen in the Palace had depressed rather than enlivened him. Somehow a note of sordid insincerity pervaded the place. The men at the bar were drinking too much, talking and laughing too loudly. At the gambling devices the tense, strained faces showed that the bets were too high, that the men were playing for more than they could afford to lose. And in the dance hall the gaiety seemed forced, the tempo was too fast, the men whirled the girls too high.

"It's almost as if — as if they were afraid this is the last night they'll ever be there," he muttered. Then his eyes lighted as they encountered a sign, TIVOLI SALOON. "That's the place Moosehide mentioned. He was telling Jack Gorman about a poker game they had in there."

Stepping inside, he was instantly struck by the sharp contrast to the Palace. Men were drinking at the bar, and in the rear other men were grouped about a faro layout. But there was no dance hall, no jangling piano. And the men were drinking quietly. Toward the rear end of the bar a small group of older men were laughing in evident appreciation of a story told by one of their number — but the laughter came in low, belly chuckles, not in raucous guffaws. The atmosphere of the Tivoli breathed sincerity — where the atmosphere of the Palace had, in its every aspect, flaunted insincerity.

94

As he crossed to the bar a man motioned him toward the group. "Well, by God, if here ain't Tom Jorden now! He's the lad I was tellin' you about — him that's got guts an' luck enough fer two men! An' I'm predictin' that when he gits the savvy he's goin' to be hard to beat! Come on over here, Tom. I want you should meet the boys."

Tom grinned and flushed slightly as he encountered the appraising glances of these shrewd-eyed men. Then Moosehide was introducing them: "This here is Bettles, who's been in the country ever since the mountains wasn't no bigger'n igloos an' kin drink more licker, an' show it less, than any two men in the house. This here is Camillo Bill, which he's got more good claims than any one man ort to have. Beside him stands Swiftwater Bill, who owns the only genuyne bald-faced shirt in Dawson. The next one is Porcupine Jack, whose name comes, not from any quills he's got, but from the Porcupine River, 'cause his faith in the lower country has got even God guessin'. An' the other one is Burr MacShane, who onct staked out a claim on the North Pole an' never panned out nothin' but codfish."

Tom smiled. "I'm mighty glad to meet you men," he said. "I've heard Moosehide mention some of you."

"Don't never believe nothin' that old walrus tells you," Bettles chuckled. "Hell — he learnt to lie even before he could talk! An' now mebbe you'll give us the straight of that there Battle of Lake Lindeman, as he calls it. Accordin' to him, this here naval battle raged ontil night come down so black a man couldn't see a match when he lit one, an' right in the middle of the lake them two boats run together an' you got knocked off on the peak of a forty-foot wave an' come down right plumb on top of one of the damn pirates that stole yer boat, squshin' him flat, an' you wind up by capturin' the other pirate with his own rifle an' sailin' the boat back to camp."

Tom chuckled. "Well, allowing for Moosehide stretching that wave a bit, the facts are about as you've stated 'em. I sure had a lot of luck. What will you have? I'm buying a drink."

"A lot of luck an' a lot of guts," Swiftwater said.

"I've heard whisky recommended as a beverage," Bettles grinned, reaching for the bottle. "Guess I'll try a little of that."

When the drinks were poured Burr MacShane raised his glass. "Here's to Tom Jorden, boys — may his luck hold."

"Bein' a cheechako, that-a-way," Bettles said as the glasses were returned to the bar, "how come you'd hit fer the Tivoli instead of the Klondike Palace?"

Tom smiled. "Oh, I stopped in at the Palace first. Heard the piano going, and it sounded kind of lively, so I went in. But I didn't stay long. I didn't like the place. It seemed somehow — well, sort of — of tawdry, and insincere."

"If Black John was here he'd prob'ly know what them words means," Moosehide grinned. "But I guess it biles down to you meanin' — it stinks. An' it goes to prove what I was tellin' the boys before you come in — yer one cheechako that don't have to wait to see the ice go out of the Yukon before becomin' a sourdough."

"Guess that's right," Swiftwater Bill agreed. "But that damn dive is doin' a real service fer them cheechakos, at that. 'Cause when Cutter Malone gits through with 'em down to the Palace, they're shore goin' to appreciate hell when they git there."

Camillo Bill cleared his throat. "Now yer here, what do you aim to do?" he asked, shooting Tom a glance. "I don't make a practice of grubstakin' cheechakos. But I wouldn't mind takin' a chanct on you."

"Not by a damn sight!" Moosehide interjected. "I found him first — an' by God, if anyone grubstakes him, I do! Cripes, with the luck he's got, I couldn't lose!"

Porcupine Jack, who had scarcely taken his eyes off the younger man, spoke up. "If you brought in enough money to grubstake the two of us for a trip to the lower country, I've got a proposition on the Porcupine River that's got 'em all skinned."

Bettles grinned. "Hell, Porcupine, I'll grubstake you fer a trip down there any time you want to go."

Porcupine Jack shook his head. "Nope. This ain't a grubstake proposition. She's a two-man trip. Equal partners."

Bettles shook his head. "I'm doin' all right here. The lower country'll get along if I never see it again."

Tom smiled. "I thank you men — all of you. I sure appreciate your willingness to deal with a greenhorn — a cheechako. But the fact is, I've agreed to work for Sam Brandon until I'm ready to strike out on my own. He's the man I threw in with at Lindeman. Moosehide, here, knows him. He's an older man, and he brought in

**97**

some money to invest. He needs someone to sort of look after his interests — do the outside work. I don't know a thing about mining. I've got to learn as I go along. Brandon's idea is for me to go around to the different creeks, ask questions — watch the work — in fact to learn all I can. You men are all sourdoughs — men of experience. I'd be mighty obliged if you'd allow me to visit your workings and learn what I can — probably pester you with a lot of questions. If I get to be too much of a bother, just kick me off the works."

Camillo Bill grinned. "I've got goin' propositions on a dozen different cricks — an' no two of 'em jest alike. Yer welcome to hang around any one of 'em er all of 'em — an' ask all the questions you want to. It won't bother me none — nor no one that works fer me. There's quite a bit to learn — what with flumes, an' sluices, an' test pannin', an' all — but nothin' that you couldn't pick up in a summer. You've hit here jest at the right time, too — we're right now startin' to sluice out our dumps."

The others nodded approval, and Bettles included the others in a wave of the hand. "Right here at the bar stands a bunch of men whose combined savvy includes every damn situation that a man could be up against, both in the upper country an' in the lower country too. An' there ain't a damn one of us that ain't glad to help an up-an'-comin' young fella get along. Cripes — we all had to learn! Why the hell wouldn't we help?"

Moosehide Charlie grinned and jabbed a thumb into Tom's ribs. "Shore we'll help. An' when the rest of the boys see what I've saw, they won't be blamin' you none fer throwin' in with Brandon instead of us old badgers. You see, boys, Sam Brandon's got a daughter. She's jest as much sourdough as Tom here. An' believe me — she ain't hard to look at, neither!"

# CHAPTER
# FOURTEEN

## Porcupine Jack

During the next four weeks Tom Jorden spent very few nights in Dawson. Every moment of the ever-lengthening days found him on some creek, absorbing the details incident to the operation of sluices, riffles, grizzlies, sumps, flumes, shafts, and dumps. He learned the art of collecting "flour gold" from the riffles with quicksilver, of test panning, of burning in for winter mining, of sniping bars in summer. He memorized the laws applicable to the business of placer mining, the size and location of claims — discovery, inland, creek, and river — and their legal staking and recording. He visited Quartz Creek with Swiftwater Bill, Bonanza with Bettles, Ophir and Hunker with Camillo Bill, Squaw Creek with Moosehide Charlie, and Shorty Creek with Burr MacShane.

To a man the sourdoughs liked him — went out of their way to explain or to offer advice, generally in an offhand, roundabout manner. As on the occasion he and Swiftwater Bill were camped on the Klondike and a canoe rounded a bend, its two occupants paddling furiously to force the craft against the current. Another followed it, and another, and another. Then a line of pack-laden men streamed past on the foot trail. Swiftwater grinned. "Stampede," he grunted.

"A stampede!" Tom cried, his eyes lighting. "Gosh, I wonder if I oughtn't to get in on it? My agreement with Brandon leaves me free to hit out on my own any time I want to. I'd sure like to make a strike!"

Swiftwater nodded. "Yeah? Well, who the hell wouldn't? Look 'em over, son. You don't see no sourdoughs amongst 'em, do you? I ain't seen a damn one of 'em that looks like he know'd which end of an owl the hoot comes out of. Some damn-fool cheechako prob'ly panned out some colors on some sand bar, way to hell an' gone up some crick, an' then busted a gut gittin' back to Dawson to file him a claim. Then he most likely went to the Klondike Palace an' throw'd a few ounces of dust around an' done a lot of loudmouthed braggin' — an' now half the cheechakos in Dawson is follerin' him to his location. They'll come dribblin' back in a few days, cussin' their luck, an' they'll hang around the Palace waitin' fer someone to fool 'em again. An' when they git broke they'll go to work choppin' cordwood fer wages — an' that's about their speed, at that. Don't never pay no heed to no stampede that ain't got anyways a sprinklin' of sourdoughs in it."

Tom grinned. "You old-timers sure hate the cheechakos, don't you?"

Swiftwater shook his head. "No, we don't hate 'em. It ain't nothin' agin a man that he's new to a country — if he wasn't a damn fool along with it. We jest sort of despise 'em, that's all. Look at 'em — the ones that's goin' past. They're like a lot of damn sheep. One hits out, an' all the others foller — they don't know where they're goin' — nor why — but they go jest the same. They come pourin' into the country to find gold — an' not one in a thousan' of 'em takes the trouble to learn how to find it when they git here. But, by God, a cheechako'll eat as much an' drink as much as a good man — an' the result is grub an' licker's gittin' so scarce we've got to pay ten times what it's worth to git it."

Toward evening, a week or so later, Tom stopped at a claim on Hunker Creek, where three men were engaged in sluicing the tail end of a dump. One of the men he recognized as Porcupine Jack. "Hello," he said. "I didn't know you had a claim around here. I thought you pinned your faith in the lower country."

The older man eyed him from beneath the brim of a dilapidated felt hat. "This ain't my claim," he replied. "I'm workin' it fer Camillo Bill. I wouldn't fool around with this upper country."

"The claim's not much good, eh?"

The older man shrugged. "Good enough, I guess. Good as any on the crick. Camillo picked it up for forty thousand, an' he'll take out maybe a hundred an' fifty thousand before he's through with it. Good investment — for the upper country."

"Most of the sourdoughs have more faith in the upper country than they have in the lower," Tom said.

"Yeah — an' most of 'em call Forty Mile the lower country. Hell, everyone knows that Forty Mile and

Birch Crick are worked out. Bettles, and Burr MacShane, an' I are the only ones that have really been in the lower country. I mean the real lower country — north of the Circle. Bettles did all right on the Koyukuk. Made enough there to buy in on Bonanza. And Burr MacShane went way to hell an' gone beyond the Endicotts, an' he did all right too. You can't blame those fellows for sticking around here — they've both picked up good propositions here, and this is an easy country to live in. Down there, on the Koyukuk, and the Chandalar, and the Porcupine, it's tough. I've got a proposition on the Porcupine — if I can ever find it — that's got this upper country backed off the map." The man paused, walked over to the sluice, and gave an order to the two others. He returned and glanced at his watch. "About quittin' time. You'll stop over for the night. We've got an extra bunk in the shack. Throw your pack in there, and we'll be with you in a few minutes."

Tom strolled over to the shack a short distance away and kindled a fire in the cookstove. In a few minutes he was joined by the others. The older man introduced him. "Boys, this is Tommy Jorden — came into the country this spring along with a fellow named Brandon. And, Tommy — that's Mike Casey, and the other's Pete Moss."

As the introductions were acknowledged Moss picked up the empty water pail and stepped to the door. "Jorden," he repeated. "Know'd a fella named Jorden onct. Run a hardware store in Big Falls, Minnesoty. I worked around there one harvest shockin' wheat."

"He's my uncle," Tom replied shortly, and turned to Porcupine Jack. "You say you've got a good proposition on the Porcupine, if you could find it," he said. "You're a sourdough. I should think any of the old-timers would grubstake you for a trip in there."

Porcupine Jack nodded. "Yeah, they would — if I'd ask 'em. In fact, most of 'em has offered to do it without my askin'. But I refused to take 'em up."

"Don't want to let 'em in for a half interest, eh?" Tom smiled.

"Hell, no! It ain't that! I'd give any one of 'em the shirt off my back. It's — I think maybe you can understand. None of 'em have any faith in the Porcupine. There's never been a big strike there — never even a middlin' big one. A few men have taken out a little better'n wages on some of the cricks. But after you pass Rampart House there's no tradin' posts, an' it costs too much to haul in your supplies. Once a strike was made, things would be different. There'd be a stampede, an' it wouldn't be long till there'd be another Dawson way up the Porcupine. Hell — there wasn't a shack where Dawson is now — till Carmack made his strike on Bonanza. And down around Forty Mile the sourdoughs laughed when anyone mentioned the upper country.

"I've put in a good many years in the lower country, an' because I've never found what I'm after, the sourdoughs think I'm kind of cracked. They don't think I know what I'm talking about when I tell 'em there's coarse gold on a crick that runs into the Porcupine, way up. But because I'm one of 'em — because I'm a sourdough — any one of 'em would grubstake me. An' if I failed on that trip, another one would — an' they'd keep on doin' that. But — don't you see? — it would be charity — not business — from their angle. And I don't want charity! That's why I'm here on Hunker workin' for Camillo Bill. He pays me good wages to run this outfit for him. And I accept those wages because I know I earn 'em. This job'll be finished in three, four days, an' I'll hunt another one. In about two years I'll have enough to outfit myself for another go at the Porcupine. I'll hit it yet. The gold's there — just as sure as God made little apples. An' when I find it I'll have earnt it — no one will have handed it to me. I think you'll understand."

Tom nodded. "Yes, Porcupine," he said, "I think I understand."

# CHAPTER
# FIFTEEN

## Brandon Buys Some Claims

Sam Brandon entered the Tivoli Saloon one day and stepped to the bar, where Moosehide Charlie stood drinking with old Bettles, dean of the sourdoughs. "Just the man I wanted to see, Moosehide," he said after acknowledging his introduction to Bettles. "I need some advice. I've bought two locations from a man named Jack Fisher, one on Hunker and the other on Ophir Creek. Mr. Rumsey, at the bank, and others, including Corporal Downey of the Mounted Police, speak highly of Fisher as a man of integrity."

Bettles nodded. "Yeah, you can go on what Jack Fisher tells you. I've know'd him for years. He's prob'ly lettin' go some of his scattered locations so he can put in all his time on a big proposition he's bought into on Bonanza."

"That's exactly what he said. So, after making inquiries, I took these locations over. Now I've got to find a man who can operate them. I thought maybe you could recommend someone."

"What's the matter with Tom Jorden?" Moosehide asked in surprise.

"Why, nothing — except that I need a man of experience. I'm paying Tom a salary to go out on the creeks and learn all he can about the country and about mining. And I've scarcely seen him in the past four weeks. The fact is, I'm contemplating a rather extended prospecting trip myself, and I'd like to leave a man in charge who could attend to the cleaning up of the dumps on these Fisher properties. I can't expect Tom to have acquired the necessary knowledge in so short a time."

"Can't, eh?" replied Moosehide dryly. "Well, tellin' you about me — if I was looking fer someone to run an outfit, an' I found out I could get holt of Tom Jorden, I wouldn't hunt no further."

"What! Do you mean to say you believe him capable of —"

"Listen, Brandon," Bettles cut in. "I know this here Tom Jorden. Know'd him ever since the first night he hit Dawson an' passed up the Klondike Palace to have a couple of drinks in the Tivoli. An' I know what Moosehide told us about what come off there on Lake Lindeman. An' I watched him the four, five days he spent on my workin's up on Bonanza, an' I've heard what the other boys has said about him when he was visitin' their outfits. He ain't ben in the country long. But, by God, the way he goes at things — eighteen hours out of every twenty-four — he don't have to be. There ain't nothin' goes on that he don't see it — an' if he don't know the why of it, he ain't ashamed to ask. An' he don't ask no damn-fool questions, like most cheechakos, neither. Everything he asks is right to the pint. He's learnt more in four weeks than half the old-timers has learnt in four years. I'm like Moosehide.

If I could get holt of Tom Jorden to run a proposition fer me, I wouldn't hunt no further. By cripes, he can handle anything that's likely to come up right now! An' if he run up agin somethin' he didn't savvy, he'd find out the how of it before he had to tackle it — an' don't you fergit it!"

"Surprising! Astounding!" Brandon exclaimed. "Of course I knew Tom was smart, and willing, and seems capable enough as far as he knows. That's why I hired him. But I had no idea he could absorb the requisite knowledge in so short a time. But if you men recommend him, it certainly takes a load off my mind."

Bettles grinned. "Whenever you get through with him, jest turn him over to me. I've got some scattered propositions, here an' there, that I'd like to have him lookin' after. He's the best damn cheechako I ever seen — bar none."

One evening several days later Tom Jorden stepped into the dining room of the hotel to find Sue Brandon seated alone. As he crossed to her table the girl's eyes lighted.

"Oh, Tom! It's about time you showed up! Where in the world have you been?"

Tom smiled and dropped into the vacant chair opposite her. "Here, there, and pretty much everywhere. I've been out soaking up savvy."

The girl returned the smile. "I hope you soaked up a lot of it, because you're sure going to need it."

"What do you mean? Where's your dad?"

"He's gone."

"Gone! Gone where?"

"Off on a prospecting trip. Said he was tired sticking around town. I could see that he was getting restless, so I encouraged him to go. And he hit out and left you and me to run the outfit."

"The outfit! What outfit?"

"Oh, we're a going concern. We've got two locations to work. One on Hunker and the other on Ophir. I'm the office man, and you're superintendent in charge of operations."

"You mean he bought these locations? Bought 'em without having them investigated?"

"Yes. He investigated the man instead of the locations. Everyone — including the banker, and Corporal Downey, and Moosehide and Bettles — speaks very highly of him, so Daddy bought the locations on his representations. So now you've got two dumps to clean up."

Tom's brow wrinkled. "It's a wonder your dad would trust the job to me. You'd think he'd pick up some man with experience."

Sue smiled. "He thought so too. So he hunted up Moosehide and Bettles and asked them to recommend someone who could fill the bill."

"And they couldn't?"

"They could."

Tom flushed slightly. "You mean they — they recommended me!"

"They did — both of 'em. What's the matter? You look scared. You can do it, can't you?"

"Sure I can do it! And I'm not scared. Just surprised." A waiter brought the girl's supper and took Tom's order. "Go ahead and eat," he said. "Don't wait for me. I'll be through by the time you are. You've got the descriptions of those locations, I suppose?"

"Yes. We'll go over them tomorrow. And —"

"Tomorrow! Tomorrow I'll be on Hunker! I know just the man to run that outfit — an old fellow they call Porcupine Jack. He's been cleaning up a dump for Camillo Bill, and he ought to be through right now. I want to grab him before someone else does. I'll run the Ophir job myself. We'll go over those papers just as soon as I can throw this grub into me!"

"But, Tom," the girl said with just a hint of reproach in her tone, "surely tomorrow will be time enough. You're tired. You've just come in off the creeks. There's a show in town tonight. Local talent, and they say it's a scream — those who've seen the rehearsals. That young Dr. Sutherland is in it, and they say he's a wonderful female impersonator. Why, the other night, in one of the dance halls, he ran into old Dr. Lemoine, who has the reputation of being quite a lady's man. The old doctor was a bit tight, and Dr. Sutherland was in costume for rehearsals, and he enticed the old doctor into a booth and teased him up till he spent all his dust — and the next day he returned the old doctor seventy-five dollars in percentage checks he had collected on what the old fool spent."

Tom laughed. "I'd sure like to see the show," he said, "but I'll have to wait till some other time. Your dad isn't hiring me to go to shows."

"But, Tom — I — I thought we'd have this evening together. Why, I've hardly seen you since we reached Dawson. I thought you'd take me to the show, and we could enjoy it together."

"We'll spend the evening together, all right — part of it — going over those locations and whatever instructions your dad left. Then I'll hit out. The moon will be up by ten o'clock. The show won't be starting till then, and you can take it in. I'll be on the trail."

The girl made no answer, and the meal was finished in silence . . .

Leading the way directly to her room, Sue handed him the deeds to the locations and a typed memorandum. "I have some expense money for you too," she said.

Tom made a note of the locations and glanced over the memo. He handed the deeds back. "Better keep these here," he said. "I'd suggest leaving them at the bank. These instructions are plain enough — simply to clean up the dumps on the two claims. Never mind the expense money. I've got enough for the present. Porcupine Jack has two men working with him, and I hope to get all three of 'em. Then I'll find a couple of more to work with me on Ophir. I'll slip out and look the ground over. Have they got shacks on 'em — these claims?"

The girl shook her head. "I'm sure I don't know. Dad said something about building sluices, but he didn't mention any shacks."

"Okay. I'll be back as soon as I can make it. I'll need money for sluice lumber — and maybe for shacks. When is your dad coming back?"

**111**

"He didn't say. He hired a man named Jim Devine, who has a canoe and claims to know the country. I don't expect them back very soon because Daddy said the man promised to show him some likely creeks that the cheechakos haven't found yet."

Tom frowned. "If he knows so many good creeks, why isn't he prospecting them himself?"

Sue shrugged. "I wondered about that too. But the inaction of sticking around town was getting on Daddy's nerves, so I didn't say anything. The trip will do him good — and he can afford the twenty-five dollars a day he's paying the man."

"Whether he can afford it or not," Tom said, "I hate to see anyone put anything over on him. Well, so long, Sue. I've got to stop at the store, and by the time I get my supplies to the canoe the moon will be up. Have a good time at the show."

The girl held out her hand. "Good-by, Tom — and good luck." As his fingers closed about hers the girl felt them tighten, then suddenly her hand was free, and as Tom turned abruptly and disappeared through the doorway she saw that his face had flushed deeply.

"He does care," she murmured as she listened to his footfall descending the stairs. "But — he might have taken me to the show."

# CHAPTER
# SIXTEEN

## A Frame-up

Tom reached Hunker Creek just as Porcupine Jack and his men were cleaning up the tailings of Camillo Bill's dump. He hired the three, bought the shack on a claim that had petered out on a small feeder, and set the men to tearing it down. "By the time you get the lumber packed over to our location, I'll be back with tools and nails and whatever you'll need to put it together again," he told them, and struck out for Ophir.

Within a week he was back in Dawson. Going straight to the hotel, he found Sue in her room and handed her a penciled memorandum. "I bought a secondhand shack on Hunker for seven hundred dollars and have my crew tearing it down and packing it to the claim. It'll cost another hundred and fifty to rebuild it. On Ophir I bought new lumber from a man who has a small portable mill. That shack will cost more. I bought the lumber for sluices too. Our pay roll for the two jobs will come to twenty-eight hundred dollars a month. You've got the estimate there. Better give me about six thousand in cash. I'll be hitting out in the morning. I've got that shack and the lumber to pay for, and I'll take the first month's pay roll. Might not be back before it's due. I've got a lot of supplies to arrange for. See you at supper."

During the afternoon Tom purchased the supplies. In the Tivoli he found several of the old-timers at the bar.

Burr MacShane beckoned him to join them and shoved the bottle toward him. "I hear you're operatin' a couple of claims for Sam Brandon," he said.

"I will be pretty quick, if I have any luck," Tom replied. "Got to build a couple of shacks and sluices first."

"You'll make out, all right," Bettles said. "Jack Fisher's square as a die, an' he told me he sold these locations to Brandon reasonable. Take most of the old-timers, an' a man can go on what they tell him."

"Speaking of old-timers," Tom said, "did any of you ever run across a man by the name of Jorden — John Jorden — in this country?"

The men shook their heads. "John Jorden," Moosehide repeated. "Some kin of yourn?"

"My father."

"Yer father!" exclaimed Swiftwater Bill. "Is he s'posed to be here — on the Yukon?"

"On the Yukon or some other river — here in the North someplace."

"How long ago was he s'posed to of come here?" Camillo Bill asked.

"Fifteen years ago."

"Fifteen years!" cried Burr MacShane. "Cripes — there wasn't but damn few white men in this country then, barrin' a few traders scattered along the rivers. No one here but Bettles has ben in the country that long. How about it, Bettles? Ever run onto John Jorden?"

Bettles shook his head. "Nope — never heard the name. I was up on the Koyukuk them days. There wasn't no white men here in the upper country then, except fur men — traders an' maybe a few trappers."

"She was a hell of a country to git into them days," Swiftwater explained. "You had to come in by way of St. Michaels, an' on up the river from there. Ain't that so, Bettles?"

"Yeah — an' no way to git to St. Michaels except on some damn whaler. A lot of them ships started out that wasn't never heard from agin. The chances is, Tom, yer pa never got here. I know damn well if he'd ben anywheres in the country fer fifteen years, I'd of heard of him."

"You might ask Downey," Moosehide suggested. "The police keeps a pretty good check on folks."

"Police — hell!" Bettles exclaimed. "Cripes, the police never seen this country till eighteen ninety-five!"

Tom nodded. "I asked Corporal Downey, but he'd never heard of him. It's probably like Bettles says. He never got here."

"By God, I know'd Tom wasn't no common cheechako!" Moosehide exclaimed. "His dad was a sourdough!"

Burr MacShane smiled. "He would have been — if he'd got here."

"By cripes, he was one!" Moosehide insisted. "What I claim — if a man even started fer here them days —

**115**

THE WAY OF THE NORTH

he's a damn sight more of a sourdough than the ones that gits here now!"

"Anyways, it shows Tom comes of damn good stock," MacShane opined.

"It ain't who a man's dad was, er what he done, that cuts any figger in this country," Bettles said. "It's what he does after he gets here that counts. If Tom's a good man, it's because he's got guts an' savvy — not because his dad got to someplace — er didn't git there."

"I've hired Porcupine Jack and a couple of men to work the Hunker claim," Tom said. "But I've got to find a couple of more to work with me on Ophir. Where do you fellows pick up men when you need 'em?"

"Over to the Palace, mostly. That's where the cheechakos hangs out. Most of 'em ain't worth a damn when you git 'em. But it's the best you can do."

"I'll drop in there after supper and see what I can do."

The talk became general, a few more drinks were had, and Tom left the saloon and proceeded to the hotel. As he passed the open door of the Klondike Palace a squat, thickset man drew back quickly and jerked his companion from sight.

"That's him now!" he exclaimed under his breath. "I don't dast to let him see me. He'd put the police on me shore as hell."

The other, a tall, spare man with a receding chin and pale, vacuous eyes that flickered uncertainly above a scraggly yellow beard, watched Tom enter the hotel. "What's the police got on you?" he asked.

"They ain't got nothin' now. But they would have if he set up a squawk. He claims I an' another guy stoled his boat on Lindeman, an' he turned me over to the constable. But he was in a hurry to git here, so he wouldn't wait to file no complaint. He'd had to go back to Summit an' be a witness. So all the cop done was to take me back to the line an' shove me acrost. But I snuck back."

"Did you steal his boat?"

"Yeah, we tried to. But we run into some bad luck. An' on top of that, the damn bastard helt my own rifle on me an' made me help sail the boat back, an' then he throw'd the rifle in the lake. An' not only that, I've got a score to settle with him fer knockin' hell out of me down to Sheep Camp."

"How do you know he's goin' to hit out with this here dough?"

The squat man winked. "I know my way around. I use' to be janitor in a bank back in Chi, an' many's the job I've tipped the boys off to — like when pay rolls was draw'd out. I'd give 'em the office, an' they'd clip off the dough an' slip me my cut. When I got here I was broke, so I worked on the cricks awhile an' then hit the bank fer a job. I was in there sweepin' out, couple of hours ago, when this skirt come in an' draw'd out the money — seven thousan' in bills. An' I heard her tell the cashier it was fer expense money an' pay roll that Tom Jorden was takin' out to the cricks in the mornin'. She mentioned Ophir Crick — an' right then I know'd we had somethin'. I know the trail to Ophir — worked a couple of days fer a guy out there. By jeez, I didn't come to this damn country to break my back on the end of no shovel. There's easier ways than that to make a livin', if a man keeps his eyes open. There's an empty shack on a feeder a few rods back off'n the trail. We kin knock him off an' hide out there till the stink blows over. There ain't no other shack nowheres near."

"Who's this here frail that draw'd out the dough — his wife?"

"Naw. Name's Brandon. Him an' her old man's pardners."

"You mean we'll foller him out, an' when we come to this place we'll knock him off?"

"We won't have to foller him, 'cause you'll be right there with him."

"Me!"

"Yeah, you. It's like this — I seen him go into the Tivoli a little bit ago, so I follers him in, keepin' back whar he can't see me. When he gits to talkin' with a bunch of guys, I picks up a paper an' sets down to a table clost enough to hear, holdin' the paper in front of my face, like I was readin' it, an' I hears him tell these guys he's got to hire a couple of hands to work on a claim on Ophir, an' where'll he git 'em. An' they tells him over to the Palace, an' he says he'll go there after supper an' see if he kin find someone. So, when he comes in, you hire out to him an' ask him where his claim's at. An' when he tells you it's on Ophir, you tell him you got a pardner that's workin' on Ophir but he'll be through in a few days an' he'll come to work too. Then he won't hire no one else from here — see? I'll hit out ahead an' pack enough grub to that shack to last us while the heat's on, an' when you come to the place you slug him with this here blackjack I'll give you, an' we'll grab off the dough an' hit fer the shack. Cripes, it's like takin' candy from a kid!"

The other's eyes flickered nervously. "What's the matter with you sluggin' him? I ain't never did no strong-arm work. My grift's pocket pickin' an' dope peddlin'."

"You ain't goin' to git no chanct to pick his pockets — nor yet to sell him no dope," the other growled. "An' as fer me sluggin' him — how the hell could I? I don't dast to show up. If he seen me, the hull thing would be off."

"But — I don't know where this shack's at. How would I know when to slug him?"

"You can't go wrong. It's where the trail makes a bend around a big rock that looks like a face — got a nose an' a chin to it, an' a kind of slit fer an eye that water is tricklin' out of — looks like the guy was cryin'. It's the only rock like it, an' if he hits out in the mornin', like she told at the bank, you'd ort to be gittin' there jest before dark. You kin see this rock quite a while before you git to it, an' then you drop behind, an' when you git there let him have it. Fetch the jack down on his noggin — an' don't be afraid to lean on it, neither, 'cause believe me, that guy's tough. If you don't knock him plumb out, there'll be hell to pay."

The other fidgeted and licked his lips. "I — I don't believe I'll tackle it," he said. "I mightn't —"

The squat man leered at him. "You'll tackle it, brother — don't never think you won't. You'll tackle it, er, by God, I'll drop the word to the police about that there guy you rolled the other night out back of Harry Ash's place."

"What! How'd you know about that?"

The other grinned. "I know, all right — an' someone else knows too. If we told what we know — you'd be in fer a hell of a stretch — an' the police ain't slippin' no dope to prisoners in this man's hoosegow. Jest think that one over."

# CHAPTER
# SEVENTEEN

## The Fight in the Cabin

After Tom's brief report and abrupt departure Sue Brandon sat for a few moments slowly drawing the slip of paper he had handed her back and forth between her fingers. She arose, crossed to the window, and watched until he was lost to view among other pedestrians. Then she glanced over the memorandum. "He's certainly got things going," she murmured, and, crossing the room, pigeonholed the memo in the little desk that stood in the corner. "But — I wish . . . I don't see why he has to be *all* business. He might have told me more about his trip."

The little clock ticked off the passing minutes as she sat there staring straight ahead at the row of pigeonholes in the ugly little desk. Her thoughts drifted back to the first time she had ever seen him — staring at her as she stood at the rail of the boat — and again as he fought the thug who was robbing the old man on Dyea Beach — and again on the outskirts of Sheep Camp, when he had stepped out of the gloom in the nick of time, at the moment of her abysmal terror. Other highlights in long sequence passed before her mind's eye. But in no slightest instance did any act reflect to his discredit.

"Daddy likes him," she murmured, "and the sourdoughs all respect him. And — yes, I do — I love him! I can't help it. And he loves me too. I know it! But why doesn't he tell me he loves me? There've been times when — when he has almost told me, evenings on the long trip down the river — and other times too — but . . ." Vaguely her brain groped for an answer. It's not that he's afraid — he's not afraid of anything. But why has he never mentioned his past? What is the barrier that lies between us, that keeps us apart? Why doesn't he make any close friends? At Lake Lindeman there were dozens of young men, but always he seemed to avoid them, to distrust them. Can it be that, in spite of his conduct since we've known him, he has a discreditable past, even a criminal past?

She glanced at the clock, slipped a checkbook from a drawer, and drew a check. "I'll have to hurry," she said aloud, "or the bank will be closed," and, putting on her hat, she stepped from the room.

At supper Tom again seated himself opposite and smiled at her across the table. "Did you get the cash?" he asked.

The girl nodded and, opening her purse, drew out a neat packet and slip of paper which she pushed toward him. "I did it up in a waterproof package," she said. "I found some material at the store — membrane from a seal's stomach, the man said — or maybe a whale's. They even use it for windowpanes."

Tom nodded. "I got some for the shack windows. Good idea. You can't see through it, but at least it lets in light — and glass would be hard to pack to the creeks."

"I didn't like to leave the money in my room, so I carried it with me," she said. "It's your worry now. Just sign that receipt. Daddy's a stickler for receipts and things like that. And if I'm going to be 'office man,' I'll have to be too."

Tom signed the receipt and slipped the packet into his pocket. "Your dad's right," he said. "Get a receipt for every cent you put out. And be sure and file all the estimate memos too. I'll want to go over 'em from time to time, to see how they check out with actual expenditures."

"What are you doing this evening, Tom?" she asked at the conclusion of the meal.

"Got some odds and ends of supplies to get, and hire some packers to get 'em out to the cricks within the next few days, and hire a couple of men to help work the Ophir claim."

"But — will that take all evening?"

"You bet it will! Men are hard to find — especially good packers. And the damn cheechakos won't work unless they're broke. When I get my crew lined up I'm going to hit the hay. I've been on the go pretty steady lately, and I need some sleep. I want to hit the trail with my Ophir crew at daylight — and daylight comes mighty early this time of year."

Was he purposely avoiding spending the evening with her, or was he just plain dumb? Sudden rage flared in the girl's brain. The blue eyes flashed angrily. "You want to hurry back to the saloon, Tom Jorden!" she said. "You've been drinking! I smelled it on your breath when you first came in!"

Tom smiled into the angry eyes. "That's right," he said, "so I have. And you're right about my hustling back, too. The saloons are about the only place where you can find men when you want 'em." He pushed back and rose to his feet. "So long, Sue. I'll be seeing you — but it may not be for a month."

Furious, the girl watched him pass between the tables and disappear through the doorway. With seven thousand dollars in his pocket, would he be seeing her again? Had he purposely fixed the date of his return so he would have a month's start before any inquiry would be made? Abruptly she left the table, hastened to her room, and threw herself on the bed. Gradually her anger subsided and her face flushed with shame. "I — I was a fool," she muttered. "Suppose he had taken a couple of drinks? He certainly didn't show it. But — he knew I was angry — and he just laughed!" The words ended in a sob, and, burying her face in the pillow, she sobbed and sobbed.

Leaving the hotel, Tom entered the Klondike Palace and stepped to the bar. "Know anyone that wants a job?" he asked of the beaproned figure that faced him across the mahogany.

A man who ranged himself beside him spoke before the bartender could answer. "I do," he said. "Where's it at? An' how much you payin'?"

The speaker was a tall man, and Tom noted the pinpoint pupils that met his glance out of a pair of faded blue eyes above a scraggly yellow beard.

"It's on Ophir," he said. "And I'm paying going wages — an ounce a day."

"Ophir, eh? Say, you don't want to hire another guy too?"

"Yes, I can use two men. You got a partner?"

"Yeah — an' it works out all right. He's up to Ophir right now. Feller he's workin' fer's jest finishing up his dump. Ort to be through by the time we git there."

"Okay. We'll pull out at daylight. Where'll I meet you?"

"Right here's good as any place. I'll go home an' git me some sleep an' be here by daylight."

Swinging along under light packs, the two made good time. The long-legged man seemed tireless, and as they halted at a tiny creek for a noonday snack Tom grinned. "If you're as good on a shovel as you are on the trail, it looks like I've hired a top hand. Is your partner as good as you are?"

"Yeah, you won't never have to fire us. You'll find out both of us is tougher'n hell."

Long shadows cast a gloom over the little valley they were threading as Tom, who was in the lead, paused at the top of a sharp rise and wiped the sweat from his forehead. "We'll camp pretty quick," he said. "We've had a long day."

"Oh, we kin keep on yet awhile," the other replied. "Seems like we'd ort to git as fer as we kin before we quit."

"It's all right with me. I thought you might be getting tired." Tom glanced at the trail ahead. "Look at that

**125**

rock that sticks out almost over the trail," he said. "Looks like a face. See the forehead and nose and chin."

"Yeah," the other answered, wetting his lips with his tongue. "Yeah, that's right — looks like a face. An' — an' there's water drippin' off'n it — like the guy was cryin'."

"That's right," Tom laughed. "You've got a pretty good imagination."

"Yeah," the other repeated somewhat vaguely, "yeah — pretty good."

As Tom rounded the huge rock a blinding flash seared his eyeballs — and the next thing he knew he was lying on the ground and Burr MacShane was bending over him, splashing cold water in his face. His head ached fiercely, and he passed his hand over his eyes several times, as though to rid them of some obstruction. "Is — is it getting dark?" he asked. "Or — am I going blind?"

"It's pretty dark, Tom," MacShane said. "What the hell happened?"

"Where's the other fellow?"

"There ain't no one here but you. I come around the bend there an' damn near stumbled over you."

Tom rose to a sitting posture and felt in his pocket. "What happened," he said, "is that I've been robbed."

"Robbed! Who done it?"

"The man I hired to help me on the Ophir claim. I drew six thousand dollars for expenses, and we hit out at daylight."

"Did this guy know you had the money on you?"

"No — that is, I don't see how he could have known. I sure as hell didn't tell him. Sue Brandon drew it out of the bank yesterday afternoon and turned it over to me at supper in the hotel dining room. Then I went over to the Klondike Palace and hired this bird."

"Hum. He could have seen her draw out the money, an' followed her, and seen her turn it over to you. You weren't alone in the dining room, were you?"

"No. It was right at suppertime. There were a good many in the room."

"An' — in the Palace — did you hunt this fella up? Or did he hit you for the job?"

"Well — since you mention it, he struck me for it. I asked the barkeep if he knew of anyone who wanted a job — and this jasper spoke right up. He was standing beside me at the bar and overheard me."

MacShane nodded. "He knew you had the money, all right. What fer lookin' guy was he?"

"Tall and thin, with long legs, and a yellow beard that sort of grows in patches all over his face, and pale blue eyes with the smallest pupils I ever saw — just like pin points."

"Hophead, most likely. Their eyes is like that. Come on, if you can stand up. We'll find a campin' place. I'm hittin' fer Dawson. The moon'll be up directly. I aimed to keep on travelin'. But I can't leave you — the shape yer in. Cripes, there's a knot at the back of yer head as big as my fist. The bastard fetched you a hell of a crack."

Tom rose to his feet and took a few tentative steps. Finding that he could navigate, he turned to

**127**

MacShane. "You go on to Dawson," he said. "I'm not going. If you run across him on the trail, nail him. If you don't, report the robbery to Downey and give him the guy's description."

MacShane hesitated. "But — hell, Tom — you ain't in no shape to go on! Besides — what the hell can you do? Chance is the bird hit back to Dawson. You'd stand more show of runnin' acrost him there."

"If he hit back for Dawson, you may overtake him on the trail. We've been hitting a good pace all day, and he'll be tired. And he can't have much of a start. It was already growing dark when he socked me. If you don't overtake him, Downey may pick him up. He can't miss him — I never saw another guy that looked just like him."

"But — where are you goin'?"

"On to Ophir. He claimed to have a pardner working there for some fellow that's just finishing up his dump. There's a chance that he may have shoved on to connect up with this partner. I suggested that we camp a while back — but he wanted to keep on for a while. If he'd figured on going back to Dawson, he wouldn't have urged me to keep on going away from there."

MacShane nodded. "There's somethin' in that, all right. Well, good luck, Tom. Sure you're all right?"

Tom laughed. "Sure. Except for a headache, I'm okay. But man — if I ever lay hands on that son-of-a-bitch — he'll know what a headache really is!"

Tom started on up the trail through the darkness. His arms hung heavily from his shoulders, and the light pack on his back seemed to weigh a ton. It required a conscious effort to put one foot before the other. A short distance farther on dizziness and a slight nausea assailed him and he sat down on a ledge of rock. The dizziness and the nausea passed and he raised his eyes to the eastward where the light of the rising moon threw the serrated skyline into bold relief and accentuated the deep gloom of the narrow valley. As he lowered his gaze his shoulders suddenly stiffened. A gleam of light caught his eye — a light that came from somewhere deep within the spruce and birch undergrowth of the valley. He rose to his feet for a better view, and the light disappeared. He took a few steps to the left, then to the right, peering into the blackness of the valley. But there was no light. Slowly he passed a hand across his eyes. "Am I going nuts?" he muttered. "Did that crack on the head knock me cuckoo or something?" He sank again to the ledge, and the light appeared. He stared at it for a long time. It was not the flickering light of a campfire. It was a steady yellow glow — the light of a lantern or of a lamp. He moved his head a few inches to the right and to the left, and the light disappeared. And he realized that by a freak of chance he had hit upon the one spot on the trail from which the light was visible. "Must be a shack over there," he muttered. "Maybe the guy's got an extra bunk. Guess I was kind of optimistic when I told Burr I was all right. My head feels kind of fuzzy, and I'm too damn tired to go much further, anyway."

Stepping from the trail, he made his way through the thick undergrowth with difficulty. The darkness was

**129**

intense, and he had to feel for each step among the stones and fallen tree trunks. He stumbled on and on, pausing every few feet to peer ahead, but no gleam of light caught his eye. If the man had put out his light for the night, Tom knew he had small chance of finding the shack. Then the undergrowth suddenly thinned and he found himself on the lip of a low ledge of rock thickly carpeted with caribou moss — found himself staring straight into a lighted window not fifty feet distant. And as he stared the heaviness left his arms and legs and his brain cleared. Through the window he could see two men seated at a rude table, above which a lantern hung from a wire. One was the tall man with the pin-point eyes, and the other was the thick, squat man — the man who had cornered Sue Brandon on the outskirts of Sheep Camp — the man who had stolen the boat from the Lake Lindeman camp.

Tom's jaw tightened, and his lips set in a hard, straight line. Swiftly he slipped the pack from his shoulders and stood for long moments studying the setup. The window through which the light shone was devoid of glass, and the underbrush near the end of the cabin was lighted for a space of several feet. Evidently the door was missing or had been left open. The squat man sat with his back to the doorway; the other faced it. There was no wind. A deathlike silence hung over the valley, and Tom realized that one false step — the snapping of a twig, the dislodgment of a loose stone — would instantly put the men on their guard. Very deliberately he lowered himself over the four-foot ledge. Then with infinite care he began inching his way toward the shack, placing each foot so as to avoid displacing stick or stone. It was fully ten minutes before he stood at the corner of the shack. Then grimly he unsheathed his belt ax and with two quick strides stood in the open doorway.

The tall man's pin-point eyes widened suddenly. His receding chin dropped and a low, mewling cry issued from his open mouth. The squat one whirled, a pistol in his hand. The hand jerked upward, and there was a loud roar as Tom leaped sidewise into the room. Before the man could fire again, the whirling blade of the belt ax clove the man's skull almost squarely between the eyes. The next instant the tall man went down in a heap, his teeth clashing audibly as Tom's left fist crashed to the point of the receding chin. Blood reddened the floor where the squat man lay, the pistol still grasped in his hand. Crossing to the other, Tom rapidly searched his pockets and explored inside his shirt. Not finding the money, he turned his attention to the corpse, but with no better luck. A hurried search of the shack failed to uncover it, and, stepping to the water pail, he dipped into it and dashed a cupful of cold water in the tall man's face. He dashed another and another before the man came to, muttering and sputtering. Twisting his fingers into his collar, Tom jerked him to his feet, backed him against the wall, and shifted his grip to his throat. The man's eyes widened in horror, his jaw sagged open, and he gasped for breath as the fingers of steel tightened about his windpipe; at the same time they jerked his head forward and slammed it back against the wall in a series of staccato thumps.

Then suddenly the fingers loosed their grip and the heaving chest pumped air into the tortured lungs.

"Where is it — damn you? Where's the money — six thousand dollars you took off me when you slugged me there on the trail?"

The man's voice came in a choking gurgle. "I — never done it. It was him. I ain't got —"

The grip tightened, cutting off the words, and the head thumping was renewed. "You lie, damn you! Come clean — or by God you'll be as dead as he is before morning — only you won't die quick, like he did."

Again the grip loosened, and again the chest heaved convulsively, pumping air. "I — don't know where — it's at. He — tuk it. He —"

Again the fingers clamped down, and again the back of the man's head beat a tattoo against the wall. This time his face was purple when Tom loosened his grip. "I can stand this all night — if you can. And in the morning I'll be alive — and you won't."

"Don't — don't — I — I can't take it — I — I'll tell you — it's — there under the floor — that board — by the wood box."

Slamming the man to the floor, where he lay like a rag, Tom stepped to the wood box, raised a loose board, and lifted the packet from the aperture. The covering had evidently been removed and replaced. Swiftly he counted the bills, recounted them; then, with a puzzled glance at the crumpled heap on the floor, pocketed them.

Lifting the man, he deposited him on the bunk, where he lay, whimpering, choking, gasping. "They was seven thousan' — not six — like you said," he whined.

Tom nodded. "My mistake. Put your feet together while I tie you up."

"Tie me up! My God — what you goin' to do?"

"I'm going to tie you up so you can't get loose, and go back to Dawson for Corporal Downey. He'll want to know what came off here."

The man's voice rose in a thin shriek of terror. "Tie me up! You can't leave me here — not alone — with no dead man! Night'll come before you git back!"

"That's right — maybe two nights."

"I'll starve!"

"You just had a good supper. That'll last till I get back."

"My God — a dead man — in the night — I'll go nuts — crazy!"

"That's all right with me."

"Take me along! Take me anywheres away from here. You can't do that!"

"Can't I? You wait and see." As Tom talked he trussed the man, hand and foot, and bound him to the bunk with straps cut from the two packsacks and a length of old babiche line he found hanging on a nail behind the door. "I'm going to throw a good feed into me, and then I'll be on my way."

All during the meal, which Tom prepared and ate from the supplies the squat man had packed to the cabin, the man on the bunk begged and whined and raved. The meal over, he blew out the lantern and, retrieving his pack from the rock, made his way back to the trail.

# CHAPTER
# EIGHTEEN

## Tom Reports

Arriving in Dawson, Burr MacShane reported the robbery to Downey and later, in the Tivoli, recounted the incident to Swiftwater Bill, Bettles, and Camillo Bill. Still later the bartender repeated it to Jack Gorman, who shortly thereafter met Sue Brandon on the street.

"Hello, Sis," he said. "Too bad about Tom, ain't it?"

"Too bad about him! What do you mean?"

"Why, I'da thought you'd know. Burr MacShane claims he got robbed somewheres on the trail to Ophir. Got six thousan' dollars took off'n him."

"Robbed! Where is he now?"

"Who — Burr? He pulled out couple hours ago."

"No — Tom!"

"Why — I don't know. I guess Burr didn't say. Accordin' to the barkeep, Burr wanted Tom to come back to Dawson with him — but Tom wouldn't."

As the girl made her way to the hotel, icy fingers seemed closing about her heart, fingers of doubt. Had Tom really been robbed? If so, why in the world hadn't he come straight to Dawson to report the robbery to the police, and to her? She went to her room, threw herself on the bed, and, for what seemed hours, lay there staring up at the ceiling.

Two days later she met Moosehide on the street. "Have you heard anything of Tom Jorden?" she asked.

"Heard anything of him! No. What you drivin' at?"

"Why — he was robbed."

"Robbed! When?"

"Three or four days ago — somewhere on the Ophir trail."

"An' — you ain't seen him sence?"

"No. I haven't seen him since I turned over several thousand dollars to him to be spent on the Hunker and Ophir claims. That was the day before he was robbed."

Moosehide's brow drew into a frown. "That's funny," he said, "that you ain't seen him."

"Why?"

" 'Cause I seen him last night right here in Dawson. Jest on the edge of dark. Him an' a couple other fellas was hittin' out of town. I hollered at him, but he never turned around. Seems like he didn't want to hear — er he was in a hell of a hurry er somethin'. I thought it was kinda funny at the time."

The girl was silent for several moments. "Are you sure it was Tom?" she asked.

"Shore's I'm standin' here."

Sue Brandon walked slowly down the street, her eyes straight ahead. Tom Jorden in Dawson — only yesterday — and he had avoided her — avoided Moosehide. There was a lump in her throat, and her heart seemed like a dull weight in her chest. They had been fools to trust him, she and her father, not knowing any more about him than they did. Oh well, it cost only seven thousand dollars to find it out. It might have been much more.

Then one day a week later she looked up from her menu to see Tom Jorden threading his way among the tables, heading straight for her. She felt the color drain from her cheeks, knew that her eyes were staring as he drew out the chair and seated himself opposite her. She knew that his lips were smiling, and in her ears was the sound of his voice.

"What's the matter, Sue? You look like you'd seen a ghost. Well, I've got everything going okay. Porcupine Jack and his men will have the shack finished by the end of the week and will get to work on the dump by Monday. I've got a couple of men working on the Ophir shack. That'll soon be done, and the sluice too. Then we'll find out how good a deal your dad made with Fisher." He drew several papers from his pocket and tossed them across to her. "There's the receipts for the shack and lumber payments, and —"

The girl suddenly found her voice, found that it came in jerky sobs — found, also, that tears were coursing down her cheeks. "But — Tom — they said — Burr MacShane said you'd been — robbed." She fumbled in her purse, found her handkerchief, and dabbed at her eyes.

Tom grinned. "Oh — that! Sure I was. Forget it. Gosh, Sue, it's nothing to cry about. I got the money back, all right. And listen here, lady — the next time you make up a package of money, be sure you count it right! I asked for six thousand dollars — and receipted for six thousand — and you made a mistake and put seven thousand in the package. That's damned careless. Here's the thousand. Better stick it back in the bank."

The girl was smiling now, smiling through the tears that persisted in welling into her eyes, blurring the face across the table.

"Yes sir," she said in mock contrition.

"I mean it, Sue. If you're going to handle your dad's money you've got to handle it right. There's no harm done this time. And I'll never mention it to him. But stop and think what a spot I'd have been on if the mistake had been the other way — and you'd only put five thousand in that packet and I'd receipted for six. Either you'd have thought I got away with a thousand or I'd have had to dig it up out of my own pocket — and I haven't got many thousands to spare."

The girl's eyes were dry now, and the blue eyes met the gray ones squarely. "We wouldn't have thought you took the money, Tom. We — we *know* you are honest. But — there's something I don't understand. Moosehide Charlie told me he saw you in Dawson one evening, only a couple of days after the robbery. He must have been mistaken."

"No, I was here that evening. I had to hire a couple of hands for the Ophir job and report to Corporal Downey."

"But Jack Gorman said that Burr MacShane reported the robbery."

"Yes — the robbery. But I had to report killing one of the robbers and tying the other one up. By the way, the one I killed was that damn scoundrel who followed

**138**

you out from Sheep Camp and later stole our boat. I had to kill him — he'd taken one shot at me and was about to take another. I heard Moosehide holler at me that night, but I was in a hurry — wanted to get my men on the job — and wanted to overtake Downey — he'd gone on ahead."

"Oh — it must have been terrible! Tell me all about it. How could you have killed him — if he had a gun?"

Tom shrugged. "There isn't much to tell. A guy I hired slugged and robbed me on the trail. Burr came along, and I told him to report the robbery to Downey, and I went on. I located the man and our squat friend in a cabin and started in to get the money back when Squatty took a shot at me. I dodged it and caught him between the eyes with my belt ax — used to practice throwing a hatchet and sticking it in trees when I was a kid. Then I punched the other one in the jaw and choked him a bit, till he told me where they'd cached the money. That's all there was to it. Downey gave me a clean bill. We buried Squatty and he brought the other one down with him. He's crazy as a loon."

"All there was to it," the girl repeated slowly. "And then you went on with the job."

# CHAPTER
# NINETEEN

## "I'll Never Marry You!"

Tom swung around to Hunker Creek before returning to Ophir to find the shack and sluice finished and work already started on the dump. Porcupine Jack filled his pipe and squatted beside the pile of gravel. "She's runnin' pretty good, Tommy," he said. "But Jack Fisher had so many irons in the fire that he skipped work on a lot of his locations. This is no hell of a dump, and we'll clean it up in a few days. I expect after that we'd better put in some time cuttin' wood for next winter's minin'. You can tell your boss that he's got a good thing here."

"Sure — go ahead with the woodcutting when you finish the dump. I'll tell Brandon what you said when he gets back."

"Back? Where is he?"

"Off on a prospecting trip."

"Prospectin'! What does he know about prospectin'?"

Tom grinned. "Nothing. He hired a fellow to take him around. He's an old-timer, or claimed to be. Name's Jim Devine, and he claimed to know where there's a lot of likely cricks, way back."

Porcupine Jack laughed. "Jim Devine!" he snorted contemptuously. "He's an old-timer, all right — an' about the only one of the old-timers that ain't worth a damn, anywhere you put him. I wouldn't trust him around the first bed of a crick. Better tell Brandon not to go buyin' any claims off him."

"I don't think it's a question of buying claims. He's paying Devine twenty-five dollars a day as a guide. This Devine probably won't show him anything worth while, but at least Brandon's learning how to get around the country, and that's probably worth what it's costing him."

The old sourdough nodded. "Yeah, most likely. But speakin' of prospectin' trips, I'd shore like to have another go at the Porcupine before someone else hits in there an' locates my crick."

"But how do you know there's anything up there? Most of the sourdoughs don't think much of the lower country."

"If they knew what I know, they wouldn't be sayin' that. I've got a map. An' I've got nuggets that were taken out of this crick — right on the surface!" Pausing, he thrust a hand into his pocket and withdrew a small, dirt-caked moosehide pouch. Loosening the string, he dumped its contents into the palm of his hand. "Look at them. You ain't seen any nuggets like them here in the upper country, have you?"

Tom's eyes bulged as they stared at the irregular, slaglike slugs that showed dull yellow in the man's hand. "Good Lord!" he exclaimed. "Have you showed those to the others?"

"Do you think I want to start a stampede? You're the first one that's seen 'em. Six of 'em — an' if they don't go thirty ounces, I'll eat 'em."

**141**

For a long time Tom stood looking down at the misshapen nuggets. In his visits to the claims of the sourdoughs he had seen much gold, but never nuggets like these. When he spoke his voice betrayed his excitement. "You told me that evening in the Tivoli that if I had money enough to grubstake the two of us for a trip up the Porcupine —"

"That's right!" the other interrupted, his shrewd old eyes lighting. "An' I meant every word of it. Have you got enough?"

Tom nodded, his eyes still on the gold. "Yes," he answered, "I have."

"Your money or Brandon's?"

"My own. I've got four thousand dollars."

"Okay," the oldster replied. "Like I told you, I wouldn't take a grubstake off any of the sourdoughs — it would be charity. But this ain't charity, Tommy — it's business — an' damn good business, too. When can you start?"

Tom considered. "My agreement with Brandon allows me to quit on a moment's notice. I told him I didn't want to be tied down by a contract, that I wanted to be free to hit out on a stampede or hit out on my own at any time. But I can't go till he gets back. I can't leave Sue with these two operations on her hands."

Porcupine nodded. "Shore you can't. An' I've agreed to clean up this dump — an' I'll clean her up. It's the first of July. Of course the sooner we start, the sooner we'll get there. But if we didn't hit out till the first of August, we'd prob'ly make it all right. If we can locate the crick before winter sets in, come spring, we'll have a dump of our own to work — an' believe me, she'll be a dump worth workin'!"

"All right. I'll go on over to Ophir and clean up that dump. If you finish the dump, go to work on the wood, and I'll cut loose from Brandon as quick as I can."

The dump on the Ophir claim was also a small one, and two weeks later Tom weighed up and sacked the last ounce of dust, set his two men to cutting wood, and carried the dust to Dawson.

He stepped into the hotel to meet Sue and her father coming down the stairs. Brandon grasped his hand and pumped his arm heartily.

"By George, Tom, you've done a great job! Heard all about it from Sue and the sourdoughs — and Corporal Downey too. Good work!"

Tom smiled. "Glad you're satisfied," he said. "I've got the Ophir cleanup with me. It wasn't a very big dump, but it panned out all right. Next year you ought to take plenty out of that claim. I've got the men working on the wood now. And I expect Porcupine Jack will have finished the Hunker dump by this time. I'll slip out there and see. How did you make out? And when did you get back?"

"Got back a week ago. Located a couple of propositions on a creek, way back off the river, and recorded 'em. But I had a streak of real luck. I figured on outfitting and hitting right out again. I paid off this guide I had — Jim Devine — gave him seven hundred and fifty dollars for his month's work guiding me, and he got pretty drunk that night, and the next morning he told me he'd decided he'd better go out to his claim and sluice out his own dump before someone beat him to it. He says that with so many cheechakos in the country, some of 'em are apt to slip out there and do some sluicing on their own account if they knew he was off on a trip. His dump isn't very big. He was sick for a long time last winter and couldn't work. But he says his claim is a good one, and he'll probably take out plenty.

"I offered to buy the claim if it was any good — but he just laughed at me — said it was so good he wouldn't sell at any price. I thought it was the whisky bragging and thought no more about it till this morning, when he came here to see me. And what do you think he showed me? A receipt duly signed by the police for nineteen hundred and twenty dollars that he'd paid in as taxes at fifteen per cent on the dust he'd sluiced out of his dump in one week! Just think of it, Tom! He took out twelve thousand, eight hundred dollars in a week — that's better than fifty thousand a month!"

Tom grinned. "That's right," he agreed. "Some claim! But where does your luck come in? I thought you said he refused to sell."

"He did at first. But today the poor fellow is all broken up over a letter he got from his old mother back in Iowa. She begs him to come back home at once. His father is dying, and she'll be left all alone. So he agreed to sell me the claim — but not until he works that dump for another week. He wants to get that much more dust out — and also to prove to me that he hadn't just sluiced out a rich spot in his dump. He's going to

**144**

bring this next week's tax receipt to me, so I can see for myself what he took out."

"Did he name a figure for the claim?"

"Three hundred thousand. That is, providing this coming week's cleanup is as good as last week's. Why — it's a bargain! We can take out that much in six months!"

"You're sure he isn't trying to put something over on you?"

"Certainly I'm sure! I know he was broke when I paid him off. Where else could he have got more than twelve thousand in dust within a week? I verified his tax payment to the police — just got back from detachment. He had the dust, all right — the police weighed it in."

Tom nodded and turned over the little sacks of dust. Brandon pocketed them. "I'll have 'em weighed in at the bank. That seems to be a good claim on Ophir — but dust like this will be chicken feed when we get that Devine claim going!"

"Could be," Tom admitted, and turned toward the door. "Well, I'll be trotting along. Going up to Hunker and see how Porcupine Jack made out."

"But surely, Tom," Sue said, "you're not hitting out today! There's doings at the log church tonight, and —"

Tom shook his head with a grin. "Never put off till tomorrow what can be done today. I learned that in school when I was a kid. So long. Be back in a week."

Tom visited the Tivoli Saloon and had a drink or two with the sourdoughs, then, after stopping for a few moments at the bank, he hit out of town.

145

★ ★ ★

A week later Tom stepped into the hotel practically on the heels of Jim Devine. Brandon, who happened to be in the office at the time, welcomed the two and introduced them, then led the way to his room, where Sue was busy over some papers.

"Well," Brandon asked eagerly, "how did you make out this week?"

Devine handed him the police receipt. "Paid royalty on thirteen thousan', four hundred dollars — eight hundred an' thirty-seven an' a half ounces. That dump's a-holdin' up, all right — gittin' a little better, even. I shore wisht I could stay here an' work it out. But a man can't stay away an' leave his old maw all alone whilst his paw's a-dying that-a-way — could he, Mr. Brandon?"

"Certainly not! I — er — believe you named three hundred thousand as your figure?"

"Yeah, that's what I offered it to you for. Wisht I hadn't. Got another party offered me three-fifty fer it today. But I turned him down. I'm a man of my word, Mr. Brandon. That is," he added, a hopeful gleam in his eye, "if yer still in the notion of buyin'. If you ain't, it's all right with me. I kin git fifty thousan' better fer it inside half an hour."

"Of course I'm in the notion of buying! A bargain's a bargain, Devine. As you say, you're a man of your word."

"All right, Mr. Brandon. Let's git it over with. The *Sarah* pulls out fer White Horse at five o'clock — an' I aim to be on her. Here's the description of the claim — make out the deed, an' I'll sign it."

**146**

Tom picked up the description paper. "This claim's on Moose Creek, I see — a feeder to Squaw Creek."

"That's right. It's the only claim on that there feeder."

"And the dump you've been panning is on this claim?"

"Why, shore it is! Wher' the hell would it be?"

"I was just wondering. And you took this eight hundred and thirty-seven and a half ounces out of that dump this week, eh?"

"That's right."

"Work alone?"

"Shore I did. If I'd had help, it would ben more."

Tom laughed. "If I were you, Devine, I'd take up that other fellow's offer of three hundred and fifty thousand and then hit out on the *Sarah* before he finds out what a damned liar you are. Mr. Brandon isn't interested."

"What do ya mean?" snarled Devine. "Mr. Brandon knows I was broke two weeks ago. An' I fetched in that dust, didn't I? Them tax papers proves it!"

"Certainly they do, Tom!" Brandon exclaimed. "What do you mean by insulting Devine this way?"

"He paid duty on the dust, all right," Tom grinned. "But he didn't get an ounce of it off this claim — or any other. He bought it at the bank — the day after you paid him off."

"But — impossible! The man only had seven hundred and fifty dollars! The idea's preposterous!"

"That may have been all he had when you paid him off. But I stopped in at the Tivoli the other day, after you'd told me about him, and found out that he cashed your check there and started in to play the wheel. He had a remarkable run of luck — both on the wheel and at the faro table — and ran his seven hundred and fifty up to twenty-six thousand, five hundred. Then he quit and got pretty well oiled. Next morning he took the cash to the bank and bought dust with it. It is this dust that he paid the duty on. He went back to his claim, all right, and hung around there all week. So did I — watching him from the rim. But he didn't do a tap of work. In fact there's no dump on the claim — only a little pile of tailings that he had worked dry before he hit out with you on the trip." He paused and turned to Devine, who was edging toward the door. "Don't forget your location papers, Devine," he grinned. "And you might step around to detachment and try to explain to Downey that you paid duty on the same bunch of dust twice. Maybe he'll rebate you — but I doubt it."

When the man had gone, Brandon turned to Tom. "Why — why, the damned scoundrel! But it was a pretty smart trick, at that. And the devil of it is, if it hadn't been for you, it would have worked! How did you happen to suspect him?"

"Porcupine Jack tipped me off that he'd bear watching when I told him you'd gone on a trip with him. So, after I heard his spiel last week, I made some inquiries and followed him."

"By George, Tom, you're all right! I don't know what I'd do without you!"

"Oh, you'll get along all right. Just keep your eyes open, that's all. The fact is, you're going to have to get along without me — for a while, at least."

"What do you mean?"

"I'm going on a prospecting trip with Porcupine Jack. We're going to try our luck in the lower country."

"The lower country! Don't be a fool, Tom! All the sourdoughs say the lower country's petered out!"

"Porcupine Jack don't — and he's a sourdough."

"Probably some addlepated old mossback who's wedded to one idea! Have nothing to do with it. Stay on with me. I need you — and Sue — I'll see that you never regret it. I — I'll double your salary!"

Tom shook his head. "No, my mind's made up. I promised Porcupine I'd go with him after we finished cleaning up the dumps. You'll do all right without me. Remember our agreement called for my quitting whenever I wanted to hit out on my own."

"Yes, I know. But, damn it, Tom — I hate to see you go. I think you're making a mistake. But if your mind's made up — I won't stop you. I will, however, call your attention to an understanding we had — that if you should fail in any venture you undertake, you'll come back to me."

"I'll be back — if I fail. That's a promise."

Brandon stepped from the room abruptly, leaving Tom alone with the girl. The blue eyes raised from the papers on the desk and regarded him intently. "I've never seen Daddy so upset," she said. "Oh, Tom, why do you go? You've got a good thing here — with us. Daddy will see that you have every possible advantage!"

Tom nodded. "I know that, Sue, and it's one of the reasons I'm going. I'm not asking any advantage. I want

**149**

to make my own way. I don't want to be carried along on Sam Brandon's money."

"But — he needs you! And — and — oh, Tom, I need you too! Don't I mean anything to you at all?"

Tom's face flushed a deep crimson. "I — yes, Sue, you mean a lot to me. A lot more than I thought any girl would ever mean to me. And — that's another reason I'm going. Sometime I'm coming back — and I'm going to marry you — but when I do we'll stand on our own feet. We won't ask any odds of your dad — or anyone else. No one can ever say I got along because I was Sam Brandon's son-in-law!"

The blue eyes seemed to deepen as they gazed into his own. Then her lips moved. "I — I will marry you, Tom. But on one condition — that you give up this harebrained trip and stay on with Daddy."

Tom shook his head. "No, Sue. I'm going."

The blue eyes flashed in sudden anger, flashed as they had flashed across the prostrate man that day on Dyea Beach. "Tom Jorden — if you go, I'll *never marry you!*"

Tom walked slowly across the room. In the doorway he turned. "Someday," he said in a low, steady voice, "I'm coming back — and you'll change your mind."

# CHAPTER
# TWENTY

## Down the Great River

Early in the morning of the last day of July, Tom Jorden and Porcupine Jack shoved off in a Strickland canoe on their long journey down the Yukon and up the Porcupine. The sun was already up and a mist hung over the river. For in July night is night in name only on the Yukon.

As the light craft slipped easily along with the current, Tom cast a wistful glance over his shoulder. He wondered when he would see Dawson again — when he would see Sue Brandon. And — would she change her mind? Was he making a mistake in throwing in with Porcupine Jack, as Brandon had told him? Were the sourdoughs right about the lower country? Was Porcupine Jack the addlepated old mossback Brandon had dubbed him? He felt a strange sinking sensation in the pit of his stomach as the unanswerable questions crowded his brain. Doubt assailed him, and an uncomfortable foreboding, as his eyes sought to penetrate the mist ahead — the mist that veiled the foreview and seemed to engulf his future in a vast gray void.

Again he turned for a last look at the familiar wooden buildings, but the mist had closed about them.

**151**

THE WAY OF THE NORTH

He was alone on the river — alone with Porcupine Jack. Just those two, in a world of their own.

In the stern Porcupine Jack, noticing the glances, divined what was passing in the younger man's mind. "Figure it'll be kind of lonesome, eh — just you an' me? Well, maybe it will. We didn't get much of a send-off, Tommy. But when we come back, believe me, they'll all sit up an' take notice. We're goin' to make good, Tommy. We're bound to make good."

At the absolute conviction in the older man's tone Tom's doubt vanished, even as the mist swirled and vanished in a light breeze that sprang up from the south.

"You bet we'll make good!" he replied heartily. "We'll show 'em!"

They were traveling light, carrying only enough provisions in the canoe to last from one trading post to another.

Some four miles below Dawson they passed a collection of shanties and shacks, each with its accumulation of net reels in all stages of disrepair, racks for the drying of fish, and empty meat caches. Numerous boats and canoes lined the beach, and dozens of dogs prowled about or lay stretched in the sun on the sloping embankment.

"That's Moosehide," Porcupine Jack explained. "It's a Siwash town."

"They've sure got dogs enough," Tom opined. "How in the world do they feed 'em all?"

"They ain't only about half fed. Most of 'em don't belong to the Siwashes. They summer 'em for prospectors — cheechakos, mostly. The sourdoughs rather pay a little more an' summer 'em with some white man, so they'll have some meat on their bones when they want to use 'em in the fall. All they get down here is dried fish — an' damn little of that. The Siwashes get more shiftless every year. When I first hit this country there were only a few tradin' posts an' the Siwashes were all trappers, except a few company men. They got along fine too. The men wore company shirts of good wool an' either wool or caribou-hide britches, an' the klooches dressed in druggets an' strouds an' squaw cloth that had some body to keep out the cold. An' now look at 'em — the men in cheap shirts that's got more cotton than wool in 'em, an' overalls. An' the klooches — well, look at the stuff floppin' on those clotheslines! Dresses brought in from outside — flimsy cotton stuff made to sell to Alabama niggers. But it's bright colored, an' the nearest thing they can afford to what the dance-hall girls rig themselves out in.

"Time was when a man could go into any Siwash village an' find some klooch that could make a damn good pair of mukluks, or a moosehide parka, or a rabbit robe. But just try it now! Since the country settled up, the trappin' has gone to hell — an' the Siwashes along with it."

At Forty Mile they replenished their supplies, had a drink or two in Bergman's saloon, and shoved on. At Eagle, on the American side, Doc Hamilton and Bob Steel asked the latest news from Dawson and in return told of the hanging of three men at Circle. They took aboard a Swede who was nursing a hang-over incident

**153**

to a week's debauch, during which he had blown in the eight hundred dollars Al Mayo had paid him for chopping cordwood on a steamboat contract he had at Star City. The picture of dejection, he sat humped up amidships, broke and sick, returning to the job. He uttered no word until, with his destination in sight, Porcupine Jack offered a word of encouragement.

"You'll be all right in a day or so, Ole."

The man raised his face from his folded arms and blinked his bloodshot eyes. "Ja. Oh vell — eesy come, eesy go. Vot de hell!"

"Easy come, easy go," laughed Porcupine Jack as they shoved off after landing the man at the cordwood pile. "If there's any harder, more backbreaking work than chopping cordwood in the summertime, I don't want any of it. Fifty days' hard labor gone in a week! But it was his money — an' if he thinks it was worth it, I suppose it was."

In Circle City, Jack McQuesten greeted them across his counter. "Where you headin', Porcupine?"

"Same country. I'll find that crick yet."

McQuesten shook his head. "Better fergit the Porcupine country. I'm tellin' you this lower country's worked out. Me an' Al Mayo's ribbin' up fer a trip up the Stewart. Better throw in with us. By God, the upper country's where the gold is! I was through there a year ago — an' I know."

"What did you fetch back?"

"It ain't what I fetched back — it's what I know is there. I run onto plenty colors on a crick way back off'n a branch of the Stewart. I wasn't fixed to winter, that trip, er I'd of shore hit it. I'm tellin' you, my crick's got Bonanza backed off the map!"

"So's mine, on the Porcupine, whenever I find it. I hear how you hung a couple of fellows down here."

"Yeah — three of 'em. Windy Smith, an' a couple of more dirty bastards. They murdered a fella up on Birch Crick. Called a miners' meetin' an' give 'em a trial, an' strung 'em up. That's the gallows out there in front of the store. They begged like hell, but it didn't do 'em no good. By God, they learnt their lesson, all right! They can't go murderin' folks around here.

"Better change yer mind an' throw in with me an' Al. Yer a damn good man, Porcupine. I hate to see you wastin' yer time in the lower country. They tell me Dawson's grow'd, this year, till a man wouldn't know it."

"Yeah. Jumped from two thousan' to forty thousan' — an' thirty-nine thousan', nine hundred an' fifty of 'em's cheechakos! Flour's a dollar a pound, an' petrol an' whisky's fifty dollars a gallon, an' everything else in proportion. Yer welcome to the upper country. I don't want no part of it."

On an island in the "flats," halfway between Circle and Fort Yukon, they found Joe Manook, of Rampart, with three white men and half a dozen Indians working to haul a little stern-wheel steamboat off a bar with a Spanish windlass. Here the mighty river, unrestrained by the mountains that hold it to its regular channel, widens and spreads out for two hundred miles into innumerable shallow channels and dead snyes that were the bane of the early navigators of the river.

The two pitched in and helped, and by evening the boat was afloat. That night, about the smudge, Manook nodded approval of Porcupine Jack's decision to have another go at the Porcupine.

"I know that ever sence Carmack made his strike on Bonanza the sourdoughs has all ben cussin' the lower country. But you mark my words — what with folks pourin' in there like they be, the upper country'll peter out, an' then the wise ones'll be comin' back down here. I'm doin' all right around Rampart — an' I'll keep on doin' all right. An' you'll do all right on the Porcupine, if you ever locate yer crick there. A man's got to foller his hunch. You've rode that hunch a long time, Porcupine — an' this might be the time you'll hit it. Me an' you's about the only sourdoughs that's still got faith in the lower country — an' we'll stick to it. By God, I know we're right!"

At Fort Yukon, located at the confluence of the Porcupine and the Yukon rivers, they found that prices had not skyrocketed as they had in Dawson. They took on some supplies and pushed on to Rampart House, one hundred and fifty miles up the Porcupine, where they loaded the canoe to capacity and learned that a free trader had established a post somewhere up the river.

"This is the country," Porcupine Jack said as he pointed to the wares on the shelves. "Good honest trade goods — not the damn cheap outside stuff they're handin' out in Dawson. Look the stuff over — rabbit robes, genuine Yakutat moccasins, and King Island mukluks — stuff that was made by klooches that makes

**156**

'em to wear — not by some damn factory that makes 'em to sell. I'm tellin' you, Tommy, we're goin' to hit her this time shore! We'll keep on goin' till we do!"

# CHAPTER
# TWENTY-ONE

## On the Porcupine

As they camped one evening, some forty miles above Rampart House, Porcupine Jack pointed to a huge rock mass that loomed in the distance. "That's Boundary Mountain," he said. "When we pass that we'll be back in Canadian territory again. We've been on the American side ever since Eagle."

"How far beyond here have you been?"

"Close to a hundred miles, I reckon. I've been as far as the mouth of Old Crow River. It's a good-sized river that runs in from the north."

Tom looked puzzled. "It's funny," he said, "that if you've put in several years prospecting this river, you never got any farther than that. It's only thirty-two days since we left Dawson."

"That's right. But you've got to remember, Tommy, the summer's short up here above the Circle. And I had to prospect every river that run in from the north. Accordin' to my map, the crick where he took out those nuggets runs into a river that runs into the Porcupine from the north."

"But — don't it show which river? Who made the map?"

"An old fellow who was in here years ago. But it ain't a very good map. He must have made it as he went along, comin' down the river. Some of the rivers ain't where he's located 'em on the map. An' some of 'em that look big on the map are hardly more than cricks — an' others that look little are quite a good size. This trip we're goin' to explore the Old Crow. Accordin' to the map, this crick runs in not over two or three miles above the mouth. We ought to be able to locate it soon after we hit the Old Crow."

"Aren't these rivers named on your map?"

"No. The fellow that made it didn't know the names of any of the rivers. I learnt 'em off an old Hudson's Bay Company map that I ran across at Rampart House ten, twelve years ago."

Some forty miles beyond the boundary they rounded a bend to see a long, low building of logs on a flat at the mouth of a river that ran in from the south.

"That'll be the Bluefish River, accordin' to the H.B. map," Porcupine said. "And that's prob'ly the outfit of that free trader we heard about at Rampart House. There wasn't anything here when I came down the river two years ago."

"A trading post in here will be a break for us," Tom opined. "If we locate that crick it'll save us a long trip back for supplies."

Porcupine shrugged. "I'm not countin' much on what we can get from him. Mostly the stuff these free traders handle ain't worth packin' off — cheap, shoddy goods, an' bad whisky for the Siwash trade."

"I should think the police would put a stop to it."

"They do, wherever they can. They know what every sourdough knows — that these hooch peddlers are the orneriest skunks in the country. They trade the Siwashes out of the fur they need for grub an' blankets an' traps an' ammunition. Not only that, but they trade 'em out of the fur that ought to go to the reputable traders to settle their debt — to pay for supplies that have been advanced to them on credit. Of course when they don't show up an' pay their debt, the trader has to refuse 'em credit for the next season. The hell of it is, it's the women an' children that have got to suffer. If it was only the ones that drink the damn rotgut who freeze an' starve, it wouldn't be so bad. The police knock hooch runners off wherever they can, but — take this outfit here — we've come through four hundred miles of American territory to get here. It must be a good two hundred miles from here to Dawson, as the crow flies — an' the police ain't crows. If there's any overland short cut from the Klondike to the upper Porcupine, no one's ever found it. They've got to come up the river from the Yukon or down it from the Mackenzie, and either way the Siwashes would tip the trader off long before they got here, an' he'd have his liquor cached where the police could never find it. An' if his tradin' license was in shape, there ain't a damn thing they could do."

The two beached their craft beside several other canoes and a poling boat and ascended the slight rise to the log trading post, set a few yards back from the river. Beside the building was a meat cache elevated on poles and numerous racks upon which fish were drying in long rows. Sounds came from the rear — sounds of curses, and blows, and snarls, and deep, throaty growls. The two rounded a corner of the building to see a man unmercifully beating a huge dog chained to a post while two Indians looked on in stolid silence.

Tom stepped forward. "Hey, what's going on here?" he asked.

The man whirled to face the two newcomers. He was a large man, heavily bearded, with a cast in his left eye that imparted a diabolical expression to his face. "Who the hell are you? An' whose damn business is it what I'm doin'?" The wry eye glared off at an angle while the other blazed with an insane fury. "This is my dog! The son-of-a-bitch bit me onct too often! I'll break every bone in his body! I'll kill him where he stands!"

"Not that way, you won't. Not with that club. Not while I'm here."

At the words the man's rage broke all bounds. He leaped forward, swinging the club in a blow that, had it landed, would have crushed Tom's skull like an eggshell. But it didn't land. Tom ducked it easily, and as the man spun halfway around with the force of it, he kicked his feet out from under him, and as he went down another well-directed kick from his pac landed squarely on the man's wrist, sending the club spinning to the feet of the huge dog who was lunging against his chain in a vain effort to get at the man on the ground. But the man was up in an instant and again lunged in, arms flailing and fists flying. Then followed several minutes of furious fighting with the two slugging it out toe to toe.

**161**

The trader was no mean antagonist; the very power of his blows rocked and jarred when they landed — but most of them landed harmlessly on Tom's guard, whereas Tom's accurately placed blows landed where they hurt. Blood gushed from the man's nose, dyeing the blond beard, and from the corner of his cocked eye. A powerfully driven blow that landed just above the paunchy belt line sent him to his knees, and as Tom stepped in for a finishing punch he toppled sidewise and buried his face in his arms.

"I got enough," he whined. "Lay off! I'm licked!"

Tom stepped back, then turned toward Porcupine Jack, who, with the two Indians, had been an interested spectator. The next instant, at a sharp cry from Porcupine, he whirled just in time to dodge a heavy stick of firewood that missed his head by inches. The man had regained his feet, and as he stooped for another stick Tom's heavy pac caught him in the groin and he sank to the ground with a scream of pain.

"You asked for it, damn you! If you want to fight that way it's okay with me — I'm tough." Again the pac shot out, catching the prostrate man in the jaw. The blood-soaked beard dropped into the dust, and he lay very still.

Tom strode to the canoe, picked up his rifle, and, returning, shot the dog between the eyes. Then he turned to Porcupine. "Come on," he said, "let's get to hell out of here before this bird comes to and shoots us in the back. At least he won't be able to take it out on that dog."

162

Porcupine Jack grinned. "He damned near got you, Tommy. But you learnt a lesson. When you fight with the likes of him, a fight's a fight to the finish — an' no rules. Never give a rat like him a break. Give him all you've got — an' then some. An' never quit till you've got him licked — an' damn good an' licked."

# CHAPTER
# TWENTY-TWO

## Tom Jorden Tells a Story

Day after day the two pushed on upriver, camping now and again to pan the gravel on a likely looking bar or to prospect a promising creek. They frequently consulted Porcupine's map — a crude affair sketched on a fragment of very old canvas. The main river depicted on the canvas was fairly easy to follow, but the nameless tributaries, sketched in with what appeared to be either berry juice or blood, much faded, were almost impossible to correlate with the mouths of the rivers and creeks they passed.

"As a matter of fact," Tom said one evening as they strove to identify a blurred red mark on the map as a flat-topped mountain that showed in the distance, "this main river here might not even be the Porcupine. The man that made this map certainly knew nothing of map making. How do we know that the top of this map is north? It might be south or east or west, for all we know."

Porcupine Jack shook his head. "There ain't no one that wouldn't know the top of a map was north," he opined. "We've got to believe that, Tommy, if we believe anything. If it ain't true, then all the years I've put in up here have been wasted. But there's another thing that goes to show that this is the right river — all these smooches are on the north side way back from the river — an' they must mean mountain chains — they couldn't mean anything else. And if they do — then this is the river, all right, because there ain't another river in the country that I ever saw or heard of that has mountains only on the north side. The rest have mountains on both sides — or no mountains at all."

"But there are mountains on the south side of this river."

"Only a few stray ones here an' there. But the regular chains are to the north. Then here's another thing — see those two marks there, runnin' parallel with the river — they're in the right place to mark a canyon that we'll be comin' to in a few days. This is the river, Tommy. And we'll hit that location sure, this time. An' when we do, we'll have another Bonanza! It ain't far, now, to the mouth of the Old Crow River. An' this crick we're huntin' ain't only a little ways up it."

"It better not be far," Tom said, only half convinced by the oldster's argument. "The freeze-up's going to hit us pretty quick. There was ice on the backwaters this morning, and the little lakes have been frozen for a week."

"That's right," Porcupine admitted. "But there's a Siwash camp at the upper end of the canyon. We'll pick up a sled an' four, five dogs, an' when the river closes up we'll make better time on the ice, an' do it easier."

In his heart Tom Jorden was pretty well discouraged. He realized that had he suspected how vague and

**165**

unreliable Porcupine's map was he would never have financed the venture. The long winter would be upon them within a few days, and here they were, nearly a hundred miles beyond the nearest trading post — not counting the hooch-peddling trader, who probably wouldn't sell them supplies at any price now — with only a very old and a very faulty map to guide them. That — and Porcupine Jack's indomitable faith. Yes, and the little sack of big nuggets in Porcupine Jack's pocket. Tom tossed another stick on the little fire. Faith — and nuggets. The two words repeated themselves in his brain, and he glanced across the fire into the face of the old man, whose shrewd gray eyes were fixed on the little flames that played about the stick of wood. There was nothing of discouragement in those eyes — only contentment, and an abiding certainty that this time they would strike it.

A wave of shame mingled with anger swept through Tom's brain. Shame at his own discouragement — anger at his lack of faith. Porcupine Jack had put in fifteen years on this river with never a thing to show for it, and his faith was unshaken. Yet his own faith was tottering in less than two months! Faith and nuggets. Another Bonanza. That was Porcupine Jack. *That was the North!*

The anger subsided, and as he sat there he realized that he was infinitely richer for this trip even if they never found the creek they sought — richer for the hard days of the river trail and the long talks over the campfire in the evenings. People were different, here in the North, from those he had known in the small

Midwest town. Here were men and women of vision — vision and a high hope. The Brandons and the sourdoughs were real people — people who gladly staked their lives and their fortunes on the chance of making a strike. People who went broke with a laugh — and tried again. He had seen men sell properties of known value for a tithe of what they were worth, merely so they could hit out and make another strike on another far-off creek. *"We might find another Bonanza!"* That was the hope that lured them on, and on, and on.

And as he compared these men with the men he had known back home, with their petty jealousies and their petty aims and accomplishments, he pitied rather than resented their attitude toward himself. He knew that of them all only old Dr. Leroy was the equal of these men of the high North — the only one of them all who would have fitted in.

Tom realized, as he sat staring into the little fire, that from Porcupine Jack he had learned much wisdom — much forbearance, and tolerance for the frailties and the shortcomings of others. In all these talks the old man had never mentioned his past, nor had he ever questioned him about his. Tom suspected that there had been a past, either unsavory or sad — one that the oldster strove either to forget or to ignore. His own past he was willing to forget, as one would forget a bad dream. Even so, as he sat there, an uncontrollable urge came over him to talk — to tell this old man of the bitterness and the aloneness of his life among those

**167**

who either pitied or scorned. Instinctively he knew that Porcupine Jack would understand.

"When I was a little kid," he began, his eyes on the licking flames, "I had the finest dad any kid ever had. We lived in a little town in Minnesota, where he and his brother owned a hardware store. Sometimes in the summer he'd knock off early and we'd go fishing in the lake, and just on the edge of dark he'd row ashore on some sandy beach and we'd go swimming. He taught me to swim before I was five years old. Other evenings we'd walk in the woods and along the creek, and he'd tell me all about the things we saw — birds, and animals, and snakes, and frogs. And winter evenings he'd read to me until I fell asleep, and then he'd carry me upstairs and put me to bed. I had no mother — she died when I was a baby. You know, I'll always remember those days and those evenings — as long as I live I'll always remember them." He paused, and beyond the fire Porcupine Jack nodded, his lips clamped tightly about the stem of his pipe, his eyes on the little flames that threw the shadow of his hat-brim over his upper face.

"Yes," he said slowly. "A man would."

"And then one day my dad was gone — and I never saw him again. I was too little to understand at the time — but I learned. My uncle and his wife and two kids moved into our house, and I lived with them. The house was the same — but it was a different world I lived in after they came, a damned sight different.

"I picked up the story of my dad's disappearance — a little here and a little there — as the years went by. He had skipped out because of a crime. It was a crime he never committed. But in the whole town there was only one person besides me who believed he had not committed it — old Dr. Leroy. I think that with the exception of my dad, he is the finest man I ever knew.

"It seems the town banker was a young man named Joel Stowe. And on one of my dad's business trips to Minneapolis he learned from a broker friend that Stowe was an inveterate gambler in wheat and that he had been losing heavily and steadily of late. The broker was worried about Stowe's account and inquired about his resources.

"Dad was worried, too, as both his personal funds and the funds of the store were deposited in the bank. So when he got home he went at once to Dr. Leroy and reported what he had heard. The doctor agreed that it would be well to draw their money from the bank, saying that he would draw his in the morning. But Dad wouldn't wait till morning. He hustled over to the bank just before closing time and presented a check covering his entire deposit and another for the funds of the store — some ten thousand dollars in each account.

"Knowing that the bank was in trouble, and that there was not sufficient cash on hand at the moment to honor the checks, the cashier stalled, telling Dad he'd have to see Mr. Stowe in the morning.

"According to the cashier, Dad got mad and demanded the money then, and when he was refused payment he swore he wouldn't wait till morning and wanted to know where he could find Stowe right then. The cashier told him he had gone out to his farm, some five miles into the country. Stowe lived in bachelor's quarters over the bank but owned several farms he had taken over on mortgages. Dad left the bank, saying he was going out to the farm and bring Stowe back and get his money right then — or else. Dad evidently went home, hitched his mare to the runabout, and headed for the farm, as several people saw him drive out of town in that direction shortly after banking hours.

"Later the sheriff learned that shortly after noon on that same day Mr. Kay, the local manager for the Peabody Grain Company, had gone to the depot at traintime to get a package of money to be used in paying for wheat drawn to the elevator by farmers. The company paid in cash, and not by check, in the small towns, each elevator having an iron safe in the office. The express agent turned over the package containing twenty thousand dollars in bills to Kay, who receipted for it. As he did so, the telegraph operator told Kay he hoped he'd have better luck with the money than the elevator man a few stations up the line had had the night before. He said he got the report over the wire that yeggs had blown the safe and got away with eight or ten thousand dollars.

"Just at that moment Stowe stepped into the depot on some errand on his way to the farm, and Kay told him of the robbery and asked him if he'd mind slipping the package of money into the bank vault for the night, as he was afraid the yeggs might try to repeat. Stowe agreed, counted the money, receipted for it, walked out of the depot with the package under his arm, stepped into his rig, and drove away.

"The tenant on Stowe's farm told the sheriff that Stowe had arrived at the farm about the middle of the afternoon, stopped at the house to give some instructions, and had driven on to the back pasture, half a mile distant, where they were building an underpass to allow the cattle to go under the railway track that bisected the farm. He said that there was only one laborer at work on the underpass at the time — a tramp who had asked for a job a few days before.

"This man said that a couple of hours later Dad had driven up as he was busy about the barn with his evening chores and inquired for Stowe. He said that Dad had seemed mad about something, and when he told him where Stowe was, Dad drove on out through the wood lot in the direction of the back pasture. He said that about three quarters of an hour later, as he was eating supper, he looked out the window and saw Dad drive back through the farmyard. He said he was driving fast and his face looked kind of grim.

"He said the tramp didn't show up for supper, and when darkness fell, and neither Stowe nor the tramp had appeared, he lighted a lantern and walked back to look for them. He found Stowe's horse, hitched to the buggy, tied to a fence post near the underpass, but saw nothing of either Stowe nor the tramp. He hollered, and, getting no answer, he hunted around and finally came upon the badly mutilated body of a man lying on the railroad track. The man had evidently been run over by a train. One glance at the blood-soaked seersucker suit told him the body was Stowe's, although the body

**171**

had been decapitated. The head, by the way, was never found.

"The man said he jumped into Stowe's rig, hit hell bent for town, and notified the sheriff, who returned with him at once.

"They investigated as best they could by lantern light, and removed the messed-up body from the track. Then the sheriff returned to town, sent the undertaker for the body, and questioned Dad, who told him that he had driven to the underpass where he found Stowe giving orders to the man who was working there. He said he demanded his money from Stowe, telling him that he knew of his losses in the wheat pit. He said that Stowe promised him he could have it the minute the bank opened in the morning, that it was impossible to get it sooner, as the time lock on the vault was set for 9 a.m. Dad told the sheriff that he had then driven back to town. He said the tramp who was working there could verify his story of his short conversation with Stowe, though of course he couldn't have overheard what they said.

"The next morning the bank didn't open its doors, and thorough search of the vault failed to turn up the package of money Kay had turned over to Stowe. The cashier also admitted that there was only eleven hundred dollars in cash on hand. He said that Stowe had recently made heavy drafts on the bank from Minneapolis.

"About noon the sheriff arrested my dad for the murder of Stowe, several people having identified the body. No trace of the grain company's money was

**172**

found, nor was the tramp ever seen again, although news came later in the day from the next town, only a few miles beyond the farm, that a tramp had been seen boarding a westbound freight the night before.

"Further inquiry brought out the fact that the engine crew of a fast freight coming downgrade just on the edge of dark said that they swept around a curve at the underpass and saw an object lying across one of the rails. The engineer said he applied the brakes but the heavy train couldn't be stopped until it had passed over the object. He said they hadn't stopped to investigate because they were behind time, and both he and the fireman were sure the object they had run over was a dog.

"Dad stuck to his story, pointing out that the tramp could have murdered Stowe and made off with the package of money that Stowe was supposed to have had with him. He also pointed out that the farm tenant could have murdered both Stowe and the tramp and disposed of the tramp's body altogether.

"They held a preliminary hearing, and the evidence they produced made things look mighty bad for Dad. The cashier told of his demand for the cash, and of his anger when the checks were not honored, and of his threat to get it that day — or else. The tenant said that Dad seemed mad about something when he inquired for Stowe, that he drove to the pasture in search of him, and that he drove rapidly past the house on his return, and his face looked grim.

"The sheriff's theory was that Dad had demanded the money from Stowe, who, knowing the bank was

173

short of funds, showed him the cash he had got from Kay and maybe offered him part of it, but that Dad probably demanded it all, as it was the exact amount of his two checks, and that when he refused, Dad flew into a rage and killed him, took the money, paid the tramp to disappear, and then hid the money someplace between the farm and town.

"Even his own brother and partner admitted that Dad had a bad temper, once he got riled up, and that he was pretty mad when the cashier refused payment on the checks. He said Dad had stopped in at the store before hitting out for Stowe's farm and said that Stowe would hand over that money today, or he'd wish he had.

"About the only evidence in Dad's favor, and that didn't go very far, was the speech old Dr. Leroy made, pointing out that Dad had always been a model citizen and that they were fools to think that he would kill a man over a matter of money.

"But it didn't do any good, and Dad was bound over to the district court to be tried on the charge of murder. The county seat where the trial was to be held was thirty miles away, and next day the sheriff started for there in a light spring wagon with Dad handcuffed on the seat beside him. About halfway along the road Dad clouted him over the head with the handcuffs, took the key from the sheriff's pocket, and disappeared, after turning the horses loose and locking the sheriff to a wheel.

"I had kind of a tough time after that. Uncle George and his wife believed Dad guilty — or pretended to, though there were those who said he wanted him out of the way so he could have the store to himself. They had two kids, and when we quarreled, as kids will, no matter what happened, their kids were always right and I was always in the wrong.

"Everyone in town believed Dad was guilty except old Dr. Leroy. Some of 'em said it served Stowe right, and others regarded him as a common murderer for robbery. Half of 'em pitied me, and the other half hated me — and I hated 'em all, for thinking Dad was guilty.

"Uncle George let me finish high school and then put me to work in the store. He paid me fifteen dollars a week — five in cash, five that he withheld for board and lodging, and the other five he withheld to pay for my clothes and keep up to the time I started to work.

"When I read about the gold rush to the Klondike I told Uncle George I was going — but he wouldn't advance me any money — told me I couldn't go anywhere till I'd worked long enough to pay him back what I had cost him. I often wondered whether I wasn't entitled to a half interest in the store — but knowing how people felt toward Dad, and of the raw deal he'd got, I knew they'd never give me a break, so I kept still.

"I decided to hit out for the Klondike anyway, and with the few dollars I'd saved in my pocket, I started for the train the next morning and happened to meet Dr. Leroy just stepping into his buggy. When I told him where I was going and how much money I had, he told me to wait in his office. In a little while he came in and handed me five thousand dollars that he'd managed to get somehow out of Uncle George. He told me I might

**175**

possibly run onto my dad up here in the North. He said he believed that he would hit for somewhere in the Arctic because an old uncle of his who was a sailor on a whaler had been wrecked somewhere up here and, in coming out, had found gold along some river. The doctor said this old sailor had given my dad a map and some nuggets he'd picked up. And that's one of the reasons I wanted to have a go at this lower country — because it's nearer to the Arctic, and it might be just barely possible that I can run onto some trace of him. I haven't had any luck. I wouldn't even know him if I saw him. I've asked Bettles, and Swiftwater Bill, and Moosehide, and all the old-timers, but none of them ever heard of him. It's fifteen years since he pulled out, and Bettles said if he'd been in the country that long he'd surely have run across him. Swiftwater thinks that if he hit north at all, it was probably on some whaler that never got here. Gee, if I could find my dad, I wouldn't care if I never made a strike. But I guess it's no use. He's been gone too long. His name is John Jorden. You never ran across him, did you?"

Beyond the fire Porcupine held a brand to his pipe, which had gone dead. He slowly shook his head. "Nope. I never met anyone by that name. But don't give up, Tommy. You might find him yet. A man can never tell when his luck will change. If a man quits, his luck will never change — if he don't quit, it might. That's what's kept me comin' back here all these years. I might never locate the crick we're huntin'. This trip might be just like all the rest. But, if I don't locate it, you can bet your life it won't be because I quit."

**176**

# CHAPTER
# TWENTY-THREE

## At the Siwash Village

After much dickering they managed to buy four dogs and a sled from the little band of Indians whose village was at the head of the rapids. They camped for ten days at the village, waiting until Porcupine Jack judged the ice on the river to be safe for sled travel.

Above the mouth of the Bluefish River the timber thinned perceptibly, becoming smaller in size and more scattered, with only an occasional thicket of stunted spruce. They had pitched their tent within the shelter of such a thicket, a few hundred yards from the village, which consisted of half a dozen pole-and-mud hovels strung along the river at the head of the canyon.

One morning a week after their arrival a series of loud cries and shrieks brought the two from their tent to see a young Indian woman, holding a baby in her arms, running away from a man who was lashing her with a dog whip.

"Hey — cut that out!" Tom yelled, recognizing the man as one from whom they had bought two of the dogs. The woman sped past him, heading for the shelter of the spruce copse, and as the man reached him he stuck out his foot and tripped him. As he sprawled on the ground, a half-empty quart bottle fell from his pocket. Tom picked up the bottle as the man scrambled to his feet cursing. He was one of the two Indians in the village who had a smattering of English, the other being his wife, the woman he was beating, both having worked for the factor at Rampart House. The man, evidently the worse for liquor, advanced, drawing the whip back threateningly, demanding his bottle.

Tom stood his ground. "Hit me with that whip, and it'll be the last man you'll ever hit," he said. The Indian halted, stared into his eyes for a moment, and the whip arm dropped to his side. Tom turned to the woman, who had paused at the edge of the copse. "What's the trouble?" he asked. "What was he whipping you for?"

"Heem go trader, git flour, git shell for de gon. Com' back. Got no flour. Got no shell. Got hooch. Git droonk. All de money gon'. I'm geev um hell. Heem git mad."

Tom turned on the man. "Why didn't you get the flour and shells?" he asked. "We paid you eighty dollars for those two dogs. What did you do with the money?"

"Buy hooch," the man replied sullenly. "Two qua't — eighty dolla."

"Good God! Do you mean you paid eighty dollars for two quarts of whisky and didn't get any flour or shells! What are you going to eat? And how are you going to kill any meat without shells?" The man relapsed into sullen silence; lowering his eyes, he became absorbed in tracing a pattern in the dirt with the toe of his moccasin. "Who is this trader that sold you the hooch?" Tom demanded.

The woman who had stepped closer replied: "Heem nem Cronk. Got pos', Bluefish Riv."

Tom nodded. "That's what I thought. I've got a mind to go down there and smash every damn keg he's got on the place!" He turned to the man. "And you — I ought to take that whip and wind it around you a few times — just for luck!"

The woman shifted the baby and laid a hand on Tom's arm. "No wheep," she pleaded. "My man good man w'en he no git de hooch."

"Okay," he said, and turned to the man. "Where's that other bottle of hooch?" he demanded. "You said you got two bottles."

The woman answered: "All gon'. Heem dreenk wan bottle las' night."

"Cripes — no wonder he's drunk!" Tom turned to the man and held up the partially emptied bottle. "It would serve you right if I'd smash this on a rock. But along toward evening you'll be needing a good stiff drink, and another one in the morning, so I'll hang onto it. You folks go back home now and quit your scrapping. Mind you — if you hit the woman again, you don't get a drink. I'll smash the bottle and whale hell out of you besides. And you bring her along when you come for your drink."

The two turned and walked side by side toward the village, and Tom returned to the tent to see Porcupine Jack smiling in the doorway.

"From what I hear from Moosehide an' Sue Brandon, you sort of make a specialty of hornin' in on other folks' troubles, Tommy."

"Sue Brandon! Do you know Sue Brandon?"

"Oh, shore. Moosehide introduced me to her one day on Front Street. We got to talkin' about this an' that, an' she told me about you knockin' hell out of a couple of thieves down on Dyea Beach, an' again about savin' her from some thug at Sheep Camp. Then there was the trader beatin' his dog — an' now this Siwash. An' besides that, from what I hear, you've had considerable scrappin' to do on your own account, what with those fellows tryin' to steal your boat on Lake Lindeman an' robbin' you on the Ophir trail."

"It's all in the day's work, I guess. Old Dr. Leroy told me I'd run up against some tough characters. He said I'd run onto the best as well as the worst here in the North. And I guess he was right. I've run onto both. I don't mind the scrapping. When I was a kid I had to lick nearly every kid in town before they learned to quit taunting me about my dad's being a murderer."

Porcupine Jack's smile widened. "You ought to meet Black John Smith. You'd like him. An' I've got a hunch that he'd like you."

"Who's Black John Smith?"

"Oh, he's an outlaw that lives on Halfaday Crick — way up the White River somewhere. They say he knocked off an Army pay roll over in Alaska. And the talk is that he's pulled some fast ones here in the Yukon. But nothin' that Downey can lay his hands on. But at that he does a damn sight more good than he ever done

180

harm. He's the only man in the whole North that goes out of his way to straighten out other folks' troubles for 'em." Reaching out, he took the bottle from Tom's hand, removed the cork, and gingerly took a taste of the contents. He made a wry face and spat. "Forty dollars a quart for that damn stuff! Half water an' half alcohol that's had chewin' tobacco soaked in it."

"It's a damned shame," Tom exclaimed, "to cheat these poor devils that way! I ought to do just as I said and go down there and smash every barrel or keg or jug he's got!"

"We'll be goin' down past there before long. We'll have to get supplies, either there or at Rampart House. The first thing we want to do is to locate that crick where these nuggets came from, before the snow gets too deep. This ain't a big snow country down here, but we're bound to get some before long. If it stays cold, we'll be pullin' out of here in a few days."

Toward evening the Indian and the woman appeared at the tent.

"How about it?" Tom asked, addressing the woman. "Has he been good?"

She nodded. "All day lay on de bed. Git oop. Chop de wood. Puke. Lay on de bed. Git oop. Chop de wood. Puke. Giv' um dreenk. Mebbe-so kin sleep."

Tom grinned. "Okay," he said, and poured a liberal drink from the bottle into a tin cup which he handed to the man, who reached for it with a hand that trembled so violently that he was compelled to use both hands in conveying the cup to his lips. "That'll probably fix him

**181**

up, if it don't kill him. But what are you folks going to do if you have no flour or shells?"

The woman answered. "We got some flour. Got some shell. Got fur. Chrees'mas tradin' com', I go trade. I git flour. Git shell. You bet."

# CHAPTER
# TWENTY-FOUR

## On the Gravel Flat

Three days later the two pulled out. The going was excellent on the new river ice and they made good time, reaching the mouth of a considerable river that flowed in from the north by starlight. "This is the Old Crow, according to the H.B. map. I camped right here once before," Porcupine Jack said as they sat sipping tea over the supper fire. "Two years ago, it was. But I didn't dare to go on. Game was scarce that year, an' I figured I had just about grub enough left to take me back to Rampart House."

Tom nodded thoughtfully. "We haven't seen much game this year, either. Wood is scarce, too, and it's getting scarcer as we go along. That little grove of spruce we camped in at the head of the canyon is the biggest patch of timber we've seen since we left the Bluefish. And our grub is running low besides."

Porcupine nodded. "That's right, Tommy. But we ain't so bad off, at that. A man can never tell what he's goin' to run onto in this country. Just because we haven't found any game to speak of on the Porcupine is no sign we won't on the Old Crow. There might be plenty of moose up there, an' caribou, too, for all we know. An' there might be plenty of wood. I know we're pretty far north for wood, but Burr MacShane has been a lot farther north than this — way up past the Endicotts, on the Colville, he was. An' he told me that he run onto two different patches of timber on cricks up there — when he'd been travelin' for weeks without seein' a stick of timber. There's always a chance of findin' timber where no timber's supposed to be. An' as for grub — it ain't so far to that post on the Bluefish. Cripes, Tommy, we're sittin' pretty. Just think of it — a week or two weeks from now we might be scoopin' out nuggets bigger'n any of these I've got in my pocket! An' we might be livin' high on fresh moose an' caribou! An' we might find one of those patches of timber like Burr MacShane found! We might strike another Bonanza! An' then they'll all come pilin' in here — first the sourdoughs an' then the damn cheechakos. An' what'll the sourdoughs be sayin' about the lower country then? They'll be sayin' I was right. They'll be sayin' I knew more'n all of 'em put together — me an' old man Manook! Why, jest look around you, Tommy. Look at this big flat here! Inside of a year there might be a town right here where we're sittin' that will make Dawson look like a dirty deuce in a new deck! There's a damn sight more room here at the mouth of the Old Crow for a town than there was at the mouth of the Klondike — an' no slough to fill up, neither! We'll name it Jorden — that's what we'll do! We'll name it for you, Tommy!"

From beneath his rabbit robe that night Tom gazed up at the winking stars. "There *might* be moose, and there *might* be caribou, and there *might* be wood,

**184**

and there *might* be big nuggets, and there *might* be a big town here," he repeated softly. "That's faith. That's the philosophy of the sourdoughs. *We might strike another Bonanza!*"

Progress up the Old Crow River was slow. They laboriously prospected every little creek and feeder, pecking at the iron-hard gravel with the picks they had purchased at Fort Yukon. Snow came in short, wild flurries of flinty particles that piled up in wind-packed drifts and ridges, leaving the ground bare. They found no wood, except a few scattered spruce trees and stunted willows in the creek valleys, and no moose or caribou. Tom shot a wolf one day, and it furnished meat for a week. The gill net furnished fish aplenty for themselves and the dogs. And save for a scattering of tiny nuggets, they found no gold.

One evening, after two weeks of hard work, Tom lifted the kettle from the smoky, sodden fire. "There's more smoke than heat to this green willow," he said. "It's taken an hour to boil a couple of fish. I hate to be a quitter, Porcupine — but it's a cinch we can't go on like this. Our flour's all gone, we finished up the last of the wolf several days ago, and now we've got nothing but fish — and boiled fish, at that. We used up the last of the pork, so we can't fry 'em. Not only we haven't seen a moose or a caribou, but we haven't seen signs of any. And even you admitted we haven't found gold enough to bother with. Even if we did strike it lucky, we couldn't do any winter mining. We have a hell of a time collecting wood enough to cook with."

"We ain't up the river far enough to know what she's really like, Tommy," Porcupine said, spearing a fish from the kettle with his fork and transferring it to his plate. "Cripes, we ain't only four, five miles off the Porcupine. Any one of these cricks is liable to be the one we're huntin'. Course we ain't struck anything yet like these nuggets in my pocket, but take it in the summertime, when the surface gravel's thawed — a man could take out wages on most any of 'em. I don't like boiled fish any better'n you do — but boiled fish beats nothin' all to hell. It'll keep a man goin'. I don't believe the man that made this map went very far back off the Porcupine. The place he's got marked where he found the nuggets shows that. Like you say, if we don't find timber we couldn't do any winter minin', even if we made a strike. But if we do make it, we could come back next summer an' rig up a scow an' cut the timber on the Porcupine an' fetch it up here. Then we'd be all set for next winter. Besides that, we could prob'ly snipe enough of them big nuggets off the gravel bars to more than pay expenses. Those big nuggets are here — somewheres — an' it's up to us to find 'em. Tell you what we'll do — we'll keep on for a week, an' then if we don't strike it, we'll go back to the post on the Bluefish an' get us some supplies an' come back. I've got faith in this lower country, Tommy. It ain't all gummed up with cheechakos — an' the gold's here. All we've got to do is to find it."

Tom smiled. "Okay," he said. "We'll stick it out on boiled fish for another week — but believe me, if

**186**

anyone ever mentions boiled fish to me after we get out of here, I'll knock him for a loop!"

Three days later they halted at the mouth of a creek that flowed in from the northeastward. This creek was larger than any of those they had encountered, its valley was wider, and the gravel flat at its broad, deltalike mouth showed numerous old channels. Porcupine Jack's faded blue eyes seemed to sparkle with a new intensity as he pointed to a range of high mountains that loomed dimly on the northern horizon.

"Accordin' to that H.B. map, those must be the Davidson Mountains. They ain't only fifty, sixty miles away, an' the coast's about the same distance beyond them. Tommy, we're right now standin' within a hundred an' fifty miles of the Arctic Ocean."

Tom grinned. "Yeah? Well, it's all right with me if we never get any closer." He looked up to see the oldster striding rapidly across the flat toward what appeared to be a dilapidated framework of willow built against the low gravel bank of one of the ancient channels. He saw him pause and examine the structure, then turn and beckon excitedly. "Come on, Tommy! I bet we've found it! I bet this is the crick we're huntin' for!"

Hastening to the spot, Tom eyed the arrangement of sticks, dried and weather bleached by the passing of many years. "Some Siwashes probably camped here a long time ago," he said. "They stretched hides over this and made a kind of a tent."

Oblivious to the observation, Porcupine Jack was on his knees drawing something from beneath a flat rock that protruded slightly from the gravel cutbank. The object was a mouse's nest — a quart or more of matted ravelings which the old man examined minutely. After selecting a few ravelings, he tossed the nest to the ground and, reaching into his pocket, withdrew his precious map, removed the waterproof membrane covering, selected a raveling from one of its frayed edges and compared it with the ravelings he had taken from the nest. When he spoke his voice was tense with suppressed excitement.

"This is the place," he announced. "This is the crick where my nuggets came from."

Again Tom grinned. "I didn't notice any mouse's nest marked on your map," he said.

"No. But these ravelin's are the same as the ravelin' I got off the map. Don't you see, Tommy! It wasn't Siwashes that camped here. It was a white man. Those poles are lashed together with tarred rope. Siwashes would have used babiche or strips of hide. It was canvas stretched over these poles — not hides. An' it was from a piece of that same canvas he drew his map on, while he was camped here years an' years ago, that the mouse gnawed off the edges for his nest. I just happened to see it stickin' out from under that rock. We'll camp here, Tommy. Somewhere on this gravel flat we'll find where he got those nuggets!"

Despite his growing skepticism, Tom caught something of the old man's excitement as he minutely examined the ravelings the other passed to him. The threads were undoubtedly of the same texture and thickness. Then suddenly his eyes widened and he pointed to a spot a hundred feet farther along the

**188**

cutbank. "And, by gosh, I don't believe we're going to have to hunt very far, either! See that hole there in the bank? Water never made that hole! I'll bet that's his tunnel!"

Both dashed toward the spot and, dropping to their knees, peered into the aperture which extended some ten or twelve feet into the cutbank. Frost and seepage had dislodged gravel, from the roof and sides, which had fallen to the floor and lay in an irregular heap.

"We'll make camp, Tommy," Porcupine said, "an' then we'll clean out this loose stuff an' run the tunnel on in."

Tom glanced at the iron-hard face of the cutbank. "What are we going to use for wood?" he asked. "How are we going to thaw out the gravel without any fire?"

Porcupine Jack's eyes swept the barren landscape upon which not even a scrub willow showed. "That's right," he admitted. "We can't do much till next summer. We'll build that scow and set a gang haulin' in wood — an' you an' I will put in the time prospectin' this flat. Just look at it, Tommy — miles an' miles of gravel that might be just rotten with gold! We'll camp here a couple of days an' peck around with our picks. We might pick up some nuggets right on the surface. Then we'll hit back to Dawson an' record our Discovery location before someone beats us to it."

"I guess there's not much danger of anyone's beating us to it," Tom laughed, "if you've been hunting for it for years and only just found it. I'll bet mighty few white men ever saw this crick."

**189**

"Prob'ly not," Porcupine agreed. "Maybe only the man that made my map. But by the way the damn cheechakos are pourin' into the Yukon, I won't rest easy till I've got the papers for this location."

# CHAPTER
# TWENTY-FIVE

## "I'm Your Dad"

Cronk, the cockeyed trader, filled his glass with liquor from a bottle he took from his rude desk, and the glass of the Indian from another he kept beneath the counter. Then he drew a foxskin from the Indian's pack and added it to the growing pile on the wide shelf behind him. "An' you say they camped fer ten days an' then went on up the river?"

The Indian, obviously drunk, nodded owlishly. "Um-hum. Ten day."

"Sammy Long Bear was down an' said they bought a couple of dogs off'n him. They prob'ly hung around waitin' fer the river to tighten up. Likely headin' through fer the Mackenzie by way of Lapierre House an' the Bell River."

The Indian grinned. "Sammy Long Bear git dronk an' wheep he's woman, an' w'ite man knock heem down on ground an' tak' he's bottle 'way."

The trader scowled. "God damn him! I told him not to drink none of that licker whilst them two was around! It goes to show you can't trust a damn Siwash! Like as not they'll talk, an' the police'll come

up here an' put me out of business. An' where'n hell
will you fellas git yer licker then?"

"W'ite man say heem like com' down here an' smash
all you keg to hell."

"He did, did he? Which one — the old one er the
other?"

"No, not ol' wan. De wan dat geev you lickin' for
poun' de dog wit' club dat day."

"He never give me no lickin'! If he'd of fought fair
I'd knocked the hell outa him. He kicked me in the jaw
when I was down — that's what he done. You'd ort to
know. You stood right there an' seen him do it — you
an' that damn no-count brother-in-law of yourn. An'
you never neither one of you made a move to help me
— an' me furnishin' you all the hooch you kin drink. If
you two'd grabbed up clubs, the three of us could of
knocked them two cold as a snowball."

"You git pay fer de hooch," the Indian replied surlily.
"Wan dreenk, wan foxskin. Me — I'm no git pay for hit
w'ite mans wit' club."

"Is that so! Well, listen — s'pose them two was to
come back here an' smash my kags, like he claimed —
where'd you git yer hooch then? Not at Rampart House
— not on the Porcupine — an' most times not at Fort
Yukon. An' bein' as there's two of 'em an' only one of
me, they might sneak up an' git the drop on me an' do
it."

The Indian swallowed his liquor and shoved the glass
toward the trader. "Mor'," he said.

Cronk refilled the glass and extracted another
foxskin. "It's time you damn fools got wise to yerself.

Who's yer friend — me er them? I'm tellin' you they wouldn't neither one of them damn bastards give you a drink if yer tongue was hangin' out a foot. Not if you'd give 'em a dozen foxskins, they wouldn't. Long as I'm here you kin git all you want to drink. If they'd set the police on me er smash my kags, you'd go dry." The man tossed off his own drink and refilled his glass. The Indian reached for his tobacco and clumsily filled his pipe as the other eyed him shrewdly. "I said a while back that them two was prob'ly hittin' fer the Mackenzie — an' mebbe they be. But then agin, mebbe they ain't. They might be jest goin' up the river a ways on a prospectin' trip. You claim they had plenty of grub on their sled when they pulled out. But with game scurce as it is upriver, it won't last 'em no hell of a while — an' when it runs out, they might come back down the river. If they do, chances is they'll camp agin somewheres clost to yer village." The Indian puffed at his pipe and nodded agreement. "An' if they do," the trader continued, "it might be the smart thing fer you boys up there to knock 'em off."

"W'at you mean — knock off?"

"Well — you got a gun, ain't you?"

The Indian pondered the suggestion for several minutes. Then, removing the pipe from his mouth, he asked, "You mean shoot um — me?"

"What the hell do you think I mean?"

The man shook his head. "Me, I'm got wan gon. Dem got two gon."

"What if they have? There's more'n one of you, ain't there? How about Sammy Long Bear? You said that damn cuss knocked him down an' took his bottle away, didn't you? I'll bet Sammy wouldn't mind takin' a shot at him."

The Indian shook his head. "No. Sammy Long Bear no shoot um. Heem like he's woman. Heem sorry he whip her. Heem say good t'ing w'ite mans tak' bottle 'way. Heem say no goin' dreenk no mor' hooch."

The trader laughed. "That's what he says now, mebbe. But wait till he comes down fer the Christmas tradin' with a big bunch of foxskins. Wait till I slip him a couple of free drinks. When that licker takes holt, you'll see how many of them skins goes fer flour an' how many goes fer hooch. But if he won't help you, how about that damn brother-in-law of yourn? He'd kill his gran'mother fer a couple of drinks. An' there'll be a damn sight more'n a couple of drinks in it fer anyone that knocks them two birds off."

"W'at you mean — mor' as couple dreenk?"

"Listen. I don't want them damn bastards comin' down here an' smashin' my kags. Nor neither I don't want 'em hittin' back to Dawson an' settin' the police on my trail. It's worth money to me if they're dead — see? I'll give a gallon of licker to anyone that knocks 'em off. That's four quarts — a hundred drinks — a hundred fox-skins. Think how long it would take you to trap a hundred foxes — an' look at the hard work — trompin' miles an' miles through the snow, an' cold enough to freeze the tail off a brass monkey, an' then skinnin' 'em after you ketch 'em. An' I'm givin' you the chanct to git what them hundred skins would buy fer jest one little job."

The Indian reached for his glass, gulped the liquor, and shoved the empty glass across the counter. "Mor'," he demanded.

Cronk refilled the glass and took another pelt. "But, mind you, you've got to git 'em both. If a man was to knock off one of 'em an' leave the other go, hell would be to pay fer all of us. If the other didn't clean up on us, the police would."

"Mebbe-so shoot wan, odder wan shoot me."

"That's what would happen if you done it alone. The other one would shore as hell git you before you could load that old muzzle-loader of yourn. Why don't you split the hooch with yer brother-in-law? You could watch yer chanct an' nail 'em when they wasn't lookin'."

"No split hooch."

"How about usin' an ax, then — er yer knife? That's the idee — yer knife! Cripes, you could sneak up in the night, whilst they're asleep, an' slit their throats er stick 'em through the heart. Then drop 'em through a hole in the ice — an' come down here an' collect yer —"

The trading-room door opened suddenly, and Tom Jorden, closely followed by Porcupine Jack, stepped into the room. Cronk's words died in his throat, and as he turned to reach for his rifle the Indian, with a vicious snarl, jerked the keen-bladed knife from his belt and leaped straight at Tom. At the same instant Porcupine Jack, with a cry of warning, jerked the younger man back and the next instant staggered against the counter, the knife buried to the hilt in his chest.

In an instant Cronk realized that here was murder, and that he himself would be held responsible for the act of the drunken Indian. Quick as a flash he swung the rifle on Tom. Dead men tell no tales, and with both men dead and their bodies under the ice of the river, no man could say what had become of them. Let the police investigate and be damned.

But, quick as he was, Tom was quicker. His rifle roared, its muzzle almost against Cronk's chest, and the trader dropped, his rifle smashing the glass of liquor on the counter, while Porcupine Jack sank slowly to the floor at Tom's feet. As Tom bent over the prostrate form the Indian slipped silently from the room and vanished into the bush.

Stepping around the counter, Tom made sure that the trader was dead and, seeing a door standing open, glanced into a small room that contained a bunk and a chair. The bunk was a pole affair, built against the wall and piled with filthy blankets. Sweeping the blankets to the floor, Tom stepped into the trading room, jerked several new blankets from a shelf, and spread them on the bed. Then he returned to the trading room and gently raised the old man in his arms, carried him to the room, and deposited him on the bed.

As he laid hold of the hilt of the knife to remove it, Porcupine Jack shook his head. Blood oozed from a corner of his lips.

"Leave it there, Tommy. This is the end of the trail."

"No! No! I'll pull out the knife and bandage you up. You'll come through all right. Be laid up for a while, that's all."

"No, Tommy. This is the end. I know it — an' you know it. So what's the use pretendin' it's different? I'm glad we made our strike, boy. Glad my faith in the lower country was justified. You show the boys those nuggets we found there in the loose gravel. Right on the surface they were — an' God knows how far it is to bedrock."

"I'll show 'em the nuggets — Bettles, and Swiftwater, and Moosehide, and all of 'em. They'll know you were right. But don't talk. I've got to get that knife out."

The oldster shook his head. "I've got to talk now — or I'll never talk. Don't pull the knife out. It would drain me of blood — an' I need what little strength I've got. There's things I want to say. I knew I'd hit it someday. I'm an old man, Tommy. I wouldn't have needed much gold. I wanted it for you. You're a good man, Tommy. Ever since you hit Dawson I've been watchin' you. An' I'm satisfied. All the boys like you — the sourdoughs — the men who count. An' there's that girl — Sue Brandon — back in Dawson. I've kind of watched her too. She's a fine girl. She loves you, Tommy. I'm not blind. I know. Marry her."

"She hates me," Tom said in a low, dull voice. "She told me she'd never marry me."

The old lips smiled. "I figured you'd quarreled. You've never mentioned her — even that time you had the chance. You've learnt a lot since you left Big Falls, Tommy. But you haven't learnt much about women. I'm dyin' happy, boy — happier'n I ever expected to be again. Don't be a damn fool, Tommy. Marry that girl —

**197**

an' if you ever get back to Big Falls tell Doc Leroy I sure appreciate his faith in me. I swear on my dyin' bed — I didn't kill Joel Stowe. He never showed me any money. If he had Kay's twenty thousand with him, that tramp must have murdered him an' made off with it. He —"

Tom was staring, wide-eyed, into the old man's face.

"You didn't — What are you talking about? Who are you?"

"I'm John Jorden, Tommy. I'm your dad."

Tom was stunned at the words. For several moments he knelt there staring down into the faded blue eyes. Presently he found his voice: "But — but why haven't you told me before?"

The thin lips smiled. "I thought it was better not to. I've been away a long time, Son. I wanted to size you up. To — to sort of look you over from all angles. I wanted to look at you as a stranger would. An' that's the way I wanted you to look at me. I wanted to know you threw in with me on this proposition as a business venture — not because I'm your dad. Not like the sourdoughs would have grubstaked me. Not for charity. I didn't want charity, Tommy — no more than you wanted the pity of those folks back in Big Falls. I guess you'd call it pride."

"You knew who I was before we hooked up as partners — before I told you my story that night?"

"Why, sure I did. You're usin' your own name. Just to make dead sure, I got Pete Moss to mention George Jorden an' Big Falls that night you stopped with us on Hunker. He'd never been there. He just said what I told him to say. An' the way you snapped out that George Jorden was your uncle an' then changed the subject told me a lot, Tommy. Even before you told me your story that night I knew you'd lived pretty much within yourself. And I knew why. It was because most people believed your dad was a murderer — an' you hated 'em for it. When people were kind to you, you suspected it was because they pitied you — because they wanted to show that they didn't hold your dad's crime against you. There were prob'ly a lot of 'em like that. But there must have been a lot of others too — folks that would have liked you for yourself, if you'd let 'em. By suspectin' everyone you've cut yourself off from a lot of real friends, Tommy.

"Then there was the other kind — the snobs, an' the sanctimonious, an' the holier-than-thous — like George an' Margaret. George always was pretty much of a rotter. You must have had a hell of a life with him an' Margaret. They're two of a kind. I knew they'd take you to live with 'em. They'd have to. They're your only kin. I knew they'd make your life miserable. But there was nothin' I could do about it. I had to keep out of reach of the law. With the evidence they had against me, I wouldn't have had a chance. It wouldn't have helped your case any if I'd stayed there and been hanged. It would have made it all the harder for you. If I'd ever made a strike I'd have managed, some way, to send Doc Leroy the money for your education — the money to get you out of George's clutches — to send you off to school in Minneapolis or somewhere. But I never made a strike. I've been a failure, Tommy. An' that's

**199**

another reason I didn't tell you who I am. I — I guess I was ashamed to tell you. I've never made more than a livin' — an' mostly a mighty tough livin', at that. But I'm dyin' happy, Tommy. Because — you're a fine man — an' — because — at last — I — we — made our — strike —" The words came haltingly, and the voice died to the faintest whisper and ceased in a strangling gurgle as blood gushed from the mouth and splashed unheeded over the new blankets.

# CHAPTER
# TWENTY-SIX

## Back on the Yukon

Tom Jorden knelt beside the bed for a long time, gazing, dry-eyed, into the face of the dead man, trying in vain to correlate that face with the face of his father as he remembered him. He had always thought of his father as a large man, full-fleshed, with black hair and a sweeping black mustache that concealed his lips and swept upward at the ends, against full, ruddy cheeks. While the man who lay there on the bunk was spare of body and smooth-shaven save for a stubble of white beard that failed to conceal the firm-set, angular jaw. This man was gaunt — with the rugged gauntness of toil. "Fifteen years," he murmured aloud, "fifteen years of hard work, of faith, and of discouragement. Fifteen years of flapjacks, and moose, and caribou, and wolf — and boiled fish. No wonder his hair and beard are white. No wonder he's down to bone, and sinew, and muscle. But he never quit. By God, my dad was a man!"

Step by step his mind dwelt upon the all-too-short days of their association, from the present back to that evening he first met him with the other sourdoughs at the bar of the Tivoli Saloon. Then it leaped the void of fifteen years — he was a little boy again sitting on the stern seat of the boat while his dad rowed to the fishing grounds, the heaving overboard of the pair of coupling links that served as an anchor, the baiting of the hooks, and the thrill of a walleye tugging on the end of the line with the cane pole bending in his hands, and the voice of his dad in his ears, "Take your time, Tommy. Don't horse him in." And then the fish would be flopping around in the bottom of the boat and his dad would be taking him off the hook and feeling around in the pail for another minnow. And again they were walking beside the creek that wound through the woods, and his dad was telling him about the birds, and the snakes, and the turtles, and the funny black bugs that skittered about on the surface of the water and didn't sink at all. And then the tears came, and Tom Jorden buried his face in his hands, and his shoulders shook with suppressed sobbing.

Twilight was deepening as he rose to his feet. He drew the knife from his father's body, washed the blood from his face, and, carrying him into the storeroom, covered him with a blanket. The body of the trader he also dragged into the storeroom. Then he unharnessed his dogs, fed them, and toggled them in the dog shelter behind the building. As he turned back toward the trading room his glance fell upon the post to which Cronk had chained the dog he was beating to death, and the words of advice that Porcupine Jack had uttered struck him with the force of a blow. "Never give a rat like him a break . . . Never quit till you've got him licked — an' damn good an' licked."

"You were right, Dad," he muttered as he turned away. "He's licked now — damn good and licked."

Before re-entering the building he visited the meat cache, and that evening he gorged himself on moose tenderloin and an assortment of tinned vegetables he selected from the shelves. He also drank coffee instead of the everlasting tea that served them on the trail.

Later in the evening, by the light of a tin bracket lamp, while going through the meager contents of his father's duffel bag, he ran onto a packet of old letters written in a feminine hand — letters John Jorden's wife had written him, evidently, while he was away on business trips. They were addressed to him at various hotels in Minneapolis, St. Paul, Chicago. Tom sat late, reading the words penned by the hand of the mother he had never known. Enclosed in one of them was a formal letter written in a bold, masculine hand. His mother had written:

I enclose a letter that came today from Mr. Stowe. I thought you might find it useful in arranging your credit with the wholesale houses.

He read the enclosure:

Mr. JOHN JORDEN, ESQ.
DEAR SIR:
Your application for a short-term loan of two thousand dollars ($2,000) has been approved by the directors of this bank. The amount will be

credited to your account upon receipt of the enclosed note, duly signed.

Yours truly,

Farmers' and Merchants' Bank

JOEL W. STOWE, President

He placed the packet of letters in his own duffel bag, blew out the light, and, wrapped in his rabbit robe, went to sleep in the trader's bunk.

As Tom ate his breakfast next morning he considered the disposal of the bodies. He thought of wrapping them in blankets and depositing them on the elevated platform of the meat cache and returning in the spring to bury them. But, fearing the drifting snow might pile up during the winter and give the wolves access to the cache, he discarded the thought. Remembering the huge pile of dry wood ranged along one side of the building, he decided to burn into the frozen ground and bury them on the grassy slope that slanted gently to the river. He remembered that when they discussed the mining of their new location Porcupine Jack had told him that here on the upper river they would have to burn in, winter and summer, to sink a shaft, as the ground remained perpetually frozen except for a couple of feet on the surface. When he had suggested that because of the scarcity of wood this fact might shoot the expense of summer mining to a prohibitive amount, the oldster had met the objection promptly. "Sure it'll take more wood," he had agreed, "an' we'll take out more gold, too. Take it in the upper country, they've got to practically quit shaft minin' in the summer on account of seepage. But with the ground frozen the year around, we can keep right on goin' down. We'll keep a big gang choppin', an' another gang on the scows. There's nothin' to it, Tommy. This lower country's got the upper country beat two to one."

"I'll dig two graves," he decided, "even if it is more work. Damned if I'll bury him beside that scoundrel."

Later, as he stood on the spot he had selected for his father's grave, his glance took in the sweeping bend of the river, the sparse timber of its valley, and the mountains dim and elusive on the horizon. "Dad would like it," he murmured, "if he could have known that all down through the ages he'll lie here beside his beloved Porcupine. A thousand years from now he'll be the same as he is this minute. Below the frost line there can be no decay."

Then he carried wood and built his two fires. Cronk he buried out behind the dog shelter. It took five days and nights of alternate burning and digging to complete the two graves. He hauled the blanket-wrapped body of his father to the grave on the sled, lowered it gently with a babiche line, and carefully refilled the grave. Carrying water from the river, he saturated the loose dirt, thus insuring against any possibility of wolves uncovering the body.

With tools he found in the storeroom he fashioned two wooden crosses and placed one at the head of each grave. As he was about to burn the name of John Jorden into the clean white wood he hesitated, the red-hot spike poised. Then slowly he shook his head and

laboriously burned in the name PORCUPINE JACK —
just the name, nothing more. For a long time he stood
there staring down at the mounded earth. "Good-by,
Dad," he said, swallowing the lump that rose in his
throat. "I'm coming back. But no matter what happens,
I'll know that you'll be lying here beside your river —
with your nuggets and your map — and your undying
faith." Abruptly he turned away and strode toward the
low log building.

An hour's search unearthed four ten-gallon kegs
concealed behind bales of fur in the storeroom. A few
well-directed blows of his ax smashed the kegs and
allowed the liquor to splash over the puncheon floor
and disappear through the cracks. He found and
smashed all save one of the remaining bottles in a case
of good liquor he found under the trader's bunk, and
also the crock of diluted liquor he found under the
counter in the trading room. The bottle he spared he
added to his pack, together with a liberal supply of
meat and goods from the shelves. Then he stepped
from the room, closed the door behind him, harnessed
his dogs, and headed down-river.

When he reported what had happened to the factor
at Rampart House, the man nodded approval. "It's a
good job, well done, lad — the shootin' of Cronk. If
ever a man needed killin', he did. But I'm shore sorry
to hear about Porcupine Jack. He was a fine man —
Porcupine was. He'd stop here whenever he'd pass, up
er down, an' spend hours on end studyin' over my
maps, tryin' to check 'em up with a map of his own —
a poor thing, it was, an' old — drawed on a bit of

canvas an' faded till a man couldn't make head nor tail to it. But he had faith in the river — Porcupine did. It's too bad he never made his strike. You don't know the name of the Siwash that stabbed him, do you?"

"No. But I've got the knife he did it with."

The man examined the knife Tom handed him and shook his head. "It's a common trade knife," he said. "There's lots of 'em in the country. Better turn it over to Downey, though. He might find out who owned it."

And so it was at Fort Yukon, and all up the Yukon — Circle, Star City, Eagle, Forty Mile — everywhere there were sourdoughs who spoke of Porcupine Jack with respect, and of his faith in the lower country almost with reverence.

At Eagle, Bob Steel approved the shooting of Cronk. "So that's where that cockeyed son-of-a-bitch wound up, eh — back on the Yukon side? He didn't dare go upriver. Downey run him out of the upper country a year ago, an' I wouldn't let him light here. I heard Jack McQuesten took a shot at him when he caught him feedin' hooch to a couple of young klooches down on the flats somewhere. It's too damn bad he didn't get him. But I'm glad that when Porcupine's time come it happened up there. He'd have wanted it that way. His life, ever since he hit the country, was linked up with that river. It was, what you might say, his destiny."

Tom found Corporal Downey at Forty Mile and made a complete and detailed report of all that had happened, even to the locating of what Porcupine Jack believed to be the spot where, years before, his old seafaring uncle had uncovered a wealth of coarse gold.

**207**

Downey listened almost without interruption until Tom finished.

"So Porcupine Jack was your dad, eh? Well, you can be proud of that, boy. There wasn't a better man in the country than Porcupine Jack — bar none. I'm shore glad his luck turned at last. He deserved it, if anyone ever did. He had guts, Tom. He never quit."

Tom nodded. "But — it's too bad, if that location does pan out big, that he couldn't have lived to enjoy it."

"Don't look at it that way, Tom. He'd lived in this country too long to get much enjoyment out of anything gold would buy. I don't believe he'd have lived long anyway. I've often noticed, Tom, that when an old man accomplishes what he's lived for, he sort of lets down. It's like he don't want to live any longer — there's nothin' to live for any more — nothin' ahead to work for and fight for and believe in. No sir, I believe Porcupine Jack got the most out of that strike he'd ever have got — just knowin' his son would have it an' carry on."

"There's one favor I'm going to ask of you, Downey. Please don't tell anyone that Porcupine Jack was my dad."

Downey looked surprised. "But why? There wasn't a better-liked man in the North than Porcupine. When the sourdoughs found out he was yer dad it would — well, sort of give you a certain standin', sort of make you a sourdough right on the start."

Tom smiled. "And that's just what I don't want. Don't you see, Downey, I want to stand on my own feet. If I make good, I want it to be because I earned it. Because of what I am — not because of what my dad was."

Downey nodded. "I see your point, Tom. Don't worry. I'll never tell a soul."

"Will it be necessary to arrest me?"

"Arrest you! What for?"

"Why — for shooting Cronk."

"For shootin' that crooked, cross-eyed bastard! Arrest — hell! I'd pin a medal on you — if I had one!"

"Here's the knife the Siwash killed Dad with," Tom said, handing the weapon over. "I thought maybe you'd want it."

Downey took the knife and stared down at it, turning it over in his hand. "I'll go up an' investigate," he said, "but I don't expect I'll have much luck. This is a common kind of a knife — and the other Siwashes won't talk. Did you lock Cronk's tradin' room when you came away?"

"No, I closed the door, but I didn't lock it."

"Cripes — by the time I get up there there won't be a damn thing left in the post!"

Tom nodded. "Yes," he answered, "that's why I didn't lock it. When the Siwashes from that village hit there within a week or so, now, for the Christmas trading, they'll have a chance to even up the score. Cronk was charging 'em a foxskin for a drink of rotten liquor — forty dollars a quart, by the bottle. I was hoping the place would be gutted when you got there."

**209**

A slow grin overspread the corporal's face. "So do I," he said. "Chances are I can't get down there till spring nohow."

# CHAPTER
# TWENTY-SEVEN

## Back in Dawson

It was late in the afternoon of the first day of December when Tom pulled up at the hotel in Dawson and greeted the clerk behind the desk with a smile. "Hello, Alex! Is Mr. Brandon in?"

"Well, by gosh, if it ain't Tom Jorden! How'd you make out in the lower country? An' say, Tom, you've took off some weight, ain't you? Can't be they fed you very good down there."

"Boiled fish." Tom grinned. "And if you've got boiled fish for supper tonight, I'll wreck this dump!"

"Got moose steak." The other laughed, shoving the register toward him and dipping the pen. "You'd ort to stuck to the upper country. All the sourdoughs claims the lower country's petered out. Want yer same room? It's empty."

"Fine. I'll have time to wash up and shave before supper. How are the Brandons?"

"Oh, they're all right. I see him every day er so. Seen Miss Sue the other day on the street. She's lookin' fine."

"Saw her on the street! Aren't they living here?"

"No. Fergot you'd ben away. Brandon, he bought a house. Second house past the log church — er mebbe the third." The man glanced at the clock on the wall. "It might be he's still at the office."

"Office! Cripes, has he got an office too?"

"Sure — BRANDON & SHARPE. It's right on Front Street next door to the Tivoli. You'll see the sign. J. W.'s in, if you want to see him. Went upstairs jest before you come. He's in room twenty-three."

"Who's J. W.?"

"J. W. Sharpe. He's Brandon's pardner. Guess he come in after you pulled out."

"This Sharpe — is he a sourdough?"

"Hell, no! Come from Frisco. He's damn near froze most of the time. An' no wonder. Dresses like he was still in California."

"I'll go up to my room and drop around and call on the Brandons after supper. Send a boy up with some hot water."

In his room Tom bathed and shaved and changed into fresh clothing. So Sam Brandon had taken a partner. He was conscious of a slight sinking sensation in the pit of his stomach. He wondered what this J. W. Sharpe was like. Was Sue still "office man" for the concern? What did she think of Sharpe?

The sinking sensation gave way to a pang of jealousy as he thought of Sue Brandon in close association all day long with her father's partner. And this partnership — how would it affect him? He had planned it all out over his campfires on the long snow trail. He'd go back to work for Brandon this winter, and in the spring he'd show him the big nuggets he and Porcupine Jack had taken out of the surface gravel and offer him a partnership in the Old Crow property. He himself would record the Discovery claim, and Brandon and Sue would record Numbers One Above and Below. Then, with Brandon's capital, they could build not one scow, but four or five, and hire crews of woodchoppers and begin operations — work all the claims at once. In the meantime they would stake out a townsite at the mouth of the Old Crow. Why, the profit from the sale of lots in that townsite alone would be a Bonanza in itself! And then, when Sue found out that he had been right in throwing in with Porcupine Jack, that he had made good in the lower country, why, then . . .

It had been a wonderful dream — coarse gold rivaling anything the upper country could show — a big city at the mouth of the Old Crow — and Sue.

But how did this J. W. Sharpe fit into the scheme? Tom scowled into the mirror as he drew the comb through his thick mat of hair. "He fits like a glove," he growled, "like a glove would fit on a foot!" Somehow he couldn't see offering Brandon & Sharpe a partnership. The Brandons — yes. But not Brandon & Sharpe.

Oh well, he still had more than three thousand dollars. He could hire a couple of men and build some kind of a scow and float wood enough to the claim to make a start. Then as he took out the gold he could hire more men and cut more wood and take out more gold. It would take longer, that's all. There wouldn't be any stampede to the Old Crow for at least a year or two, so he'd have plenty of time to stake out his townsite. This way he wouldn't have any partner — the gold he took out would be his own. But — Sue Brandon? He wouldn't have Sue, either. And what did he want with the gold if — if he didn't have Sue? "Damn J. W. Sharpe!" he muttered aloud. "I'm going down and record my location, and maybe at supper I'll get a chance to see what he looks like."

Early in the evening he knocked at the door of a neat three-room cabin to be greeted by Sue Brandon herself. Never, he thought, had she looked so beautiful, so altogether desirable, as she did now, standing there framed by the yellow lamplight.

"Tom Jorden!" she cried. And then a peculiar, almost hysterical note in her voice: "Oh, Tom!"

Then she was crowded aside as Sam Brandon shouldered past her and thrust out his hand. "Back again, eh? By George, Tom, it's good to see you! Come on in and tell us all about your trip. Gave the lower country up as a bad job, eh? I told you you were wasting your time with that old fellow. I made inquiries about him among the sourdoughs after you'd gone. They all speak highly of him as a man. And here's a peculiar thing — a thing I don't just understand — the sourdoughs, to a man, insist that the lower country is no good, yet the very thing they esteem this Porcupine Jack for is his undying faith in the lower country. It's inconsistent. It somehow don't jibe."

Tom nodded. "I think I understand," he said.

"But certainly your trip didn't accomplish anything, did it?"

Tom smiled. "I saw a lot of country. Filed a location, too. It's on a creek that flows into the Old Crow River — way up the Porcupine."

214

"Did Porcupine Jack come back with you, or did he stay down there?"

"Porcupine Jack is never coming back. He's dead." The two listened as Tom told of his trip, omitting to mention that Porcupine Jack was his own father — omitting, also, any mention of the fabulous wealth that he believed might lie concealed in the gravel of the creek delta, saying only that they found some colors on the creek.

All during the recital Sue scarcely raised her eyes from her knitting. At its conclusion Brandon cleared his throat.

"Well, now you've got that all out of your system, how about coming back with us?"

"That's what I came to see you about. But I hear you're a partnership now. What will your partner say to the arrangement?"

"Oh, I've spoken to him about you. I knew you'd be back sooner or later. He's just as anxious to take you on as I am. Fine chap, J. W. is. Shrewd businessman, too. He came into the country the same as I did, looking for investments. Got here soon after you left. Put up at the hotel, and of course we got acquainted, and it wasn't long before we decided to pool our interests. We formed the partnership of Brandon & Sharpe. We put in fifty thousand apiece, and we're operating those two Fisher properties and one other that we picked up on Goose Creek. Besides that we've got options on several other properties, and one other that we bought outright. There's plenty of work to be done right now — investigating these options and getting the Goose Creek

**215**

project into production. And the devil of it is, neither J. W. nor I are quite up to this winter traveling. I'm going on sixty, and J. W.'s forty-five — both of us pretty old dogs to learn new tricks. We do go out when it's absolutely necessary, but we don't like it. Fact is, J. W. was going to pull out for Goose Creek tomorrow. It's a property he picked up cheap from a fellow who was pulling out for Stewart River. I warned him against buying any location outright before we'd had a chance to investigate it, but he went ahead on this one. Guess he's more of a gambler than I am. Said if it didn't come up to expectations he knew where he could unload it. Personally, I don't like the idea of 'unloading' a worthless property on some other fellow. When I told that to J. W. he laughed. 'Business is business, Sam,' he said. 'The doctrine of *caveat emptor* applies here the same as anywhere else.' He's all business, J. W. is. I think you'll like him. Fine-looking chap, too."

Tom nodded, his eyes on the girl's profile. Apparently intent on her knitting, she had not once looked up during her father's recital. The lampshade threw a soft shadow upon her cheek and her auburn hair. In her lap the hands that plied her needles looked startlingly white. "Yes," he said, "I saw him this evening in the dining room. That is, I suppose it was he — store clothes, white collar, smooth-shaven, dark hair turning iron gray about the temples. Looks more like an actor than a businessman. The clerk told me about your partnership — told me Sharpe was living at the hotel — told me where to find you."

"Yes, we got tired of the hotel. Decided we wanted a place of our own, a real home. Nothing like a home of your own, my boy. You'll realize that sometime."

"Yes, I suppose I will." Sue Brandon's eyes met his in one fleeting glance then abruptly returned to her knitting. Was it a trick of the lamplight, or was there heightened color in her cheek? And did the fingers that plied the flashing needles falter ever so slightly?

Brandon was speaking again. "Sure you will. When the right girl comes along you'll know it. And in the meantime, Tom, we want you to feel free to drop in on us any time you feel like it — don't we, Sue?"

The girl nodded. "Why, of course, Daddy. Tom knows that. Don't you, Tom?"

Again their eyes met, and again the girl's glance faltered and fell as he replied: "Yes. Thanks a lot. I — I surely appreciate that." The words sounded somehow empty, banal, and all three felt the note of constraint in his voice.

As Tom rose to go Brandon sought to gloss over the situation. He slapped Tom on the back, and his voice boomed heartily: "By gosh, Tom, you don't know how glad I am to have you back! Report at the office right after breakfast and meet J. W. I've got a hunch that you're going to be pretty damn busy from now on." He followed Tom to the door, but Sue remained seated.

"Good night, Tom," she called. "See you tomorrow."

# CHAPTER
# TWENTY-EIGHT

## Tom Goes to Work

In the office next morning Sharpe shook Tom's hand heartily as Brandon introduced them. "If you're half as good as Sam's been telling me you are, I'm certainly glad you're here," he laughed. "I haven't got the hang of this rough-country traveling yet, and I don't mind saying that a little of it goes a long way. Sam's been predicting that you'd be back when you got that lower-country bug out of your system, and he says you promised when you left that if your venture proved a failure you'd come back to him."

"That's right," Tom agreed. "Well — I'm back, and ready to go to work. What's the first job to tackle?"

"Guess we better get a report on that Goose Crick property, hadn't we, J. W.?" Brandon said.

"That's right." Sharpe turned to Tom. "Know where Goose Crick is?"

"No. But it won't take me long to find out. Let's see the description of the property."

"Miss Brandon will hand you the papers this afternoon," Sharpe said. "And after you've rested up for a day or two, you'd better run out there and look it over."

"Rest up?"

"Why — yes. Sam tells me you just got in last evening from the lower country."

Tom laughed. "That's right. But I got all the rest I need last night. Give me the papers, and I'll hit out right now."

Brandon stepped to a neat desk in a corner of the little office, unlocked a drawer, and selected a paper which he handed to Tom. "Sue divides her time between the house and the office," he said. "She doesn't get down here till afternoon. Our business isn't so extensive yet as to require all of her time."

Tom read the description and pocketed the paper. "Okay. I'll find out where Goose Creek is and go out and have a look at the property. Has there been any work done on it?"

Sharpe nodded. "Oh yes. According to Simeon Petty, the man from whom I bought it, he sank three shallow shafts on the property. He didn't locate it till spring, and during the summer he worked it but could only go down a few feet until the seepage drove him out. He intended to work the location this winter, but in the meantime some friends of his persuaded him to accompany them to the Stewart River, so he sold the property to me."

"Was the stuff any good — as far down as he went?"

"Certainly. He told me that the gravel averaged fifty cents to the pan — and that practically on the surface. He seemed to have plenty of dust. Anyway, the property only stands us five thousand. If it doesn't come up to expectations, I know where I can unload it at a profit. I made the acquaintance of a man from Chicago, coming

**219**

in on the boat, who was coming into the country to seek investments. Seems to have plenty of money — I understand he's buying right and left."

"Is there a shack on the property?" Tom asked.

"Well, now, Petty didn't say. I assume, of course, that there must be a building of some kind. The man worked it all summer."

"Probably lived in a tent," Tom said. "It doesn't matter. I've got a good tent. I may be gone two or three weeks. I'll have to clean the snow out of those shafts and cut wood and burn in to get samples of the gravel out of the bottom."

"It seems to me," Brandon said, "that if the property is any good at all he wouldn't have sold it for five thousand."

Tom turned to Sharpe. "Is this Petty a cheechako or a sourdough?"

"He claimed to have been in the country for a couple of years. Mentioned living in Forty Mile before coming here."

"The location may be all right," Tom said. "You never can tell about a sourdough. They're apt to go by hunches. This mining game gets into their blood. They're just as likely as not to sell a going proposition for what they can get for it, if their hunch says they might find a better one on some other crick. We'll know more about it after I have a look at that gravel."

A few minutes later Tom stepped into the Tivoli Saloon to find Burr MacShane talking with Swiftwater Bill. He joined them at the bar as the bartender shoved out another glass.

"Where's Porcupine?" MacShane grinned. "I thought you an' him would be damn near to the Arctic coast by now."

Tom poured his drink. "Porcupine is dead," he said, and proceeded to tell of the happenings at the Bluefish trading post.

Both sourdoughs expressed profound regret at the passing of Porcupine Jack. "He was a man — an' a damn good one," Swiftwater said. "Most of us claimed he was a damn fool fer pinnin' his faith on the lower country — an' mebbe he was. But jest the same, we don't know it all. Porcupine's hunch said his luck laid in the lower country — an', by God, he follered his hunch to the end. An' that's what I call a man. An' there ain't nothin' in the books that says that one of these days someone won't make a strike down there on the Porcupine that will make the dust we take out of this Klondike country look like chicken feed. An' who'd be the damn fools then? The hell of it is that Porcupine wouldn't be here to see it."

"Either of you fellows know where Goose Crick is?" Tom asked.

"Goose Crick? Yeah — let's see — Goose Crick — it runs into the Klondike about thirty miles up — runs in from the north."

MacShane nodded. "Yeah — ain't that the crick Tim O'Hara an' Mike Sullivan located?"

"That's right," Swiftwater said. "Doin' all right up there, too. It ain't only a short crick, an' they're right at the head of it."

"Know anyone named Simeon Petty?"

"Sim Petty! Yeah, I know him," Swiftwater said. "Used to work down around Forty Mile. Worked on the steamboats now an' then, too."

"Seen him in here a while back," MacShane said. "Claimed he'd sold a location to one of them cheechako speculators fer five thousan'. He was all dressed up — an' lit up, too. Claimed he was goin' outside. But I was up to White Horse jest before the freeze-up, an' he was sling-in' hash in a restaurant. His five thousan' was gone, an' so was most of his store clothes. That's as clost as he come to goin' outside. What do you want of Sim Petty?"

Tom shrugged. "I don't want him. I've got to go up to Goose Crick and look over a location he sold to J. W. Sharpe. I've gone back to work for Brandon. He's taken on a partner since I left."

"Yeah," Swiftwater Bill said dryly, "an' if you don't git busy, you'll find he's took on a son-in-law too. This here Sharpe looks to me like a pretty slick article — like he'd be a damn sight better pickin' women than locations. He ain't overlookin' no bets when it comes to takin' that gal of Brandon's around to shows an' different doin's."

Tom downed his liquor and refilled his glass. He nodded slowly, his mind on the events of the previous evening: Sue Brandon's surprised, almost hysterical greeting as she opened the door, and later the awkward constraint in the few words she had uttered as she busied herself with her knitting. "I guess you're right, Swiftwater," he said. "I guess I'd set my sights a little too high. She told me when I pulled out for the lower country that she'd never marry me."

Swiftwater Bill grinned. "Hell, there's a gal in this camp that's ben tellin' me that all winter. But I'll bet, by God, she'll change her mind before spring! You talk like a damn fool. With the savvy you're takin' on, you ain't set yer sights too high fer no one. Look at Porcupine Jack — he never got what he was after, but, by God, he never quit tryin' fer it! You ain't the man I think you are if you lay back an' git yer time beat by a God-damn dude!"

# CHAPTER
# TWENTY-NINE

## Sharpe Makes a Proposition

One evening three weeks later Tom stepped into the hotel dining room to be greeted by Sharpe, who beckoned him to his table. "Hello, Tom! Sit down. I've just put in my order. When did you get in?"

"Half an hour ago. And believe me, I'm hungry. Forced the trail a bit today. Didn't stop for noon lunch." A waitress paused beside his chair, and he ordered a moose steak.

"Better make it a double order," Sharpe smiled. "This man's just in off the trail." When the girl had disappeared his glance met Tom's across the table. "Have you made out your report on the Goose Creek property?"

"There isn't much to report. The claim's no good and never was."

"But the man Petty told me he averaged fifty cents to the pan, practically on the surface. Did you pan the gravel from the bottom of his shafts?"

Tom grinned. "Call 'em shafts, if you want to. I found three or four holes scooped in the gravel, none of 'em over a couple of feet deep. I panned samples from all over the place. Got about an ounce or an ounce and a half of dust to show for a couple of weeks' work. I talked to Sullivan and O'Hara, a couple of partners who are working a Discovery claim on the upper end of the crick. They tell me that Petty never did take any dust out of his claim. All the dust he ever took off of Goose Crick was the dust they paid him for working for them."

"Why, the damned scoundrel! He misrepresented that claim to me! And if these men will swear on the witness stand that he never took any gold out of that property, I've got a clear case of fraud against him! You wait till he returns from that Stewart River trip, and I'll swear out a warrant for his arrest! Rascals of that stripe should be prosecuted to the fullest extent of the law!"

"He never went to Stewart River. He got drunk and blew in part of your five thousand for some store clothes and hit for the outside. But he didn't get any farther than White Horse. He went broke there and got a job slinging hash in a restaurant. If you want to prosecute him, the police can find him there. But I don't think you'd get very far with it. How are you going to prove that he misrepresented the property to you? Did anyone hear him tell you he took out fifty cents a pan? Even if you could prove he told you that, how could you prove he didn't take out fifty cents to the pan?"

"But didn't you just say that those two men on the creek told you he never took any dust out of that claim?"

"Sure they did. But that's only their opinion. They certainly weren't watching him every minute. They had work of their own to do. I know damn well he never took any fifty cents a pan — or even five cents — out of that gravel, but I'd have the devil of a time proving it."

Sharpe drummed on the table with his fingertips. "Yes, I suppose you're right. But it's a damned shame that a rascal like that can go around perpetrating frauds and nothing can be done about it. Oh well, I suppose we must all live and learn. If we can't make any money operating that property, at least we can get out without a loss. I know a man who will take it off our hands — the fellow I mentioned meeting on the boat. He seems to have plenty of money, and we might as well get some of it as to let someone else get it. In fact," he added with a knowing wink, "we might get out with a rather handsome profit — if we play our cards right."

"How do you mean?"

"Well, suppose, for instance, you were to slip up there and — er — judiciously distribute some dust in likely places — the bottom of those holes you mentioned, and maybe a few other likely spots. Then if I should offer the property to this prospective purchaser, and he should investigate it and find this dust, he'd be inclined to pay a good price for the claim, wouldn't he?"

"You mean — salt it?"

"Well, as a matter of fact, you know, we wouldn't be doing anything out of the way, because I happen to know that this party has pulled some pretty shrewd deals himself. You see, Tom, the damned rascal would try to beat us out — would offer us a mere pittance of what he believed the property was worth when he found that dust on it. It would serve the scoundrel jolly well right."

"What would Sam Brandon say to a deal of that kind? You and he are partners. He'd have to be a party to it."

"Certainly we're partners. But that doesn't mean that Sam would necessarily have to be informed of every little detail, of every deal we make. What Sam don't know won't hurt him any. He was mighty skeptical about that deal right from the first. In fact, I put it over without consulting him. He'll be tickled to death to find we made a profit on it." The man paused, cleared his throat, and, leaning forward, lowered his voice. "And here's another thing, Tom. You play along with me now and then, and you won't lose by it. There may be cases like the present, where we could put over something of which Sam might not approve. Sam's a good businessman, all right, but he's a bit old-fashioned. He doesn't seem to realize that modern business is more or less a case of dog eat dog — and the devil take the hindmost. If you don't beat the other fellow, he's sure as hell going to beat you. The smart man, these days, is the man who comes out of a deal with the money. As I say, you play in with me, and I'll slip you money now and then, over and above your salary — money out of my own pocket. That's fair enough, isn't it?"

"Well — it seems —"

"Of course it does! By the way, does Sam know you're back?"

"No. No one does except you. I didn't even see the hotel clerk when I came in."

"Fine — splendid! We'll take care that he doesn't see you when you go out, either. I'll attract his attention while you slip up to my room after supper, and I'll give you the dust. Then you can slip out, and no one will be the wiser."

"You mean the dust to salt the claim with?"

"Certainly."

"Where did you get it?"

"Get what?"

"Why — this dust."

"Where did I get it? What difference does that make?"

"It might make a hell of a lot of difference. For instance, you couldn't salt a Bonanza claim with dust taken from Hunker. And you couldn't salt any of these upriver claims with dust from Forty Mile."

"Why not? Dust is dust, isn't it? It's all gold."

"Yes, it's all gold. But all dust isn't alike. Dust from one creek may be altogether different from dust from another crick — different in color and shape and in the size of the grains."

"Do you mean to tell me that just by looking at a sample of dust you can tell where it came from?"

"I know the difference in dust from some of the cricks. But there are plenty of men right here in Dawson that know a lot more about dust than I do."

"But this man I have in mind as a prospective purchaser is not one of them. He came into the country

228

the same time I did. And he certainly knows nothing of all this."

Tom shrugged. "Maybe not. But if he hired a sourdough to work the claim, he'd damn well know it. Even if he worked it with green hands, he'd get suspicious when the gravel suddenly went lean after they'd taken the salt out of it. Then, if he'd have you arrested, it wouldn't take a jury of sourdoughs five minutes to convict you of fraud."

Sharpe scowled. "The only way, then, would be to obtain some dust from Goose Creek. I believe you mentioned that there are other claims on the creek."

"Only one. It's a short creek, and Sullivan and O'Hara have the only other claim on it. The whole crick was staked after they made their strike. But theirs was the only location that was any good."

Sharpe was silent for several moments. "These men — Sullivan and O'Hara — if we should obtain some dust from them — could they — er — be trusted to say nothing about the transaction — that is, of course, if we should make it worth their while?"

Tom shook his head. "I don't think so. They both seem to be good square guys."

Sharpe frowned. "I want you to understand that I would not for a moment consider being a party to any transaction that savored of underhandedness were it not for the fact that I have every reason to believe that the man I have in mind as a purchaser would not hesitate to take advantage of me if he got the chance. On second thought, I'll ask you to forget the whole thing. If I can unload this property for what I paid for it, well and good. If not, we'll have to take the loss. I believe that Sam feels the same way — that we shouldn't be mixed up in any shady transaction."

"I know he does!" Tom agreed.

"To be sure. So I'm asking you to say nothing to Sam or to Sue about my suggestion of — er — salting this property. They might not understand that the plan was conceived only because I believe the man with whom I was to deal is thoroughly unscrupulous. I tell you, there ought to be some way to protect innocent purchasers from the machinations of damned rascals like him and that Simeon Petty! It's an outrage!"

# CHAPTER
# THIRTY

## On Indian River

During the following two months Tom spent little time in Dawson. He visited the properties on Hunker and Ophir, to find the work progressing satisfactorily, and investigated several other locations that were offered for sale on various creeks. He also bought a portable sawmill and set it up on a feeder to Bonanza, on one of the purchases he had approved, and set a crew to work getting out lumber for a flume. The mill also did more than enough custom sawing to pay for itself during the first sixty days of operation.

During this time he saw little of Sue Brandon. Their contacts in the office, generally with either Sharpe or Brandon present, were purely on matters of business. Tom, realizing that the girl's attitude toward him had changed completely, ascribed it to her anger at his leaving for the venture into the lower country. Each was keenly aware of the constrained attitude of the other, but neither one, either by word or act, did anything to relieve the situation.

When in town, Tom moved about, attending the occasional amateur performances and other activities, generally in company with some of the sourdoughs, and always he saw Sue in company with Sharpe. At the hotel she was frequently his guest at supper. Despite the fact that Sharpe seemed to outdo himself to show her a good time, Tom sensed that she was unhappy.

Then one afternoon in early March, when he returned from the creeks to find her alone in the office, he addressed her bluntly, almost gruffly:

"You don't have to hate me, Sue — just because you prefer going around with J. W." At her desk the girl seemed to wince at the words. She did not answer, but seemed to bend lower over the location paper she was copying. Tom continued: "When I went away with Porcupine Jack, I knew you were angry. But I thought you'd get over it. I told you that when I came back you'd change your mind and marry me. I see that I was wrong. But — I still think of all the things we went through together — the camp at Lake Lindeman — the building of the boat — and the long days and evenings on the river — and I —"

"Don't!" The word jerked hysterically from between the girl's lips. Then words poured forth in a torrent. "I think of those times too. And if you hadn't gone away — everything would be — different. But you did go. And then *he* came. We met him at the hotel. He was different from the others — the sourdoughs — and the other cheechakos. We became well acquainted, and he began taking me around. I was glad to go with him. I — I was still angry with you. Then he and Daddy went into partnership. And — and then — he asked me to marry him and I accepted. Daddy approved the match because he thinks J. W. is a good businessman."

232

Tom's question came brutally direct. "Do you love him?"

"He has plenty of money — and he certainly tries to make me have a good time."

"Do you love him?"

The girl's eyes flashed angrily. "How dare you ask me that, Tom Jorden! You, who would never take me to a show — even when I asked you to! You, who from the minute we hit Dawson began to avoid me — would never even spend an evening with me! You, who when you weren't out on the cricks spent your time in the Tivoli Saloon. You, who preferred the sourdoughs' company to mine! What right have you to ask me who I love?"

Astounded at the vehemence of the girl's attack, Tom found himself at a loss for words. "Why — Sue — I never avoided you. I — I'd have liked nothing in the world better than being with you every minute. But your dad was paying me to work for him. He was paying me to learn the business of mining. And where else could I learn it but out on the cricks? He was paying me to get those properties he bought into production. And I couldn't do that by taking you to shows — nor by spending my evenings with you — much as I'd have liked to. And as for the time I spent in the Tivoli — it was spent there because that's where the sourdoughs were — the men from whom I had to learn. You know that, Sue. You know that your dad was surprised when the sourdoughs told him I was competent to handle those properties. And you know that I'd learned enough before I went away to save him

**233**

from being gypped by Jim Devine. And I learned a lot on that trip with Porcupine Jack — a lot that I've never told you."

"Oh, you've learned, all right," the girl said bitterly. "The sourdoughs all say you're a good man. But what good is it all?" Her voice broke sharply. "You've learned — but if you loved me — as you told me you did when — when you went away — *you've paid a hell of a price* for your learning!"

"Listen, Sue! It's not too late! You can break off your engagement. You're not married to Sharpe."

"A promise is a promise. I'll not break off my engagement! I've given my word — and I'll keep it!"

The door opened abruptly and J. W. Sharpe stepped into the office, his glance shifting from the flushed face of the girl to Tom. He drew a paper from his pocket. "Do you know where Indian River is?" he asked.

"Sure I do."

"Well, I ran onto a proposition up there that looks good on the face of it. Two partners have been working a Discovery claim up there all winter and have decided to split up. The location is on a feeder that runs into Indian River about twenty miles back from the Yukon. These young fellows are newcomers — cheechakos, I believe the term is — who came into the country last fall. They are here in Dawson at the moment. I ran across one of them in the hotel, and in the course of a casual conversation he told me his troubles. It seems that the two met at White Horse on the way in and decided to throw in together. They located this property, put up a shack, and have been working it

234

throughout the winter. At first everything went well. They worked hard, their dump grew, and regular test pannings showed that the proposition was paying much better than wages. But gradually they began to quarrel. Only occasionally at first, then with increasing frequency, until now they are scarcely speaking. As far as I can make out, neither has accused the other of any serious fault."

Tom nodded. "Just got on each other's nerves, eh? It's not an uncommon situation. I've heard the sourdoughs tell about plenty of cases just like it. Two men go out in the fall the best of pals, and by spring each would gladly kill the other. It even happens sometimes among sourdoughs. But mostly it's the cheechakos."

"Just so. They stood it as long as they could without resorting to actual violence, then decided to split up. So they are here now, trying to sell the property. Several of the sourdoughs are interested and have promised to look the location over right after the breakup. But the partners want to sell now. They don't want to go back and work together. And they don't want to hang around Dawson idle until after the breakup. They each want to strike out on their own as soon as the breakup comes. Our — er — rather unfortunate experience with the Goose Creek property has taught me not to buy a pig in a poke, as the saying is. We were lucky to get out of that one with our money back. I sold it to the fellow I met on the boat for five thousand." He paused and smiled at Sue, whose slight change of expression indicated disapproval. "Oh, I know Sam didn't approve

**235**

of the deal — wanted to take the loss and forget the matter. But I'm more practical. If I was a bit optimistic in my representation of the property, that's only natural. I made no definite guarantees — nothing that he could use as the basis of a lawsuit. If he don't like the property, he can resell it. After all, business is business." The girl made no answer, and Sharpe turned to Tom. "And so I want you to run out there and examine the property. Here's the description. I copied it from the recorder's book. You'll find a shack there and — according to these boys — plenty of grub. So you can travel light. You know more about these matters than I do, but I'd suggest that in addition to examining the bottom of their shaft you also make test pannings from various parts of their dump. These lads seem honest enough, but you never can tell. Despite their honest appearance they might be rascals at heart — might try to pull off an underhanded trick of some kind."

Tom grinned. "Like salting the shaft or the dump, eh?"

Sharpe frowned. "Exactly," he snapped. "When can you start?"

"Right now," Tom answered. "I can find out all we need to know about it in ten days or two weeks. So long. I'm off."

Tom spent ten days at the Indian River property. He worked long hours tending the fires that thawed out the gravel, making test pannings, and exploring the little feeder. Dead tired, he would crawl into his blankets immediately after supper and, before sleep came, would lie there staring up into the dark. Life was a hell of a thing. He wondered vaguely whether anyone's life ever worked out the way he wanted it to. There was Sue Brandon — the only girl in the world he had ever cared for. It seemed to him, as he lay there, that he could recall every look, every touch of her hand, almost every word she had uttered since the first time he had seen her standing at the rail of the boat, her hair blowing across her face and her skirts whipping about her knees, to the day in the little office when she told him she was going to marry J. W. Sharpe. He knew now that he loved her more than he could ever love any other woman. And he sensed that deep down in her heart she loved him. But — where had he failed? Why was it that two people who were made for each other from the first must live their lives apart instead of together. Maybe if he had told her about himself — about the utter sorrow, and aloneness, and the bitterness of his life — she would have understood, would have evaluated him at his worth, would neither have pitied nor have scorned. But he had been afraid to risk it. Suppose she hadn't understood? He was happy with her, happy for the first time in his whole life. He hadn't dared to tell her — had been content just to drift on and on together, as they had drifted together down the Yukon. Was it a mistake — his decision to throw in with Porcupine Jack? He knew that she had been angry at that decision, but he thought she would soon get over it. And — no, it couldn't have been wrong. If he had not made that trip into the lower country, he would never have found his father. But on the other hand, if they had not made that trip, his father would still be alive. Round and round his reasoning took him — to decide nothing, to end nowhere. *Life is a hell of a mess!* Oh well, Sue would marry J. W. She wouldn't be happy. Eventually she would find out that under the suave exterior he was a crook at heart. She didn't love him — never could love him. But she'd stick by her bargain. And he? He would go back to the Porcupine country. And there on the Old Crow he'd take out the gold — maybe millions. But without Sue, what did he want with the gold? Anyway you look at it, *life is a hell of a mess!*

The sourdoughs seemed to have a good time, and most of them weren't married. But maybe they'd never been in love. Or maybe they had been, a long time ago — so long ago that they'd had time to forget. He wondered how long it would be before he could forget Sue Brandon. It wouldn't be long, now, till the breakup would come. He'd quit his job and go back to the lower country. He liked Sam Brandon, but he hated J. W. Sooner or later Sam would find out what sort of a man J. W. was — but it would be too late then, because he'd be his son-in-law as well as his partner.

That location on the Old Crow — he'd go back there and work it this coming summer, work it with a pick and shovel, take out enough gold so he could hire a crew of woodcutters. Then he'd build the scows, as he and his father had planned to do, and haul in wood, and put other crews to work in the shafts — and by another year he'd be a real sourdough, like Bettles, and

Swiftwater Bill, and Burr MacShane, and Moosehide Charlie. And every once in a while he'd come up to Dawson, and the cheechakos would nudge each other and say, "There's Tom Jorden, the guy that struck it lucky down in the lower country." And Sue would see him too. He'd meet her on the street and tip his hat and say, "Good evening, Mrs. Sharpe." And then he'd go on into the Tivoli and mix with the sourdoughs and drink and play stud. That's what he wanted gold for — to drink and play stud! He'd bet 'em high — five, ten thousand on the turn of a card! He wished he could drink whisky like Bettles. But after the first drink or two whisky made him sick. Oh well, he was young yet. Maybe he could learn.

On the last evening Tom was to spend in the shack he finished supper, washed his dishes, and rummaged in his duffel bag for his notebook.

Unlike the Goose Creek proposition, this property showed a real promise. Pannings from the shaft and from all parts of the dump showed uniform values that would undoubtedly increase as the shaft neared bedrock. As he dumped the contents of the bag onto the floor in search of the notebook, the string that bound his father's packet of old letters broke, scattering them about, and from an envelope slipped the letter from Stowe, the banker. Picking it up, he was about to return it to the envelope when his eyes suddenly widened, and he knelt there amid the litter of socks, shirts, and envelopes and stared at the handwriting.

Rising to his feet, he carried the letter to the table, drew Sharpe's copy of the location from his pocket, spread the two papers side by side, drew the lamp closer, and for a long time he sat staring at the two sheets — the creased one with its faded ink, and the freshly penned description. Word by word, letter by letter, he studied the two scripts. *The handwriting was identical!*

"Good God!" he breathed as the full force of the discovery burned into his brain. "J. W. Sharpe is Joel W. Stowe! That tramp didn't murder Stowe! Stowe murdered the tramp! He murdered him and changed clothing with him. They must have been about of a size. Then he cut off his head and buried it where it was never found and laid the body on the rail where that freight train mutilated it beyond recognition. Then he made his way on foot to West Union. It was Stowe who was seen climbing a westbound freight there that night — not the tramp. And he was carrying Mr. Kay's twenty thousand dollars with him."

Until far into the night he sat there, lips tight pressed, eyes raising from the two papers spread before him to stare at the blank wall of the shack, shifting back to the papers again. So this was the man — this J. W. Sharpe, his employer, Sam Brandon's partner, the man who was to marry Sue Brandon — this was the man who had ruined his father's life and had caused him all the misery he had ever known, had changed his boyhood from a time of happy memories to a hell of doubt and suspicion and hatred, and now was about to marry the only girl he had ever loved.

It was long past midnight when he placed the two sheets of paper in his pocket, blew out the light, and slipped into bed. "Maybe things *do* work out," he breathed into the dark. "Maybe life isn't such a hell of a mess after all."

# CHAPTER
# THIRTY-ONE

## J. W. Visits the Claim

Returning to Dawson, he found both J. W. and Sam Brandon in the office. Sharpe eyed him expectantly. "Well, what did you find? Sam, here, is rather skeptical about the proposition. Afraid it'll turn out to be another Goose Creek. But why he should worry is more than I can see — we got our money back on that one, even if we didn't show a profit."

Brandon frowned. "As I told you before, J. W., I'd rather have taken a loss on that property than to have foisted it off on someone else, knowing it was worthless. Legitimate trading in unknown values is perfectly honorable if a man cares to take the chance. But deliberately selling a worthless property is something else again. That resale was none of my doing."

Sharpe laughed. "You'll have to get rid of some of your old-fashioned notions, Sam. Get the other fellow before he gets you is my motto. And, if I do say it myself, I haven't done so badly." He turned to Tom. "What do you think of this Indian River proposition?"

Drawing a paper from his pocket, Tom handed it to Sharpe. "There's the figures on thirty-five test pannings, taken from the shaft and the dump. As you can see, they're not bad. In fact, I'd say they're very good. They run better even than the pannings from the Fisher properties, and they've showed a good profit. Of course it depends on what you pay for the location. Take it all in all, I'd say it was a good buy — providing the price is right."

Sharpe scanned the figures. "Okay," he said. "I'll guarantee the price will be right. I'm going out and close the deal right now. The breakup can't be so very far off, and I don't want any of those damn sourdoughs horning in ahead of us. By the way, how's travel on the river now?"

"It couldn't be any better. I left the shack, twenty miles up the Indian, at five this morning — and it's only four o'clock now, and I've put up the dogs and fed 'em. I made the run in a little over ten hours — it's about fifty miles."

"That's faster than I'd care to go. But do you know, I have an idea I'd like to have a look at the property myself. Not that I don't trust your judgment in the matter. But I've hardly been out of Dawson since I got here. Believe it would do me good. Besides, I'd like to see for myself what this dog-team travel is like."

Tom grinned. "It isn't like the pictures in the geography, where an Eskimo woman and half a dozen kids, all dressed in furs, are sitting on a sled with the man standing up behind cracking a long-lashed whip, and a long string of dogs are galloping over a level plain with the snow so hard-packed the sled runners don't leave a mark. In this country you don't ride the sled, you walk. And when the going is good, you run. And

**243**

when it isn't, you push, and haul, and lift, and chop, and shovel."

"Nevertheless, I'm determined to go. But first I'm going to close this deal, so I can be sure it's our own property I'm examining and not someone else's. Can we pull out in the morning?"

"Sure. We'd better figure on taking two days for it, though — soft as you probably are. There are plenty of cabins along the Yukon where we can put up for the night, if you don't mind sleeping on the floor."

Just before supper Tom stopped in at police head-quarters and borrowed a book he had seen Corporal Downey reading when he had stopped in to report the happening on the Ophir trail. The book was *Fingerprint Directories*, by an English anthropologist, Sir Francis Galton, who had written two previous volumes on the subject of identification by fingerprints. That night he read the book. The next morning he bought a fountain pen, filled and pocketed it, and an hour later headed up the Yukon, accompanied by J. W. Sharpe.

It took two days to cover the distance that Tom had traveled in one. On the third day they inspected the property. "You see," Tom explained as they ate supper that evening, "this is a short feeder, and when it comes time to sluice out the dump we're going to be up against it for water. There isn't enough drainage into this little crick to insure any supply after the first runoff when the snow melts."

"Can't we build a dam at the upper limit of the property and hold back the water till we want to use it?"

Tom shook his head. "It wouldn't work. We couldn't build the dam till the frost goes out of the ground, and by that time the snow water would all be gone. Besides that, it would be pretty expensive. I found a little lake just over the rim. I can take half a dozen men, and with a little powder, some timbers, and lumber, we can run a flume down here with a gate at the head of it and control all the water we want."

"Good idea!" Sharpe exclaimed. "Splendid! By Jove, Tom, I don't know what we'd do without you! I suppose we'll have to move the lumber and timbers up from Dawson."

"No. We can get out the timbers right here. And there's a portable mill only a few miles above here. It won't cost much to get the stuff down." Stepping to his mackinaw, which hung from a peg driven into the wall, he produced his notebook and fountain pen, taking care to shake a few drops of ink into the cap and thus smear the penholder. Handing the book and pen to Sharpe, he said: "Just write an order for the lumber and I'll slip up there with it as soon as the moon comes up, so they can be getting it out. I'll be back in two or three hours, and in the morning we can hit for Dawson, and I'll pick up a crew and what powder and supplies we'll need and get busy on the flume."

Sharpe wrote the order, picked up the paper, and handed it to Tom. "Damn fountain pens!" he groused, scowling at his ink-stained fingers. "Never saw one yet that wouldn't leak. You spoke of hitting for Dawson in the morning. D'you know, I believe I'll stick around here — for a while, at least. I'm not as young as you are, and I didn't realize I'd got as soft as I have. I've put in a pretty tough three days, and a rest will do me good. Besides that, I'm interested in seeing how you go at things. Fact is, I know next to nothing about the practical side of mining. And seeing that I've invested every cent I've got with Brandon, I feel that I ought to know something about how the money's being used."

"That's a good idea," Tom agreed. "But how will you make out here alone? It'll probably take me several days to line up a crew and get back here."

"Don't worry about me. There's plenty of food here. I'll get along all right."

"Okay. I won't bother to come back to the shack, then. I'll hit from the mill straight on to Dawson. I can be there before noon tomorrow, if it don't cloud up. The quicker we get to work on that flume, the better."

Sharpe smiled. "It's great to be young. I wish I had your energy and your endurance. No wonder Sam Brandon said you're a good man!"

# CHAPTER
# THITY-TWO

## Black John Takes a Hand

Shortly after noon on the following day Tom Jorden stepped into the little office at detachment headquarters of the Northwest Mounted Police to find Corporal Downey in conversation with a huge black-bearded man who, with his chair tilted against the wall and his heels on Downey's desk, was puffing at a brier pipe and blowing a cloud of gray smoke ceilingward.

"Hello, Tom!" the officer greeted. "Come in an' sit down. I want you to meet a friend of mine, John Smith, from Halfaday Crick — more or less favorably known as Black John."

Tom smiled and, advancing to the big man, offered his hand. "I've heard of you. But — I — I didn't know you were a friend of Corporal Downey."

Black John returned the smile. "No? Why not?"

"Well, the fact is, the man who spoke of you told me you were an — an outlaw."

The smile behind the black beard widened. "Yeah, that's what the talk is. I'll bet even Downey, here, has heard rumors to that effect. But who was this character-defamin' scoundrel?"

"Porcupine Jack. He said he thought I'd like you and that you would probably like me."

"Porcupine Jack, eh? By God, there was a man! Him an' old man Manook was the only two sourdoughs in the Yukon that still hung onto their faith in the lower country. I shore was sorry to hear he'd passed on. Got stabbed by some Siwash up on the Porcupine, they tell me."

Tom nodded. "That's right. He got stabbed because he stepped in front of the knife that was aimed at me."

"Well, I'll be damned! Then you must be the young fella that I've ben hearin' about. Got yer boat back from a couple of thieves on Lindeman, an' split a holdup's head with a belt ax on the Ophir trail, an' throw'd in with Porcupine, an' shot that God-damn Cronk up on the Bluefish. Downey run him out of here a year er so ago, an' I heard he was hittin' fer Halfaday. I hit out an' overtook the cockeyed son-of-a-bitch at the mouth of the White. Don't jest rec'lect at the moment what it was I told him, but it was prob'ly somethin' that changed his mind, 'cause the next I heard of him he was over in Alaska. I s'pose I'd ort to hung the bastard right there — but somehow it didn't seem ethical. You done humanity a service when you shot him, son. Fer a cheechako you ain't doin' so bad. How'd you an' Porcupine make out down there?"

"We found something that looks good on the Old Crow. I filed a Discovery location when I got back."

"If it works out, it's shore too bad Porcupine couldn't live to git in on it. It must of ben tough on you, son — seein' him go like he did."

Tom nodded. "Yes," he said, "it was tough. Porcupine Jack was my dad."

"Yer dad!" Black John cried. "Well, no wonder you've got guts! I never even know'd Porcupine was married!"

"My mother died before I was old enough to remember her. And when I was five Dad had to skip out on account of a crime — a murder he never committed. That's what I came to see Corporal Downey about. I've found the murderer. He's right here on the Yukon."

Both men stared at the speaker in astonishment. "You mean," Downey asked, "that you've located a man who committed a murder back in the States when you was only five years old? That must be fifteen, sixteen years ago!"

"Sixteen years, now."

Black John's shrewd gray eyes were fixed on the younger man's face. "Could you prove it, son?" he asked.

"That's what I want Corporal Downey to decide. That's what I came to see him about. It's quite a long story. It might bore you."

"If the details becomes borin' I can stroll over to the Tivoli an' hist a couple of drinks. I ain't a policeman. I ain't paid to listen. Go ahead."

Starting at the beginning, Tom told the story much as he had recounted it to Porcupine Jack beside the campfire on the Porcupine. He eyed Downey. "I've already reported to you what happened there on the Bluefish. But the rest of it — what has happened since I got back to Dawson — you don't know."

"Yes, yes — go ahead!" Downey exclaimed.

"Shore, git on with it!" Black John seconded. "Cripes, don't be like one of these here damn writers that busts off a story right in the interestin' part, so you've got to buy the next magazine to find out how it come out!"

"Well, when I got back and struck Sam Brandon for my job, as I promised him I would, I found he'd taken a partner — a man named J. W. Sharpe."

Downey nodded. "Yeah, I know him — lives at the hotel."

"That's right. They took me on, and it wasn't long before I found out that Sharpe is a damn crook. He wanted me to salt a proposition up on Goose Crick that a fellow by the name of Sim Petty stuck him with. I scairt him out of that by telling him that in case the purchaser suspected a fraud any of the sourdoughs that might be called in to testify could tell the jury whether the dust he put into the gravel came from that creek or not.

"Then a couple of weeks ago he sent me up to look over a property on Indian River. He handed me the description he had copied from the book in the recorder's office. While I was up there I dumped the stuff out of my duffel bag onto the floor of the shack to find my notebook, and a packet of old letters rolled out. They were letters that my dad had carried around with him all these years — letters that my mother had written him when he'd been away on business trips. I read them all, that night Dad died up on the Bluefish. Enclosed in one of these letters was

250

one from the local banker stating that a loan Dad had evidently applied for had been approved by the board of directors.

"Well, just by chance this letter slipped from its envelope, and as I picked it up to return it, something about the handwriting attracted my attention. There seemed something peculiar about it — something strangely familiar. I had read this letter up there on the Bluefish along with the others — but it wasn't that — it seemed that I had seen that writing recently. Then I remembered. I took the description memo that J. W. had handed me out of my pocket and laid the two papers side by side on the table. The handwriting was identical. The man who wrote that letter is the man who copied that description off the recorder's book!"

"Good God!" Downey exclaimed. "Are you sure? You mean that J. W. Sharpe is the banker yer dad was suspected of murderin' back there in Minnesota sixteen years ago?"

"That's right. And I'm sure. I studied those two papers for a long time, comparing the writing, letter by letter. Then it dawned on me that I'd been wrong all these years. I knew my Dad never murdered Stowe, and old Dr. Leroy knew it — but we figured that the tramp had murdered him and made off with Mr. Kay's twenty thousand. But it wasn't the tramp who murdered Stowe — Stowe murdered the tramp!"

Corporal Downey's brows puckered in a frown. Black John refilled his pipe. After several moments of silence the officer spoke. "I've heard of crimes bein' solved by identifyin' a person's handwritin', but the identifyin' was done by experts — men that makes a special study of it. It's quite a science, from what I've read. Mind you — I'm not sayin' you're wrong. But jest so we don't go off half-cocked, let's stop an' think it over. Yer shore you ain't sort of prejudiced against this J. W. Sharpe to start out with?"

"What do you mean?"

"Well, I know what Sam Brandon thinks of you, an' it's reasonable to suppose you think the same of him. Now when you come back from the lower country an' find out he's taken in a partner, an' you find this partner ain't exactly on the up-an'-up, couldn't it be you'd be lookin' fer a chanct to get somethin' on him — fearin' that, bein' crooked, he might lay fer a chanct to swindle Brandon out of his money?"

Tom nodded. "That's probably true. I have worried some about that very thing. But I certainly wouldn't accuse a man of a murder unless —"

"No! No! I know you wouldn't do that. But there's another angle too. Accordin' to Moosehide an' Jack Gorman, you an' Miss Brandon was mighty good pals on the way in. They both figured you two would prob'ly get hitched. But sence this J. W. Sharpe has ben here I've noticed that she's goin' around with him to all the doin's that's pulled off. Now when you come back an' see how things is, ain't it reasonable to believe that you wouldn't have no particular love fer this Sharpe? That you might have a damn good reason for wantin' to get him out of the picture?"

Tom's face had gone a shade paler. "Sue Brandon didn't want me to go to the lower country," he said in a low, toneless voice, "and when I stuck to the plan, she told me she would never marry me. The other day she told me she had promised to marry J. W. But even so, I certainly wouldn't accuse him of a crime if I didn't believe he was guilty."

"I know you wouldn't, Tom. But ain't it a fact that you could convince yerself of his guilt on a damn sight less evidence than you'd convince yerself of — say Sam Brandon's guilt — er Moosehide Charlie's?"

"Yes, I suppose that's true. But I'm not deciding on his guilt. That's up to you. And I'm not relying altogether on the handwriting, either. When I was studying those two papers I noticed that there was a distinct thumbprint on that old letter. The penholder had evidently become fouled with ink, and when he picked up the letter to fold it he left his thumbprint on the paper. That's why I borrowed that book of Galton's on fingerprint identification. I read that book — and then I went out and bought a fountain pen. Up in the shack the other night I told J. W. I needed an order from him for some flume lumber and handed him my notebook and pen — after taking care that the penholder was smeared with ink. He wrote the order, cussed the leaky pen, and handed me the paper — with a swell thumbprint on it. You've read Galton's book. You've got a magnifying glass. Let's compare those prints — and you can compare the writing. The glass ought to help with that, too."

The front legs of Black John's chair hit the floor with a thud as he leaned eagerly forward. "By God, Downey, there's a cheechako that's ben usin' his head! What the

**253**

hell you waitin' fer? Git out that glass an' let's git to work! When we git them papers spread out on the desk we ort to find some meat a man kin sink his teeth into!"

For a good half hour the three bent over the papers, studying both the handwriting and the thumbprints, passing the glass back and forth from one to the other. Finally Black John pushed back his chair.

"There ain't a chanct in the world that this here J. W. Sharpe an' Joel Stowe ain't the same person," he opined. "It was a damn smart trick he pulled back there. Knowin' his wheat gamblin' had wrecked his bank, he know'd there wasn't nothin' ahead of him but a damn good stiff prison stretch. He puts Jorden off, tellin' him he'll pay them checks in the mornin'. He's got the twenty thousan' in cash he got off'n the elevator man. So he knocks off the hobo, switches clothes with the body, cuts off the head an' buries it, an' lays the body on the track fer further mutilation, then walks the track to the next town an' hops a freight for the West."

"Looks like a damn risky play," Downey said, "committin' a murder."

"Not when you figger he didn't have nothin' to lose except, mebbe, a little longer prison stretch. With no witness to the murder, they could never have made a first-degree charge stick. He could have claimed he killed that bum in self-defense — that the hobo found out he had the money on him an' made a play for it. Then he got scairt at what he'd done an' skipped out. A good lawyer kin make a jury believe anything."

"But, even hidin' the head an' switchin' clothes," Downey said, "it looks like he took a hell of a chanct of someone knowin' it wasn't his body they picked up off the track."

"Not sech a hell of a chanct when you come to figger he wasn't married. Tom says he was batchin' it over the bank. His wife could prob'ly have spotted the fraud — but he didn't have none. As fer the rest of the folks in town went, that suit of clothes on the body was enough identification fer them. There wouldn't no one be particularly interested — 'specially with most of the folks in town figgerin' he'd got what was comin' to him fer lootin' the bank."

"I guess that's right," Downey admitted. "The matter of age seems to check all right. Tom mentioned him as a 'young' banker — that was sixteen years ago. An' this Sharpe looks like a man somewheres between forty-five an' fifty now."

"It was a kind of a dumb trick not to change his initials when he changed his name," Tom said. "J. W. S. seems a kind of a giveaway."

"That's right," Downey agreed, "but it's surprisin' how many crooks do jest that. I've noticed it, an' I've heard other policemen say the same thing."

Black John grinned. "Is that so, Downey? By God, now, that's an interestin' bit of lore! I must remember that — jest in case fer some onknown reason I might want to make use of it sometime. J. S. is my initials. I shore as hell won't never change my name to — say, Joshuay Snood!" He turned to Tom. "Do you happen to know the amount of this here Sharpe's investment in the Brandon pardnership?" he asked.

"Yes, Brandon told me they'd put in fifty thousand dollars apiece."

Drawing a pad toward him, the big man figured for several minutes. "The sum seems equitable," he announced, returning the pencil to the desk.

"What do you mean?" Downey asked.

"Meanin' that, accordin' to what Tom told us Porcupine Jack lost in that bank failure, includin' the hardware-store loss, it was twenty thousan' dollars. An' accordin' to my figgers this sum, with accrued compound interest, would amount to fifty-one thousan', seven hundred an' forty-eight dollars an' ninety-four cents."

"But listen, John — I'm afraid there's no use even arrestin' Sharpe at this late date. In the first place, any embezzlement charges that might have ben laid against him, either by the defunct bank or by the grain company whose money he stole, would most likely be outlawed by this time. The murder wouldn't outlaw — but after sixteen years, how the hell would they ever prove it? There was no witnesses. An' it's likely that most everyone that know'd anything about the facts would be either scattered or dead. I couldn't arrest him without a request from the Minnesota authorities, an' even if I was to notify 'em I had the man, I'm doubtin' if they'd care to assume the expense of bringin' him back on such a slim chanct of gettin' a conviction. He'd fight extradition with everything he's got. An' on top of that, Tom would have no way of establishin' any claim he's got on Sharpe's money in a civil suit here. An' to get him into the jurisdiction of an American civil court would be next to impossible."

Black John grinned. "That'll do, Downey. You don't need to set there an' think up reasons why the law can't help Tom git jestice. It would take from now till midnight. You've thought up four er five legal obstructions to jestice without half tryin', an' I'm willin' to take yer word fer it that there's plenty of more — an' to concede that Tom ain't got no legal redress whatever. That's the way of the law. An' that's the reason I shun it. It obstructs more jestice than it dishes out. So, that bein' the case, we'll handle this here matter in the way of the North."

"The way of the North? What do you mean?"

"I mean we'll substitute common sense fer legal quibblin' — an' see how that works. Jest look at the facts, Downey — a bank got wrecked an' a lot of folks lost every damn cent they had because its president stole the funds an' gambled 'em away. A grain company got robbed of twenty thousan' dollars. I can't shed no tears over that loss. But a pore, friendless hobo got murdered, an' the crime laid on an innocent man. Now, we know the man who is guilty of all them pranks. We know he's livin' right here in Dawson, well-to-do an' respected, enjoyin' his freedom, an' ondoubtless livin' off'n the fruits of them an' other crimes whilst plannin' future ones — an' there ain't a damn thing the law kin do about it!"

"Guess that's so — if Tom's got his facts right," Downey admitted.

"He's got 'em right. You're no damn fool. You kin tell when a man's lyin', same as I kin. I know'd Porcupine Jack. He was a good square shooter. An' I know this lad's a square shooter too."

Downey nodded. "I believe him. But there don't seem to be anything we can do about it."

"The hell there don't!" Black John turned to Tom. "If I was you, son," he said, "I'd jest make out a bill fer fifty-one thousand, seven hundred forty-eight dollars and ninety-four cents an' present it to Sharpe, with a demand fer the money."

"But he'd never pay it!"

"Shore he would. He'd be glad to when you showed him that there letter he wrote yer pa an' let him compare the handwritin' with that description he copied. An' then show him that lumber order he give you an' explain to him about them thumbprints. You see, murder's a thing a man can't never git off his mind — onct he's committed one. Sharpe won't know they prob'ly couldn't convict him. He'd be afraid they could — seein' his identity has ben established. Besides that, he prob'ly wouldn't know that them embezzlement charges has outlawed. Bankers ain't necessarily up on criminal law — though God knows they ort to be. He would remember, though, that there'd be a hell of a lot of people back in that town who lost their money in that bank failure who would be mighty glad to testify agin him. An' plenty of 'em would fight fer the chanct to set on the jury that tried him. He wouldn't want to hear what a jury like that would have to say — by a damn sight."

258

Corporal Downey grinned. "But, John — doesn't that sort of savor of blackmail?"

"Blackmail! Why, damn you, Downey, are you hintin' that I'd connive at blackmail? Sence when has it ben called blackmail to present an honest bill fer collection? Er has the law made that a criminal offense too?" He turned to Tom. "Where's this here Stowe, er Sharpe, er whatever his name is, at now?"

"He's up in the shack on that Indian River property. Said he'd stick around there till I got back."

"That seems as good a place as any to dun him fer this little account — seein' it's past due. I'll go along with you — jest in case he mightn't onderstand about them thumbprints, *et cetry*. I'll be ready to start in an hour. Stop fer me at the hotel."

# CHAPTER
# THIRTY-THREE

## In the Office

When the office door closed behind the big man, Tom glanced at Downey. "Who is this Black John Smith, anyway? As I said, my dad mentioned him up there on the Porcupine. But he said he was considered an outlaw. At that, he said he was about the only man in the North who goes out of his way to straighten out other folks' troubles for 'em."

The officer nodded. "I guess Porcupine Jack was about right, at that. Black John is — well, he's Black John. It's said that he's wanted in Alaska — but, as far as I know, no United States marshal has ever tried to take him back there. At least," he added with a grin, "none has ever succeeded in taking him back. An' we certainly have never had any request to hold him for the American authorities. He's a sort of a law unto himself. Besides straightening out a lot of folks' troubles for 'em, as Porcupine said, he also manages to deal out a pretty levelheaded brand of justice up there on Halfaday Crick. He's got a mighty effective mode of procedure — and mighty conclusive, too. When someone arrives on Halfaday that Black John figures rates a hangin', he simply calls a miners' meetin' an' hangs him."

"Hangs 'em! Isn't that a pretty highhanded procedure? How does he know they're guilty of murder?"

Downey shrugged. "Murder — hell! That's only one of the things he hangs 'em for. A man can get hung on Halfaday for anything Black John considers hangable. I've known of a lot of hangin's up there — but I've got to hear of the first one yet that was a miscarriage of justice. Damned if I know how he knows they ort to be hung — but he does. An' mostly they're men that, fer one reason or another, the law couldn't touch. I do know that he's saved me many a headache. He'd give a man the shirt off his back if he thought he needed it. He can be gentle as a woman or hard as chilled steel. But he gets results. He's sure helped me out plenty of times."

"But what does he do for a living?"

Downey smiled bleakly. "Oh, John gets along. He claims to work a location up there on the crick. But I've never caught him at any harder work than shakin' dice with Old Cush. I've got my own good guess. He's turned in thousands of dollars to the police that was stole from individuals by some of them rascals he's hung — but never a damn cent that was stole off some big company, though I know some of those birds must have had plenty of it on 'em when they hit Halfaday. But somehow it always seems to mysteriously disappear."

"Sort of a Robin Hood, eh?"

"Yeah — that's about it. An' I guess when the books is all balanced it might turn out that the Robin Hoods

**261**

of this world do a damn sight more good than a lot of other folks."

"But do you think it would do any good for me to go up there with him and present that bill? I'd hate to make a damn fool of myself."

"Officially, I'd ruther not answer that question one way er another. Personally, I'd say that I never heard of anyone makin' a damn fool of himself by followin' John's advice. An' I might add, offhand, that even if a thing don't do no good — it don't do no harm to try it."

"Thanks, Corporal," Tom grinned. "I guess we'll be pulling out for Indian River."

Stopping in at the office of Brandon & Sharpe on his way to the hotel, Tom found Sue Brandon alone. "Back already!" she exclaimed. "You must have just about killed J. W. He isn't used to the trail."

"Oh, he stayed up there. Claimed he needed a rest. Said he'd just loaf around and wait till I get back." The girl answered nothing, and as she turned toward her desk Tom noticed an unwonted droop to the corners of her lips. "Cheer up," he grinned. "J. W.'s all right. Couple of days' rest and he'll be good as ever."

"I wasn't thinking of J. W.," she said in a low, dull voice.

"Wasn't thinking of him! Then what are you looking so sad about? I thought you were worrying because he'd got all tired out."

"I'm worrying, all right — but not because he's tired. Oh, I don't know. I — I'm afraid."

"Afraid! Afraid of J. W.!"

"Not afraid that he'll harm me — it's more of a distrust than a fear. From little things I've heard here and there — I — oh, I can't explain it exactly — it's all vague and indefinite —"

"Then — you don't love him?" Tom interrupted fiercely. "You don't love him — but you're going ahead and marry him anyway?"

"No, I don't love him," the girl replied in the same dull voice. "There — I've told you now. I don't love him — and I never could love him. But I'm going ahead and marry him anyway. Daddy trusts him — thinks he's a good businessman. And he favors the match." Something — some inner dam — seemed suddenly to let go, and the next instant words were pouring from the girl's lips in a torrent of pent-up emotion. "Oh, why did you go away? Why didn't you stay on with Daddy — with *us?* You had a good job! And we — we — Oh, you just ruined everything! I promised to marry him soon after you left because I was angry at you for going! I don't love him! I can never love him! He's been after me to name our wedding day, and I've kept putting it off till I couldn't put it off any longer! I don't love him — but I could have loved you, Tom! I — I did love you! And I know you love me! I knew — long before you — you told me — that day you went away! I know that Daddy intended to take you in as a partner — you to do the field work and he to furnish the money. And, oh — we could have been so happy together. But now —"

"When is this wedding day?" Tom's words crashed into her unfinished sentence.

**263**

"Why — it's — it's the first day of April! And — oh, I despise J. W.! But Daddy wants me to marry his partner."

"April Fools' Day, eh! Fine! That's great! And — oh boy — will somebody get fooled! Remember — that's a promise! You'll marry your dad's partner on April Fools' Day! And I'll be there! And, believe me, I'll hold you to that promise! In fact, I can hardly wait! You bet I'll be there!"

The girl stared at him in wide-eyed astonishment. "Tom Jorden — are you drunk?"

"Not drunk. Just happy. It's the way of the North. So long. I've got to see a man!"

The door slammed behind him, leaving the girl standing there staring in blank amazement.

# CHAPTER
# THIRTY-FOUR

## J. W. Arbitrates

Early the following morning Tom, closely followed by Black John, opened the door and stepped into the little shack on Indian River as Sharpe was finishing his breakfast.

"What! Back already!" J. W. cried. "And this man — is he — er — one of your crew?"

"This is Mr. Smith," Tom replied, and, turning to Black John, he said, "Mr. Smith, meet Mr. Joel W. Stowe — alias J. W. Sharpe."

"What? What's that?" The man leaped from his chair and glared from one to the other.

Tom continued, ignoring the interruption: "Mr. Stowe was at one time a resident of Big Falls, Minnesota. He used to be president of the Farmers' and Merchants' Bank there — until he skipped out with twenty thousand dollars of a grain company's money, after looting the bank and murdering a tramp."

In the semidarkness of the little room Sharpe's face had gone paper white. His mouth sagged open, and his tongue trembled visibly as he strove to speak. "What — what — are you — saying? I — I don't know what — you're — talking — about."

"Oh yes, you do. You know exactly what I'm talking about."

"Who — who — *are* you?"

"I'm Tom Jorden — John Jorden's son. You remember the last time you saw John Jorden — there in your pasture — where the tramp was building the underpass. He asked you to honor a couple of checks, and you promised to do so the minute the bank opened in the morning. But you weren't at the bank in the morning, Stowe — you were riding a freight, headed West — with the twenty thousand dollars on you that Mr. Kay entrusted to you for safekeeping — safekeeping, Stowe — that's a huge joke, isn't it? Almost as good as the joke you played on John Jorden when you skipped out and left him to face the charge of murdering you!"

As Tom talked the man's eyes never left his face, but Black John noticed that he was rapidly gaining control of himself.

"It's all a damned lie! You're crazy! Raving, ranting crazy! I never heard of Big Falls, Minnesota. I never heard of a John Jorden! I was never president of a bank! I —"

Black John interrupted. "Hold on, Stowe. It ain't —"

"My name is Sharpe — not Stowe! I never knew a Stowe!"

"Mebbe not. But you ain't sharp as you try to make out, neither. As I was goin' on to say, it ain't no use to stand there an' tell us all the places an' the folks you never heard of, an' name all the banks you never was president of. It would be a waste of time."

"Who are you?"

"Me? Smith is the name. An' by way of further identification, you might take a look at this." The big man turned back the front of his shirt to disclose the badge of a United States marshal — a badge, be it known, that he had purloined from a misguided American official who had made the mistake of showing up on Halfaday Creek a year or so before. "It ain't no use in you resistin' arrest, Stowe. You might better come along peaceable."

"Arrest! What are you arresting me for?"

"Well — murder will prob'ly be the main item. There'll be several other charges of a minor nature. I wouldn't worry about them, though, if I was you. What the hell do you care how many years they soak you fer — after yer hung?"

"You mean — you're arresting me! Taking me back to — to —"

"Yeah — you might as well say it — to Big Falls, Minnesota. There's lots of folks back there that'll be mighty glad to see you, Stowe. Fact is, when I left there, after Tom, here, let us know that he'd located you, folks was practically mobbin' the jedge to git put on the jury list fer yer trial."

"But — this is Canada! You have no authority to arrest me here! A United States marshal has no authority in the Yukon!"

"Well, now, Stowe — I'm glad you brought that pint up. Yer contention seems to have a modicum of merit. We ain't bloodthirsty folks — me an' Tom ain't. Whilst we'll have to admit we'd delight to see you kickin' around on the end of a tight one, we're willin' to forego the pleasure an' sort of arbitrate this thing."

"What do you mean — arbitrate?"

"I mean arbitrate — you know — like the government used to arbitrate with the Injuns. When they wanted some more of the land that belonged to the Injuns, the President, he'd call the chiefs together an' arbitrate. The government would get the land — an' the Injuns would get a promise."

"But suppose I refuse?"

The big man grinned. "It's all the same to us — as a matter of hist'ry, I might pint out that all them Injuns that refused to arbitrate is dead."

"What is there to arbitrate?"

"Well, Tom, here, has got a little bill agin you. It's fer fifty-one thousan', seven hundred forty-eight dollars and ninety-four cents. That amount bein' the twenty thousan' dollars you stole off'n John Jorden by not honorin' them checks, together with accrued interest to date. There ort to be another thousan' added fer my expenses up here — but if you come acrost without no bickerin', we'll let the Minnesota authorities worry about that."

"This is an outrage! It's blackmail! It's a holdup! It's illegal!"

"So's murder an' embezzlement illegal — as you'll damn well find out if you don't dicker."

"How do I know that this is not sheer bluff?"

Black John turned to Tom. "Show him them papers — the letter he wrote yer pa — an' the description he copied off'n the location record, an' that order he wrote out fer that lumber. You'll note, Stowe," he continued as the man scanned the scripts with staring eyes, "that the hand-writin' on all of 'em is the same — an' likewise them two thumbprints is identical. Handwritin' an' thumbprints don't lie. If there was ever an open-an'-shut case, Stowe, this is it. Why, any jury in the world would convict you on that evidence — even one that didn't have you already convicted before it was swore in."

Stowe's face had gone dead white again. He made one more attempt at defiance. "But — I still maintain that you can't arrest me! You have no authority! I'll fight extradition with every cent I've got in the world!"

"Yeah? Well, believe me, brother — money's a damn pore weapon to fight burlap extradition with."

"Burlap extradition! What's burlap extradition?"

"It consists in tunkin' a man on the skull with any handy blunt instrument, an' wroppin' him in a gunny sack, an' draggin' him acrost the line. It's quicker than the other kind, havin' ben devised to do away with red tape."

"But — it's illegal! It's not according to law!"

"That's ondoubtless true. But it's accordin' to the way of the North. An' I'll pint out that it ain't goin' to be no hell of a chore. The line ain't only three quarters of a mile back of here, an' you'll drag easy on the snow."

"It's impossible to pay that bill. I have no such amount of cash. Every cent I own is invested in a partnership with Sam Brandon — fifty thousand dollars."

"That'll be okay. Jest set down there to the table an' Tom'll loan you his pen. Here's some paper I fetched along from the hotel. You jest make out an assignment in full of all yer holdin's to Tom — lock, stock, an' barrel — so help'e God, an' we'll call it square. Of course there'll still be the item of them odd dollars an' cents — one thousan' seven hundred and forty-eight dollars and ninety-four cents. But Tom'll have to take that out of the profits, if any. An' before you write, I might warn you to look an' see if that there penholder's clean. If you'd done that on a couple of previous occasions, you'd be a happier man today, Stowe — an' a richer one too."

The man made the assignment as dictated by Black John, signed it, and handed it to Tom, who pocketed it.

"An' now," Black John said, "if I was you, I'd hit fer the outside as fast as God would let me. I'm givin' you a tip, gratis. Don't never show yer face in Dawson again. If you do, Downey'll pick you up shore as hell. An' that there hangin' down to Big Falls will come off as planned. You see, the governor of Minnesota notified the Mounted to be on the lookout fer you — jest in case somethin' might happen to me. Downey was talkin' to me an' Tom about you last evenin' — claimed he'd prob'ly pick you up today. That's why we snuck up here in sech a hell of a hurry — figurin' it was more to Tom's interest to git his pa's money back than to see you hung. So if I was you, I'd git goin'."

"But — I have no dogs — no food — no money!"

"You can take Tom's dogs — an' there's plenty of grub here in the shack. As fer money — you'll have to

270

shift fer yerself — an' I'm warnin' you — there ain't but damn few banks an' grain elevators along the road you're goin'."

As the two headed back toward Dawson, Tom glanced at the big man who strode at his side. "Are you really a United States marshal?" he asked.

"Hell, no! What ever put that idee into your head?"

"Why — that badge you showed Stowe!"

"Oh, that! Hell, that's jest a trinket I picked up somewheres. A man can't never tell when a little thing like that'll come in handy."

"And another thing — I didn't know the line was anywhere near Indian River."

"It ain't. You cheechakos gits the damnedest idees!"

"But you told Stowe it was only three quarters of a mile back of the shack."

"Did I? By cripes, Tom, I believe yer right! My mistake. I must of thought I was up to Cush's! That's jest the distance the line is from the back door of his saloon!"

"I don't know how I can ever thank you for what you've done for me. I never in the world could have put that over alone. And there didn't seem to be any legal redress."

"There hardly ever is any. But you don't need to thank me. Hell — Porcupine Jack was a friend of mine! An' from what I hear, you're pretty much of a man yerself."

"Will you promise to do me one more favor?"

The big man grinned. "I will, providin' it don't involve no moral trepitude."

271

Tom laughed. "It don't! I want you to come to our wedding — Sue Brandon's and mine. It'll be on April first. She told me she'd promised to marry her dad's partner on that day. And I'm holding her to that promise. And I want you to meet my wife."

"Good fer you, son! Don't worry! I'll be there!"

# About Author

James B. Hendryx was born in Sauk Center, Minnesota. He attended the University of Minnesota and his early career was in journalism. Later he found work as a cowboy in Montana and work as a construction foreman. It was during this time that he began what would prove to be an extremely rewarding career as an author of Western fiction. His earliest books are set in Montana, but soon the location changes to the Northwestern regions of the Dominion of Canada and occasionally Alaska. *Downey of the Mounted* (Putnam, 1926) featured what became his first popular character creation, Corporal Cameron Downey of the Royal Northwest Mounted Police. At a time when other writers were writing Western fiction set in the American West, Hendryx created what was to be virtually a sub-genre, stories set in Canada with vivid local colour and distinctive Canadian dialogue. His books appealed not only to American readers but to Canadian and English readers throughout the British Commonwealth. To maximize his income from his fiction, Hendryx would publish most of his fiction first in magazines. In "Justice on Halfaday" in *Short Stories*

(8/23/31), Corporal Downey was joined by another character, Black John Smith, who would become equally popular. Halfaday Creek was located on the Yukon/Alaska border, and this location would expand the variety of characters in Hendryx's fiction. Often he would put several of his short novels first published in magazines into book-length adventures, unified by the Halfaday setting and Black John Smith. Typical of these were *Outlaws of Halfaday Creek* (Doubleday, 1935) and *Badmen on Halfaday Creek* (Doubleday, 1950). Jarrolds published early titles in British editions, as later did Hammond. Hendryx depicted Canada with a notable police force, effective English law in the courts, and a belief that the rule of law prevails even in remote, wild regions. This is frequently in dramatic contrast to the cynicism regarding law enforcement in American Western fiction. Hendryx's Northwestern fiction over his long career certainly remains an impressive literary achievement.